ONE FINE DAY
THE RABBI
BOUGHT A CROSS

ONE FINE DAY
THE RABBI
BOUGHT A CROSS

□

Harry Kemelman

WILLIAM MORROW AND COMPANY, INC.
New York

Library of Congress Cataloging-in-Publication Data

Kemelman, Harry.
One fine day the rabbi bought a cross.

I. Title.
PS3561.E39805   1987   813'.54   86-23571
ISBN 0-688-05631-8

Printed in the United States of America

First Edition

1 2 3 4 5 6 7 8 9 10

BOOK DESIGN BY BERNIE SCHLEIFER

IN CELEBRATION OF
The twenty-fifth of Ruth and George
The fifteenth of Arthur and Ziona
The tenth of Diane and Murray
And our own fiftieth anniversary

ONE FINE DAY
THE RABBI
BOUGHT A CROSS

1

When at sixty-five, Barney Berkowitz decided to retire—why should only wage earners retire?—he sold his small chain of three Army and Navy stores, and entrusted the money, well over two million dollars, to a money management firm. Then, since his employees had not thought of it, he bought himself a gold watch and had the back engraved, "To our beloved B.B., on his retirement, from his grateful employees."

As a person of means, he had always been involved somewhat in the temple in Barnard's Crossing; he had been a member of the Board of Directors for years, but never an officeholder. Whenever it was suggested that his name be put on the list of candidates he would shake his head, lowered and turned to one side, while at the same time wigwagging a hand to express complete negation. "No, boys, no. No honors for old B.B. I'll just stay in the background." Holding office might mean getting involved with one faction or another, whereas he tended to think of himself as an independent, a kind of elder statesman giving advice to all factions.

A little potbellied man with a round head, which was balding and rimmed with sparse, mouse-colored hair, he made a point of going to the Saturday morning services just to show that he could even though his stores were open Saturdays.

9

After his retirement, however, he would sometimes even drop in on the daily minyan. But it was the Saturday services that he particularly enjoyed, especially when a Bar Mitzvah was to be celebrated. He enjoyed mingling with the large crowds, the boy's relatives and friends who crowded the sanctuary on those occasions, and then retired to the vestry for the inevitable collation. It was on one such occasion, a particularly lavish one, that he found himself thinking of his own Bar Mitzvah. His father had taken him to the tenement that served as a house of prayer in their neighborhood. It was on a weekday, and he had gone to school immediately after. His father had whispered to the *shammes* who was in charge of running the service, and when his name was called during the reading of the Torah, he had gone up to the reading table and recited the blessings he had been taught by an itinerant rebbe. The passage from the Scroll was read by the official reader, after which he gave the second blessing. And that was all. He had not been taught to read the passage for himself, nor did he read the section from the Prophets. There was no party afterward. No celebration. His father, restive and glancing repeatedly at his watch, hurried him out as soon as the service was over, only nodding shortly to the two or three who wished him *mazel tov,* good luck. Then he went off to school and his father to his job.

That had been his Bar Mitzvah, and he had never been sure that he had actually undergone the rite. Had he really and truly been initiated into the tribe? Well, now he could settle the question once and for all. He would have a real Bar Mitzvah. He came to think of it as his Great Idea. A Bar Mitzvah that one could not possibly cavil at. In Jerusalem. At the Wall.

Characteristically, he went not to David Small, the rabbi of the congregation, but to Alvin Bergson, the president.

"Why don't you check it out with the rabbi?" asked Bergson.

"Well, I had in mind to have it done in Jerusalem, at the Wall, and since you're in the travel business . . ."

"I see." Bergson was instantly alert. This was business. "When were you planning on going?"

"I thought maybe July."

"July is a good time," Bergson agreed. "And you'll be able to fly El Al direct from Boston then. So you'll want a ticket to Israel. And Mollie?"

"Of course."

"So that's two round-trip tickets to Israel."

"And the rabbi, I'd want him along to conduct the ceremony. I'll even spring for a ticket for his wife, if he doesn't want to leave her here."

Bergson mentally rubbed his hands. "And a minyan? You'll need eight besides you and the rabbi."

"No. B.B. is no fool. He doesn't go tossing his money around like a drunken sailor. A minyan I'm sure I can get in Jerusalem. Of course, I'm planning a party afterward, and anyone who comes from here is invited, but I'm not picking up the tab for a free vacation for them."

"Oh, sure, no trouble with getting a minyan. I just thought you'd like to have your friends with you. Tell you what, maybe I can get up a charter, and that will cut expenses all around and—"

"Now, that's an idea. And you'll take it up with the rabbi?"

"Leave it to me."

"How would you like a free trip to Israel, David?" was the way in which Bergson introduced Barney Berkowitz's plan to the rabbi. Bergson called the rabbi by his first name, one of the few presidents of the temple who did, partly because they were the same age, but more because he genuinely liked him.

Although his shoulders had a scholarly stoop, his hair was beginning to recede, and he was beginning to develop a middle-aged paunch, Rabbi David Small looked younger than his forty-odd years. His face was unlined and his eyes behind his thick-lensed glasses were innocent and candid.

As he listened to Berkowitz's plan, his face relaxed in a broad smile. "And what am I supposed to do, Alvin? Make a

11

little speech, saying, 'Today, Barney Berkowitz, you are a man'? Didn't you tell him that it was unnecessary, that he was Bar Mitzvah when he reached thirteen, whether he had a ceremony or not? All it means is that he has come of age and is responsible for his own sins, just as in our secular society one comes of age at eighteen."

Bergson grinned. "I'm in the business of selling travel. Here's a guy who is willing to spring for four round-trip tickets to Israel. Am I going to discourage him? I even suggested to him that he'd need a minyan, but the shrewdness that made him such a hotshot in Army and Navy store circles asserted itself, and he turned me down. Look, David, here's a guy who has worked all his life, and now for the first time he has money and leisure and wants to enjoy himself, but he doesn't know how. He wants to travel, but he can't just pick himself up and go. He has to have a reason, a mission. He's made that way. He's willing to give you and Miriam a free trip to justify it. So how about it?"

Still smiling, the rabbi shook his head slowly. "I'd love to go to Israel, to live there for a while, but I can't swing it right now and I can't accept his offer. My conscience wouldn't let me." His smile broadened. "If Barney feels that he has to rededicate himself to his religion, why don't you tell him he became party to our contract with God when he was circumcised, and it would be more in keeping with his plan if he had himself recircumcised."

Bergson laughed heartily. "All right, I will. But look, David, I'm planning on arranging a charter for the occasion. How about coming along as a tour guide? That would give you and Miriam a free ride."

"No, thanks. I don't know the country that well, for one thing. But even if I did, the idea of sleeping in a different hotel every other night for a couple of weeks, and riding on a tour bus every day, doesn't appeal to me."

When Bergson reported the conversation to Berkowitz, he took the rabbi's refusal philosophically. "Well, he doesn't

12

want to, so he doesn't have to. I'm sure we'll be able to find a rabbi in Jerusalem who will officiate."

To the suggestion of recircumcision offered with a straight face, he said, "How can I? The ladies—" And then as Bergson smiled, he said, "Oh, I see. It's a joke. Ha-ha."

Nevertheless, he was annoyed. As he explained to his wife, Mollie, "I offer him and his wife yet a free trip to Israel. So if he couldn't go for some reason or other, couldn't he at least call and explain, and thank me?"

"But you didn't offer him, Barney. You sent Al Bergson. How would he know it wasn't some kind of joke on Al's part?"

"Aw, he knew, all right. But he doesn't like me, so he won't accept a favor from me."

2

THE MORNING SERVICE, *SHACHRIS*, WAS SCHEDULED FOR seven, and for once, perhaps because it was a bright, sunny June day, there were ten men, the number required for a minyan, present, and they were able to start on time. Half an hour later, Rabbi David Small was back at home for his breakfast while his wife, Miriam, was in the kitchen wrapping sandwiches and filling the thermos for the lunch they would take with them on their journey, since they could not eat in a restaurant and it might be late afternoon before they got back. She was small and quick in her movements, exuding an air of brisk efficiency. Her blond hair (nowadays occasionally "touched up" at the hairdresser's) was piled on top of her head as though she had hastily pinned it up to get it out of the way. In blouse and sweater and jeans, she could have passed for a high school senior, except that there were now tiny lines at the corners of her eyes, and her firm skin showed not only purpose and determination but also maturity.

Upstairs, in her bedroom, their fourteen-year-old daughter, Hepsibah, square-faced and to her despair unmodishly stocky, was still trying to decide whether to wear her relatively new jeans and pack the old ones with a tear on the knee, or to pack the new and wear the old. And whether to wear her badly scuffed sneakers or her new moccasins. They were driving up to New Hampshire to drop her off at summer

14

camp, and it was important that she make the right impression, although that depended on who was already there. She finally settled for the torn jeans and the sneakers and came down to announce that she was ready.

Her father stared blankly. "Are you going like that? With a hole in your pants?"

"Oh, Daddy, it's a camp in the woods. You want me to wear a gown?"

"She can change when she gets there," said Miriam soothingly. "Now, bring your duffel bag out to the car, Siba. Daddy mustn't lift it because of his back. We want to get started right away."

The rabbi did not enjoy driving and regarded with dread any trip of over ten or twenty miles. He constantly worried about a flat tire, the ignition shorting out, losing his way. He reflected morosely as he got behind the wheel that if he had inquired, it might have been possible for Hepsibah to take a bus to a town near the camp, where she could have been met. Or even that he might have arranged matters so that his son, Jonathon, who was a counselor at a camp in New York, could have delayed his departure by a few days so that *he* could have driven Hepsibah to New Hampshire.

He drove with both hands clutching the wheel, looking straight ahead. Miriam, beside him, did not try to engage him in conversation, speaking only to direct him, from the map on her lap, when to turn and approximately how far they would have to drive before they reached the next point that might present a problem. Hepsibah, in back, had been gazing out of the window and had then dozed off.

They reached the camp well before noon. They made a cursory inspection of the main buildings and the hut to which Hepsibah had been assigned—they were familiar with the place from the year before—refused the offer of lunch by the director, saying it was much too early, and then made their farewells to Hepsibah. She had met a girl who had been there last year, and to their mild disappointment was not at all averse to their leaving.

The rabbi was much more relaxed on the trip back. He

had accomplished his mission, and he had the whole long summer day to get back home. Shortly after noon, they found a picnic site by the side of the road, and they stopped to have their sandwiches and coffee. He stretched luxuriously. "Now we've got the whole summer free," he said.

"And what do you plan to do?" Miriam asked.

"Do? We'll do nothing. Just relax. No kids around. No religious school to watch over. No sermons to give."

"And you'll be just as busy as you were last summer, when we also had Hepsibah and Jonathon at camp. People will come to see you with their problems. You'll still have to go to hospitals to visit the sick, and to the homes of the bereaved to sit with them during their *shiva*. No, David, if you really want to relax and take it easy, you've got to get out of Barnard's Crossing. Because while you're there, people will come to you."

"And when we went to that place up in the mountains, people still came to me. As long as they know you're a rabbi, they come to you with problems."

"We could travel," she suggested.

"You mean drive across the country?"

"I thought we might go abroad."

"One of those twenty-one-day tours? No, thank you. We'd end up exhausted. Even those we've taken to Israel, I've found were more tiring than pleasurable."

"But when you took a sabbatical and we spent the whole winter there—"

"Ah, that was different. But we were able to do that only because your Aunt Gittel managed to get us an apartment. You kept house and we didn't have the expense of a hotel room or eating in restaurants all the time."

"Well, maybe she could get us an apartment again."

He shook his head. "I doubt it. That was in the winter, but now we'd be going in the summer, at the height of the tourist season."

"We could try."

He shrugged.

But when they got home, there among the dozen or so letters on the floor under the mail slot was a letter from Gittel. Miriam tore open the envelope and read rapidly, handing over each sheet as she finished it to her husband. He pushed his thick-lensed glasses up on his forehead and peered nearsightedly at the tiny script. It was a typical letter from Gittel.

She gave news of her family, of her son who had married the religious girl and of how meticulous her daughter-in-law was in her observance of the religious regulations; of their young son who was attending a religious school instead of a secular school in spite of all her arguments and protestations—"and, of course, he always sides with his wife"; of the child's precocity—"and I'm not saying this because he's my grandson." She spoke about the economic conditions that prevailed since the "new administration" got in—although it had been in for six years already.

"But the big news" (it was on page three) "is that I am now a Jerusalemite. His Lordship" (by which she obviously meant the prime minister, of whom she disapproved) "has decreed that our office must be moved from Tel Aviv to Jerusalem. Never mind that most of our work is concerned with the Tel Aviv area. We must establish facts of our presence! It is a beautiful city, I admit it, but it is for Jews, whereas Tel Aviv is for Israelis. If you don't care for synagogue services, what is there to do?

"I managed to rent my apartment in Tel Aviv to an American professor who is teaching at Tel Aviv University for the year. But what do I do next year?" So she had come up to Jerusalem and rented an apartment. The real-estate people had suggested that she sell her apartment in Tel Aviv and use the money to buy one in Jerusalem. "But what do I do when the government falls and the regular government" (by which she meant the Labor Party, of course) "comes back into power and they decide to move my office back to Tel Aviv? So I'll have to sell again and buy again, which means more commissions for them, which is what they're really interested in."

17

It was not what she had hoped for. It was much too big. What she had wanted was a small, modern apartment that would be easy to take care of, but she had gotten a very good deal on this one—"through a friend"—and so she had taken it for a year. "About next year, we'll see."

"So if you could come for a visit, a few weeks or months, or as long as you wanted, you could stay here and not have to pay the ridiculous prices of the fancy hotels. And I can assure you that everything is strictly kosher, so that your David wouldn't have to worry because if it satisfies my daughter-in-law, believe me, it will satisfy him. I go along with all this foolishness because I am all alone, and if I want my son and his family to come here for a meal on occasion, I have to. Even then, if it were just my son and his wife, believe me, I wouldn't mind if they had only tea or a cup of coffee and maybe some fruit in my house. But can I let my grandson grow up feeling that he must not eat in his grandmother's house?"

When he finished, Miriam said, "Oh, David, it's—it's as though it's ordained."

He looked at her quizzically. "Ordained? From Heaven? You didn't have anything to do with it?"

She blushed. "Oh, I wrote to her a couple of weeks ago. You know, just a newsy letter telling her how we were. I may have mentioned that Jonathon and Hepsibah would both be off to camp and that we—"

He laughed. "All right, I get it."

"Then can I write and tell her we might come?"

"Sure. Or you might even call her."

3

HASSAN EL DHAMOURI, ASSOCIATE PROFESSOR OF FINE ARTS
at Harvard and curator of the Islamic Collection at the Fogg
Art Museum, was a tall, arresting figure. His thick hair,
brushed back, was peppered with gray, but his bushy eyebrows, which turned up at the corners, and his moustache
and imperial were still jet black. In spite of, or perhaps even
because of, his Mephistophelean appearance, his students
liked him; and he was an easy marker whose courses were not
demanding.

He sat behind his desk in the inner room of his offices at
the museum, teetering back and forth in his leather swivel
chair as he gave instructions to Mrs. Mills, his secretary, a
woman in her thirties who came in only mornings.

Professor El Dhamouri tossed a paper across the desk to
her. "Tell them I won't be able to make it, that my calendar
is full for the month, but if possible next month . . ."

"Yes, sir. Next month, or the month after?"

"Even better. You might look through my engagement
book and suggest a couple of dates."

"Very good."

He glanced at another letter, and tossing it across the
desk, said, "The usual on this one. And on this one. And
likewise on this one, but a little more buttery."

Her thin lips twisted into a smile. "The best grade of butter?"

"I would say so. The man is a professor. Make it sound as though I know of him, or am at least familiar with his work, if he's done any. Look him up and see if he has. On this one— no, hold off. I'll be talking to him in a day or two. Let's see, that's about it. You'll have the tape on my last lecture typed up, won't you?"

"I'll finish it tomorrow and I'll have these ready for your signature at the same time. I'm leaving now."

As she opened the door, a young man who had been waiting in the outer office rose and said, "I am Albert Houseman. I have an appointment with Professor El Dhamouri."

She turned to the professor and said, "A Mr. Houseman? He says he has an appointment."

"Oh, yes, send him in."

She stood aside for him to enter, and then called out, "Till tomorrow, then."

He was about thirty-five, short and thin, with eyes so dark they seemed all pupil. His nose was long and thin and parrotlike and seemed to bisect his black moustache. The professor went to the outer door, poked his head out, and looked down the corridor at the retreating figure of his secretary. Then he closed the door, set it on the latch, and returned to his seat behind the desk. He surveyed his visitor, taking note of his tweed jacket, his flannel slacks, and his polished brown loafers, and said, "Blue jeans and sneakers would have been better."

Houseman said, "I thought in the East, especially at Harvard, I'd be less noticeable if I were properly dressed."

"Well, we're improving—a little—but most graduate students would still be apt to wear jeans. Your name is?"

"Abdul Ibn Hosni, but I Americanized it—officially."

"That's the name Ibrahim used when he called to tell me you were coming. He probably forgot that you had changed it—officially."

"It's what he always calls me."

20

"And you're staying . . . ?"

"As you suggested, at the Holiday Inn."

"For how long?"

"That depends on you. If you can help us, I'll go back as soon as everything is arranged. If you can't, I notify Ibrahim, who will have an alternative plan that I may have to implement."

"I see. Ibrahim told me very little of what was involved. He said you would fill me in. All I know is that he wants something transmitted to his brother, Mahmoud, in Jerusalem. He suggested that if we were going to be together for a while, I could pass you off as a graduate student in my department. Normally I would have had you stay at my house as my guest, but I sensed—more from his tone than from what he said—that the matter is of—er—very serious importance. That's why I suggested you stay at a hotel and come to see me here rather than at my house. My house may be watched."

"By whom?" Ibn Hosni asked quickly.

El Dhamouri shrugged and smiled. "By the FBI, by Mossad, by the PLO, by almost anyone. Any Arab who achieves some prominence here in the States and who continues to be Arab is apt to be approached by any one of a dozen Arab organizations for help with some special project, for a contribution, for permission to use his name on a petition, or just for a handout. So I assume that my house may be watched from time to time, and I'm careful about whom I invite. But here, my office is at least semi-public. Anyone can drop in, and dozens do. There's safety in numbers. Perhaps I'm a little paranoid. If a Jew enrolls in one of my courses, I suspect he might be an agent of Mossad. And if it's an Arab, I wonder is he really Arab and which faction, one of Arafat's boys or one of the Syrians? Is he Lebanese or Jordanian, or maybe even a Libyan? It's not a good way to live, Abdul."

The younger man shrugged and spread his arm deprecatingly. "It's the way things are, Professor, the way they've been ever since the Jews came into our midst and set up their accursed state."

"You think so? I wonder. We have always fought among ourselves, we Arabs. Seemingly, when two Arabs get together it's to plot against a third. Then came Israel, and for the first time we were united because there was now someone we could hate more than we hated each other. All the brothers against our cousins—that's what the Israelis call us, you know, the cousins. But the plain truth is that Israel more or less made for peace among us for thirty years or more. Unfortunately, in recent years the effect has diminished, I suppose, because we have pretty much come to accept them, the fact of them, and we no longer think we can drive them into the sea. So we have Iraq fighting Iran, and Syria against Jordan, the Muslims against the Christians in Lebanon, and the Syrian PLO against Arafat's PLO, and Libya against Egypt and Chad and everybody else. If the Jews hadn't come, we would have had to invent them just to keep us from killing each other off."

Abdul looked at him doubtfully and then smiled. "You know, I can't tell if you're fooling or serious."

"Oh, I'm serious, all right. Look, Abdul, we are Druse, Ibrahim and I."

"So am I, from Lebanon."

"Very well. Now, we Druse have followed the principle of being loyal to the country where we happen to reside. So your people were loyal to Lebanon when there was a Lebanon, because that's where your people live, and I am now loyal to the United States, because I am an American. But my people come from the Galilee, from Israel, and are loyal to Israel. If I had not come here as a child, I might have fought in the Israeli army along with other members of our clan. However, with respect to the rest of the Arab world, my loyalties are primarily with the Druse in whatever country they happen to live. Right now, the Israelis are the least we have to worry about. They're out of Lebanon and are not likely to come back. We could be friends with them."

Abdul looked at him doubtfully. "That's a funny way to talk."

"Why?" He smiled, showing even, white teeth between his moustache and imperial.

"Does Ibrahim know you feel this way?"

"Ibrahim and I are like brothers. We disagree from time to time, but we have no secrets from each other. And he agrees with me that it would have been a good thing if the Israelis had allied themselves with the Druse instead of with the Christians when they invaded Lebanon. That was a mistake on their part, and they know it now. They had been so successful with Haddad's Christian army, they thought they could do the same with Jemael. But Haddad's men were farmers, whereas Jemael's are merchants, who would sell their grandmothers if they saw a profit. It did not work out well for them." He shook his head sadly. "And it was bad for the Druse. We are unarmed and subject to pressure from all sides, from the Syrians and from the Christians, and from the Sunnis and the Shiites. And anyone who supplies us with arms expects us to use them as they direct, against *their* enemies."

"That's just the point," Abdul agreed. "We need arms to protect ourselves, and we have a chance of getting them with no strings attached." He dropped his voice to little more than a whisper. "The PLO cached an enormous supply of weapons in the Bekaa Valley, enough to equip an army. They had a squad unloading tons of rifles, mortars, even small artillery, and ammunition in a cave. Then they booby-trapped the whole area."

"And then?"

"And then they assassinated the entire squad."

El Dhamouri nodded. "Not surprising, considering the makeup of the PLO. It's what pirates are supposed to have done when they buried treasure."

"But one man got away. He says he expected it and took precautions. He managed not only to get away but also to get out of the country. He made a rough map of the location of the

23

cache and of the location of the mines that were set. It's more
a set of directions than a regular map. He finally landed in San
Francisco and came to see Ibrahim."

"He gave him the map, the directions? Ibrahim has
them?"

"He sold them to Ibrahim. He will be paid when we get
the cache."

"And what if he approaches someone else with the offer?"

Ibn Hosni smiled. "No, he can't do that. Until it is found,
he will remain a—er—guest of Ibrahim's. He says his motive
is revenge, and we are inclined to believe him. But also he
needs the money for a stake."

"I see. But he might have approached someone else before he came to Ibrahim."

"He says not, but it's possible that he's lying."

"In which case, you may have been followed."

"I don't think so. I—I'm experienced at this sort of thing."

"This map, the directions, you have it with you?"

"I left them in the deposit vault at the hotel."

"I guess that's pretty safe. You'll be there until they're
dispatched?"

"That's right."

"Why couldn't you take them to Mahmoud in Jerusalem
yourself? Couldn't you get a visa?"

"I probably could. But I am known, as are the other pro-
fessionals. I'd be searched when I landed in Tel Aviv, and I'd
be watched by their Shin Bet every minute of the time I was
in Israel."

"What if you were just to mail it to Mahmoud?"

"He is known. He's sure his mail is opened. That's why
Ibrahim thought of you. Here you are a professor at Harvard.
There are archaeologists and anthropologists coming and going to half a dozen places in the Near East all the time. He
thought you might be able to persuade one of them to deliver
a letter to your cousin in Jerusalem without too much trouble.
You could tell him it's about some family matter."

"Then why wouldn't I just write to him?"

"Oh, you know, everyone makes fun of the mail. You could tell him it's important, and you don't trust the mails."

El Dhamouri canted his head to one side and took thought. "Yes, I could make that convincing, I think. Professor Wilson is going shortly to Jordan but will also visit Israel. But would I be putting him in any danger?"

"Why would anyone think of interfering with a Professor Wilson of Harvard?"

"I don't suppose anyone would. Still . . . Look, I'll speak to him. I'll be seeing him tonight at the Faculty Club. Suppose you drop by tomorrow at about this time, and I'll let you know the results. If he can't manage, there's another possibility. See me tomorrow."

The next day, when Ibn Hosni appeared, he was dressed in faded blue jeans, a tennis shirt, and well-scuffed sneakers. Professor El Dhamouri nodded approvingly as he ushered him into the inner office. Once again he latched the outer door. When he resumed his seat behind his desk, he said, "I'm afraid Professor Wilson is out. Funding problems. Maybe in the fall."

"We can't wait that long."

"Well, there's another possibility. Professor Grenish of Northhaven College—that's a small college about thirty miles north of Boston—he's making a tour of the Mideast. Greece, the islands, then Israel and on to Egypt. But planning to be in Jerusalem for a while."

"But he's going to Greece first?"

"So I understand."

Ibn Hosni shook his head vigorously. "Mahmoud would never approve of having someone gallivanting around for a couple of weeks with the map in his coat pocket or in one of his bags in a hotel room. He could get robbed—"

"Oh, my idea was not to give it to him to take along with him. We'd send it to his hotel in Jerusalem. See, it would be waiting for him when he checks in. Or it would arrive in a day or two. It would be addressed to him and would be from me,

25

or better still, from one of his students, preferably a Jewish student. When he gets the letter, he goes to the Old City, wanders around like any tourist until he arrives at the Mideast Trading Corporation. He looks at the curios in the window, and Mahmoud invites him to come inside, where there are more interesting wares, and when they are alone together, he hands him the letter."

"We-el, I don't know."

"It's safer than having the man carry it on his person. And in one respect, he's better than Wilson. Wilson knows some Arabic. He might be tempted to open my letter out of idle curiosity. Grenish doesn't know any Arabic."

"Grenish, Grenish, what's his first name?"

"Abraham."

"Abraham Grenish, sounds—"

"Jewish? He is. Which means he offers an excellent cover."

"But—but how . . . Is he a friend of yours?"

"Sort of." He smiled genially. "Some of my best friends are Jews." He chuckled as he saw consternation in the other's face. "That's an inside joke among Jews. But don't worry about Abe Grenish. I met him at a meeting of the Arab Friendship League."

"What was he doing there?"

"Showing his sympathy and support for the Arab cause. He's liberal. You know how it is with those liberals, originally they were devoted to the cause of Communist Russia. And when it became manifest to the most willing true believer that Russia was not a worker's paradise, they transferred their allegiance and hopes to Communist China. And when Chairman Mao turned out to have feet of clay, then to Castro, and then to Ho Chi Minh, and so on. It's a constant search for an underdog to support and glorify. Grenish's support of the Arab cause against Israel manifests even greater idealism, since he is himself a Jew, although I suppose he was doing the same sort of thing when he glorified Stalin. It's not an uncommon phenomenon."

"And he's a good friend of yours?"

"Well, I've maintained contact with him."

"But why?"

"Oh, it might come in handy one day to have a Jewish friend. Like right now."

"What do you propose to do?"

"I think I'll call him and invite him to dinner at the Faculty Club. He enjoys dining with me at the Harvard Faculty Club. And after dinner, over a brandy, perhaps, I'll sound him out about delivering a letter for me to my cousin in Jerusalem about a family matter."

4

WHILE THE SIGN ABOVE THE WINDOWS SAID BARNARD'S Crossing Supermarket, it was usually referred to as Goodman's. And though it was set up like a supermarket with price-marked merchandise on shelves for self-service and with shopping carts and a checkout counter, it was a small store, and its customers used it largely for last-minute purchases, things they had forgotten in their regular shopping at the large chain supermarket. It was a friendly store where the customers might stand around and gossip as they waited their turn at the delicatessen counter, and where they expected a lot of personal service, as in "Hey, Louis, you got any more of those canned peaches I like? I don't see them on the shelf." Or, "Could you have someone put that stuff in my car, Louis? I got to run next door for a minute."

And though Louis Goodman as proprietor was supposed to be engaged in purely managerial functions, nevertheless he would frequently take the bag of groceries out to the car rather than call a stockboy, whom he would have to tell in just which car the groceries were to be put. He was a tall man, loosely put together, with a flexible face permanently set in a smile. As he often said, "In this business a sour puss is worse than having your prices out of line." And his wife, Rose, plump and round-cheeked, who sat at the checkout counter, might get off her stool and dodge around the counter, and picking up a can from the shelf, call, "They're right here, Mrs. Sachs. You want one can or two?"

From the casual gossip at the store, they heard of the Smalls' intended trip to Israel. And at dinner, and afterward until they went to bed, they discussed it.

"How can I go to see him? I'm not even a member of his temple."

"So what? So does that mean you can't ask him for a favor?"

"But how do I know he's even going to Jerusalem? Maybe he's going to Haifa or to Tel Aviv. Seems to me, I heard someone say he's got an aunt in Tel Aviv. So maybe they're going there."

"Could be, Louis, but a rabbi, he'd have to go to Jerusalem, if only for a visit."

"So if he's going for a day, for instance, he'll have time to go to see our Jordon?"

"Look, you could ask. If he's going to be busy, so he'll tell you, or he'll tell you he'll try but he can't promise. The most he can do is refuse."

"The Levinsons are going to Israel. I could ask them."

"The Levinsons? What would they know about the kind of situation our Jordon is in?"

"Well, they could look him up and talk to him. They could look around and see what kind of place it is. After all, he's in the real-estate business; he can size up a neighborhood."

"Is that what we're interested in, Louis, if Jordan is living in a good neighborhood? Tell me, why are you so hostile to Rabbi Small? The other day when he came in for a carton of milk, you didn't even look at him while you were checking him out at the register."

"So I'm hostile to him. I'm hostile to him because my customers are hostile to him, that's why."

"Ah, the fancy-shmancy ladies."

"We make a living from these fancy-shmancy ladies, Rose, and don't you forget it. Besides, I got my own reasons. When

29

I made up the sandwiches for Mrs. Seltzer's meeting a couple of weeks back, the rabbi wouldn't eat it on account he said it wasn't kosher."

"What do you expect? It isn't kosher. We call it kosher-type—"

"Sure, but he didn't have to say so. Couldn't he just say he wasn't hungry or he was on some special diet? No, he had to come right out and say kosher-type isn't kosher. Everybody knew it was from our store."

"So because the rabbi tells the truth, which it is the same truth you tell if somebody asks, you won't ask him about the welfare of your own son, about his future, where he's, you might call it, a specialist on the subject?"

"All right, all right already. If he should come in the store—"

"How often does he come in the store? No, you got to call him and make an appointment."

"I'm not calling to make an appointment with no rabbi."

"So, I'll call. I'll call Mrs. Small. She's a darling. Whenever she comes in, she's nice and pleasant. She don't throw her weight around, or act like she's doing us a favor. I'll call her and ask her could we come to see her and her husband."

They sat and sipped at the tea that Miriam had served, talking of the weather and about politics, about the tourists who were beginning to arrive, and the problems they posed for the year-round residents, especially for the storekeepers.

"We're going to be tourists in Jerusalem," said Miriam, "so I'll keep in mind what you said."

"Ah, I—we have a son in Jerusalem," said Louis.

"Really? You mean he lives there? He's got a job there? He's made *aliyah?*" asked the rabbi.

"Well, I don't know if you could call it a job. It's something more in your line. He's at a yeshiva. He lives there. I guess they feed and house him while he's studying. We thought you might look him up."

"You want to know if—"

"Everything." Rose Goodman interrupted. "If he's getting enough to eat. If it's a decent place. What kind of people are they? What do they expect of him? What's his future there?"

"See, Rabbi," said her husband, "we don't know anything about it. All we know is from a letter he wrote us. It was the first we heard he was even in Israel. He writes and tells us he's in Jerusalem, and he's made arrangements to go back to his roots and his religion—"

"A Baal Tshuvah," the rabbi murmured.

"Yeah, that's the expression he used. And from what he wrote—I should have brought the letter—I got to thinking he might be in a place like the Christians have. You know, where they pray all day—"

"A monastery?"

"Yeah, something like that. Of course, I realize that from your point of view, that's all to the good. And maybe if he got to be a rabbi, that would be all right. But you don't know my Jordon. He takes on things, but he doesn't stick to them. So what happens if after a few years he gets tired of it? So then where will he be? A man has to have a trade or a profession—"

Rose took up the argument. "We're ordinary people, Rabbi. We want him to get married and make a living and have a family."

"Oh, they'll see to it that he gets married and has a family," said the rabbi. "They're strong on these things, and they arrange them. Have no fear on that score. But tell me about him. How old is he? What's his previous training?"

"He's twenty-four. Growing up, he was a good boy, never gave us any trouble, got good marks in school. He even got a scholarship to go to college, to Northhaven, which was nice because it was near so he could live at home. Naturally, we were proud. Maybe he'd become a doctor or a lawyer or a scientist. So everything is going along fine, and then in his third year, everything falls apart. He gets into some kind of trouble at the school, and first thing we know, he's dropping out and he's going out West where some friend of his from

college, his folks have a mine, a gold mine, which it is now—
at that time—worthwhile on account gold is up to eight hundred dollars an ounce.

"So it seems crazy, but he's got all kinds of figures and
statistics, and a boy twenty years old, you can hold him if he
wants to leave? Well, gold didn't stay at eight hundred dollars
an ounce, and between you, I, and that lamp over there,
maybe even a thousand dollars an ounce wouldn't be enough
to make that mine workable. So next we hear he's in Utah,
and then in California. You understand, we don't hear more
than once in four, five months. Once, he's with a group that's
getting back to the soil. Another time, he's with a group that
call themselves Children of the Sun on account everything
comes from the sun. And he sends us a picture yet showing
him wearing a long white gown with a yellow sun with rays on
the chest. Then he's someplace where they live according to
the wisdom of the East. By East, you understand, he doesn't
mean here in New England, but India or Japan, maybe. Next
we hear he's waiting for a passport, he's going to South America.

"If I could, I would have gone to see him. But never an
address or a phone number. And how could I leave Rose to
handle the store alone? And how do I know he'd be there
when I got there?"

"And could I leave Louis alone to look out for himself
while *I* went?" asked Rose.

"Next thing, we get this letter from Israel. He's in a yeshiva." He stopped abruptly and looked at the rabbi expectantly.

"Do you know where the yeshiva is? What's it called?"

"It's called the American Yeshiva, and it's in the Abu Tor
section of Jerusalem."

"How much Jewish education did your son have?"

Rose answered. "He went to Hebrew School in Salem,
where we used to live, until he was Bar Mitzvahed. How
much he learned, or how much he remembers, I wouldn't
know."

32

Louis felt it was up to him to explain. "We're not religious, Rabbi. I mean, we're not pious. My wife keeps a kosher home because that's what she was brought up to. When we go out to a restaurant, we're not so careful. We go to the Orthodox shul in Salem because that's where we always went. That's where we go on Rosh Hashonah and Yom Kippur, and on some of the other holidays, but not all, I admit it."

"I understand."

"When I go, I *daven* because that's how I was brought up. I don't know what the words mean, but I say them anyway because you're supposed to. When I was a kid, I had a rebbe come in a couple of times a week to teach me how to read, and to prepare me for my Bar Mitzvah. I would have done the same for my Jordan, but all the neighbors were sending their kids to the Hebrew School, so I did the same. But from what I could tell, he didn't learn much Hebrew there. Oh, they taught him some stories from the Bible, and about the holidays, and to read in Hebrew. But that was all. So when he wanted to quit after he was thirteen, I didn't object. What good would it have done where he wasn't interested?"

The rabbi nodded. "I get the picture. All right, I'll look him up and have a talk with him."

"Ask him if he's happy, Rabbi," Rose urged. "And if he wants to come home. If he needs money for the plane, tell him we'll send him."

It was at the Goodman store, while waiting her turn at the delicatessen counter, that Mollie Berkowitz heard of the rabbi's intended trip to Israel. When she mentioned it to her husband, he was outraged. He shook his head in disbelief. "Are you sure? He and his wife, the both of them are going? My offer of a couple of free tickets, and all expenses paid, he wouldn't accept. He was afraid maybe I might ask him to pay it back with interest someday?"

"Oh, Barney, I'm sure it's nothing like that. I heard they were planning to stay all summer."

"So?"

"So you were offering a trip for ten days, two weeks maybe. So naturally he wasn't interested."

"So he couldn't talk to me about it? He couldn't say, 'I'm planning to spend the whole summer, Mr. Berkowitz, so how about I swap your ticket for one I can return in September. I'll pay the difference.' So I would have said, 'No, you got to return the same time I do?' Forty years, forty-two years, I was a successful businessman. Somebody would come in to sell me a bunch merchandise. Say he tells me it's five hundred a gross. So do I show him to the door because I think the price is too high? No, I tell him it's very nice merchandise, but I can't pay more than four hundred. So then, does he walk out? No, he says he can maybe shave the price to four seventy-five. And I say maybe I can see my way to paying four and a quarter. So he comes down a little more, and I come up a little, and we finally settle for four-fifty. That's how you deal with people."

In the days that followed, he reverted to the subject again and again. While at table with his wife, he might say, "I keep hearing he's such a great scholar." There was no need for her to ask whom he was referring to. "So I figure when he turns down my offer, must be he's planning to spend the summer studying, take a course at Harvard, maybe, or go into Boston every day to the library. No. Turns out he's going for vacation. To the same place I invited him. Go figure it."

Or, "Time to time, on the Board, over the years, we kept hearing how we weren't paying him enough. How other synagogues were paying their rabbis more. He never looked to me like he was hungry. His wife, she always dressed nice. But every time was a vote for a raise, I went along. Why? Because a rabbi needs more than food and clothing. Like I said to some of the members of the Board, 'Boys, he's got to buy a book sometime or go to maybe a conference of rabbis in New York, for instance, or even take a trip to Israel to like recharge his batteries.' And when the vote was close, believe me my vote didn't do him no harm. So when I offered to finance a trip to Jerusalem, what I had in mind . . ."

*　*　*

And in the Small household, Miriam said, "Don't you think, David, you ought to call Mr. Berkowitz and thank him for offering to pay our . . ." She trailed off as the rabbi shook his head vigorously. "Why not?"

"In the first place, Miriam, Berkowitz didn't offer it. Al Bergson did, or rather he said Berkowitz was making the offer. As far as I'm concerned, it's only hearsay."

"Still, I think you ought to call him."

"Then he'd invite me to the celebration, and I want no part of it."

"Still . . ."

The rabbi shook his head.

5

AT FORTY-TWO ABRAHAM GRENISH WAS MADE FULL PROFES-
sor of history at Northhaven College and felt that at last he
had arrived. To be sure, Northhaven was not Harvard, nor
even Tufts or Boston University, but as he explained, not for
him were the dryasdust scholarship and the publish-or-perish
syndrome of the larger universities. He was a teacher, by
God, and he preferred a leisurely life-style.

When he had first come to Northhaven as an assistant
professor, he had managed to find lodging with a family in the
vicinity. It was far from ideal; there were children, and it was
noisy. But there were no more desirable accommodations in
the area, and ultimately he was forced to go to Barnard's
Crossing, about twenty-five miles away. There he was able to
rent a small cottage and engage a woman to come in every
day. She cleaned, and she cooked his dinner. Breakfast, coffee and a roll, he prepared himself, and his lunch he ate in the
faculty cafeteria at school. But the rent of the house and paying the woman strained his resources, and he found it necessary to piece out his salary by teaching in the Summer Session
and in the Late Afternoon Classes and even going to Boston to
give lectures for the Lowell Institute of Education.

As he advanced in rank, his salary was increased accord-
ingly, and he was able to drop first the Late Afternoon Classes,

then the Summer Session, and finally, when he was made full professor, the Lowell Institute lectures. And now at last he was able to afford and had the time to travel.

And then trouble started. He had his annual physical checkup and the doctor discovered he had an aneurysm of the abdominal aorta. The doctor arranged for an ultrasound of the abdomen and afterward reported, "It's about four and a half centimeters. We don't usually do anything if it's under five except watch it."

"And if it's five centimeters?"

"Ah, then we have to operate."

"There's no medication or—"

"That will shrink it?" The doctor shook his head. "But while it's a major operation, the success rate is somewhere between ninety-five and ninety-eight percent. However, no need to worry about it at the moment."

"But I've had no symptoms, no pain, nothing."

The doctor nodded. "No, it's usually discovered on routine medical examination. If you feel pain, bellyache or backache, it means there's seepage or a rupture. Then it's usually too late, unless you're very near a hospital and a competent surgeon at the time. We'll look at it in another four or five months—"

"And I don't have to do anything about it? No special diet?"

The doctor shook his head. Then he chuckled. "I don't suppose you do any boxing, do you?"

"Hardly. Why?"

"Well, a punch in the belly probably wouldn't do you any good."

"All right. I'll avoid fisticuffs." Grenish managed to smile.

The feeling of uncertainty and dread was lessened a few months later when he had another ultrasound taken and it was found that there had been no appreciable increase in the size of the aneurysm. And with each successive examination, taken at three-month intervals, over the course of the year, there was no change and his fear had practically dissipated. But now

37

he wondered if it would be wise to take the trip to the Mideast that he had planned. He put the matter up to the doctor.

"How long are you planning to be gone?"

"About a month."

"Oh, I think it would be all right. Where are you planning to go?"

"The Mideast, Greece, and Israel."

"Well, I can give you a report on your condition that you can show to a doctor there. I don't imagine you'd have difficulty getting competent medical help in Greece, at least not in Athens, and also in Israel. Are you going to Jerusalem? I can give you the name of a doctor there."

So Grenish confirmed his arrangements with his travel agent, who gave him further assurance that adequate medical assistance was always available.

A couple of days before he was scheduled to depart, he got a call from El Dhamouri.

"Abe? El Dhamouri. You all packed and ready to go?"

"Not all packed. I've got all day tomorrow, but I've taken care of everything else."

"And this business in the belly you told me about?"

"You mean my triple A?"

"Triple A?"

"Yes, that's what I call it, aneurysm of the abdominal aorta. It's fine. I was examined only a few days ago. No change."

"And you can eat everything? You're not on a diet of any kind?"

"No, no restrictions at all."

"Good. Do you know the Château on Route Ninety-three? It's a very nice restaurant. I'll pick you up."

"But I'm going to be here at Northhaven and it's out of your way. I could meet you there."

"No, Abe, I'll pick you up. I thought we'd have a few drinks, and we might get carried away, in which case it might not be wise for either of us to drive. I'll pick you up."

Of course, Grenish felt pleased and flattered at this evidence of El Dhamouri's regard for him. And his pride was almost bursting when El Dhamouri's chauffeur-driven limousine drew up to the Northhaven Faculty Club and several of his colleagues saw him enter as the uniformed chauffeur held the door for him.

They ate leisurely, sipping at the wines El Dhamouri ordered, so that at no time did Grenish have the feeling of uncomfortable fullness. They talked largely of academia and of their problems with their respective administrations and colleagues. In the back of his mind, Grenish had the sense that it was not purely out of friendship that El Dhamouri was giving him dinner at this obviously very expensive restaurant, that he wanted something of him, perhaps to deliver the letter he had mentioned in an earlier meeting. But El Dhamouri said nothing, and it was Grenish himself who finally brought it up over their coffee.

"Was there a letter you wanted me to deliver to someone in Jerusalem? You mentioned it a couple of weeks ago."

"Oh, yes, to my cousin. But I haven't received the information I need as yet. It may take another week or two."

"Then you'll just mail it to him?"

"No-o, I can't do that. My cousin thinks his mail is being intercepted"—he chuckled— "by his wife's sister, who lives with them and who he claims has the evil eye, and perhaps by one or more of his clerks, whom he thinks she might have subverted, and maybe even by his wife. You see, this is a matter of clan lands and . . ." He broke off as a thought struck him. "Look, according to that itinerary you showed me, you are planning to be in Jerusalem for about a week at the Excelsior, I think you said. So why can't I send it to you?"

"Okay."

"It will probably be there when you arrive, or it will arrive in a day or two. By the way, why are you spending so much time in Jerusalem? Do you have anyone there? Family?"

Grenish colored. "Hardly family. There was a girl I used to know living there. She chose to marry a religious type, and they immigrated to Israel. I thought I might look her up, maybe take them out to dinner."

El Dhamouri waggled a finger at him." An old flame, eh? And if the husband is busy, or is out of town when you come to call . . ." He smiled indulgently. "Ah, well, you'll be on vacation. But to get to my business, when you get my letter you will go to the Old City, and if you enter by Jaffa Gate, which is the one most tourists use, you will be facing David Street. You walk down David Street looking at the shop windows like any tourist until you come to Muristan Street and next is the Shuk El Lohamin. There you will see the Mideast Trading Corporation. The windows have the usual tourist goods, little carvings in olive wood and mother-of-pearl, leather bags, sheepskin vests. You show a little interest, asking prices, perhaps, and go inside to look at the better merchandise in the back."

"Your cousin will be alone in the shop?"

"No, he has several clerks, but he's sure to be around. You will give the letter only to him, and preferably when you are alone with him."

"Should I ask for him?"

"No-o, I don't think so. If you're an ordinary tourist you wouldn't be likely to know him, would you?"

"Then how—"

El Dhamouri smiled. "How would you know him? No problem. He's about my age but looks older. And he has a bad squint in one eye."

Grenish wondered if his friend wasn't being boyishly romantic about a simple matter of delivering a letter. "All right, I get a letter from you at the Excelsior and—"

"Not from me, my friend. My name on the envelope might draw attention to it by—by various people. Do you know Elmer Levy?"

"Of Harvard? The physicist? I know of him, of course, but I've never met him."

"Fine. Then the letter will come from Professor Levy. So when you get a letter from Levy—Harvard Faculty Club stationery, probably—you just take it down to the Old City and drop it off with my cousin Mahmoud."

"That's all? There'll be no reply? No message he'll want me to convey to you?"

"Nothing." He smiled. "Except that if you see something in his shop that interests you, perhaps some beads or a pin for your old girlfriend, I'm sure he'll give you a good price on it. Oh, and write me if you have a chance. Your first time in Greece, right? And you'll be there for a couple of weeks? It will be interesting to hear how the country strikes you."

6

IN A STUDIO APARTMENT IN A HIGH-RISE CONDOMINIUM THAT was already beginning to show signs of wear even though it had been erected only half a dozen years previously, two men sat playing chess. Except for a couple of cots, two easy chairs, two straight-backed chairs, and a low coffee table, the apartment was bare. In the Pullman kitchenette there was a microwave oven, a coffee percolator, and a few glass dishes.

Avram, a man of sixty, sat in one of the easy chairs, the coffee table jammed up against his knees as he studied the chessboard. Gavriel, a good twenty-five years younger, sat opposite him on a straight-backed chair. He reached forward, then drew his hand back, and then nodding, reached forward and made his move. "Check," he announced. "And if you interpose with the knight, I move my queen up and—"

"All right. You've got a win. That's, let's see, three out of seven today. Your game is improving. A coffee, maybe?"

The phone rang. Gavriel scooped it up from where it was resting on the floor. "Yes?"

He listened for a moment, said "Right," and hung up. "Yossi," he announced to the older man. "El Dhamouri picked up Professor Grenish at the Northhaven Faculty Club. In his limousine, no less. And took him to the Château on Route

Ninety-three for dinner. Very swank, very expensive, the Château."

"How did Yossi know they went to the Château? Surely he didn't follow them."

"Oh, he didn't have to. Grenish was not making any secret of it."

"All right, we'll pass it on."

"I suppose we have to, but did it ever occur to you, Avram, that we pass on an awful lot of junk that has no significance whatsoever?"

"Sure, but they feed it into a computer and you'd be surprised at what they come up with occasionally. In this case, though, we have two, each on one of our lists, and they're meeting. That's an intersection, so it's automatically interesting."

"Why? They're friends. And we've reported meetings between them several times. One only a couple of weeks ago at the Harvard Faculty Club."

"Which makes it a continuing situation, not just a chance encounter, and that makes it all the more interesting for us. Have you ever seen this Professor Grenish?"

"Sure. I attended a couple of those public lectures he gave at the Boston Library."

"And how did he strike you?"

"He didn't strike me at all. I thought he was pretty dull and colorless. I didn't fall asleep, but if I had, I wouldn't have missed anything."

"That's right. That's exactly right. A dull, colorless, mediocre sort of man. The only reason he's on our list is his membership on the Arab Friendship League. I think his name is on the stationery as a member of their Board of Trustees."

"So what? There are quite a few of these Jewish radical intellectuals who are sympathetic to the Arabs because the new Left is pro-Arab and they don't want to be shunted off as has-beens."

"Sure, and the Mossad likes to keep a general watch on them. Nothing intensive, but an occasional glance in their direction. But here we have a dull, colorless sort of fellow who is being cultivated by a rich, flamboyant personage like El Dhamouri. Why? What could El Dhamouri see in the likes of Grenish? Now, we are naturally interested in El Dhamouri because he is rich and has status and so he's bound to be contacted by various Arab groups, if only for financial help."

"Sure, but they always meet in a public place. There's no report of secret meetings."

"That's right. It's never at his home, where only someone who happened to see him enter or leave would know about it. It's always in a public place, like the Faculty Club or a restaurant, and now the Château. Why? Because he wants to be seen with him? What would he gain by it?"

"But Grenish would gain," said Gavriel, "so maybe he's the one who sets it up."

"You mean Grenish would call him and say, 'Invite me for lunch at the Harvard Faculty Club, or for dinner at the Château'? That's not very likely. Damn close to impossible, I'd say, unless Grenish has something on him. No. I think that El Dhamouri is aware of how Grenish feels about being seen with him. He's a name-dropper, is our friend Grenish—"

"Yes, even in those lectures."

"Right, so El Dhamouri not only takes him to places where a lot of people will see them together, but the right kind of people, like faculty people at Harvard. And he picks him up in his limousine at the Northhaven Faculty Club, where Grenish's colleagues will see them, and lets him know in advance that they're going to the Château, so that Grenish can mention it while waiting. I think that El Dhamouri is not merely cultivating him, he's buttering him up. And that could be very interesting."

In the Watertown section of Boston, in the back room of a mom-and-pop variety store, the elderly proprietor was having his lunch while his wife waited on trade. As he stared blankly at the curtain that separated the room from the store—the curtain billowed as the outer door opened and closed—he chewed mechanically at a bit of meat, his whole face contracting, collapsing each time he bit.

His wife parted the curtain enough to poke her head in. "Ali," she said.

"Have him come in."

A stout young man with a round red face sidled into the room. He doffed the linen cap he was wearing and held it against his chest with both hands as he looked uncertainly at the old man who stared back at him. After a moment, the old man nodded toward one of the plastic soda bottle carriers that were the sole furniture of the room, serving as both chairs and a table for the old man's lunch. Ali nodded gratefully and sat down. Leaning forward eagerly, he said, "El Dhamouri was at the Château last night. He was with another man. Not one of us."

"Did you hear what they were talking about?"

"I am in the kitchen," he said deprecatingly. "But Giuseppe waited on them."

"And did the Italian hear anything?"

"Only that the other one was going on a trip to the Mideast and would be in Jerusalem."

"And his name?"

"Giuseppe said he called him 'My dear Grenish.' "

"Anything said about when he was leaving?"

"Giuseppe got the impression that it was the next day—that is, today."

"That's it? Anything else?"

Ali's small mouth spread into a wide smile and his fat cheeks all but concealed his eyes. "Only that in Jerusalem, he will be staying at the Excelsior."

"At the Excelsior! Well, well, well. Very considerate of him. Very good, Ali. I am pleased. You will let the Italian know. Do something for him if you can. A present, perhaps. Maybe a little hashish, or a girl."

7

BETWEEN THE JEWISH RABBI OF BARNARD'S CROSSING AND its Catholic chief of police, Hugh Lanigan, there was a friendship that went back to the first year the rabbi had arrived in town. At first the relationship had been purely official, and over the years there had developed a number of situations that called for the police chief to see the rabbi on official business. But there were also any number of occasions when the police chief would ring the bell of the Small residence and say, "I was in the neighborhood," and either the rabbi or Miriam, whoever opened the door, immediately ushered him into the living room and set about brewing tea or coffee. And similarly, when the rabbi happened to be downtown, walking along Main Street on a summer's afternoon, he was apt to be hailed by Hugh Lanigan taking his ease on the front porch of his house, and when the rabbi opened the gate, Lanigan would call out to his wife, "David Small, Amy. Rustle up some drinks, will you?"

With a ruddy, square face surmounted by prematurely white hair cut in a whiffle so that at the top, pink scalp was visible, Hugh Lanigan was not much older than Rabbi Small. Although his formal education beyond high school had consisted of only a few college extension courses, he was of an intellectual and even philosophical turn of mind, and he enjoyed talking to the rabbi about their respective religions. That the rabbi's insight had occasionally been of professional interest and help to the police chief served to cement their friendship all the more strongly.

So it was not to be wondered at that the Lanigans were guests at the home of the Smalls at dinner one evening shortly before their departure for Israel. The talk had been general, but now, over coffee, they talked about the coming trip.

"It would be nice if we could make the trip sometime, Hugh," said Amy, "and see all those ancient places. You can actually go to the place of the Last Supper—"

"The Church of the Dormition," remarked Miriam. "It's in the Old City near the Wall."

"How about it, Hugh?" Amy persisted. She was a fine-looking woman, tall and trim with dark brown hair just beginning to silver. She had little wrinkles around the eyes, which were dark and protruded so that she looked somewhat surprised at all times.

"You could have gone on that trip that Father Callahan led a couple of years ago," said her husband.

"Oh, it was a bunch of old women, male and female. I want to go with you." To her hosts, she confided, "Hugh never takes his full vacation."

"I've never really had a chance to," he explained defensively. "Something always comes up that I feel I should stay on top of. Besides, I'd just as soon let some of my vacation time accumulate for when I retire so that I can take my whole last year off."

"But that's not for quite a while yet," said his wife.

"But I've got to plan for it. Then maybe we can do some traveling."

"Grace Bryant went on that trip," said his wife, "and she came back with all kinds of things she bought."

"Yeah," said Lanigan, "a bunch of junk. Jim Bryant said that whenever the bus stopped, she was the first one off the bus, buying little knickknacks they make for the tourists. She had bottles of colored sand, mother-of-pearl stuff, and little carvings in olive wood of camels and crucifixes. I'll bet most of it was made in Hong Kong or Taiwan."

"No," said the rabbi. "They have factories there, Bethlehem and Jerusalem, where they make it."

"All right, so they make it there. It still is a bunch of junk," said Lanigan good-naturedly.

"That cross she had, that was a nice thing. There were four little crosses, one at each corner—"

"Oh, yes," said the rabbi. "A Jerusalem cross. I believe the four small crosses are supposed to represent the four knightly orders that governed Jerusalem during the Crusader period. I suppose Jerusalem is where you're most likely to get them."

"Could you get me one, David, while you are over there?" asked Amy Lanigan.

"It might not be quite proper for a rabbi to buy a cross," said her husband reprovingly.

"Oh, *he* wouldn't have to buy it. He could get someone to buy it for him," said Amy.

"I'll get it for you, Amy," said Miriam. "You just tell me what you want. Is it a pendant, or a pin, or—"

"Oh, would you, Miriam? Grace Bryant got a large silver one, but if you could get me a small one, on a chain—"

"You shall have it."

The rabbi reached into the inside breast pocket of his jacket for a pencil and his notebook and jotted down a memorandum, "Amy Lanigan—Jerusalem cross."

"Look, David," said Lanigan, "don't make a big thing out of it. Just if you happen to think of it. I'm sure Amy wouldn't want you to go to any trouble."

"Of course not—"

"It's all right," said Miriam. "David makes notes because he can't remember. But then he forgets to look at the notes. But I'll remember, Amy, and since I'll be getting it—"

"I suppose you've had a lot of requests from your congregation," said Lanigan.

The rabbi smiled as he flipped the pages of his notebook.

"Pills for her sister—Mrs. Gross; psychology book—Oscar Lamed; greetings—Mandelman family; notify Ben Levy re his brother Aaron—gall bladder operation successful; talk to and size up Ish-Tov, formerly Jordan Goodman—"

"Jordan Goodman? Louis Goodman's boy. I remember him," said Lanigan. "Is he over there? He changed his name?"

"He didn't so much change it as translate it. *Ish* means man and *tov* means good, so Ish-Tov is a translation of Goodman. He's become religious. What we call a Baal Tshuvah, in a yeshiva there."

"You mean like born again?"

"Sort of. You know him? Officially, I mean?"

"Oh, it was years ago. There's a professor at Northhaven lives here in town. We've got quite a few of them—professors, I mean—living here in town: Harvard, B.U., Northeastern, that's because they're about half an hour south of here. And Northhaven, which is about the same distance north. Well, this one had a picture window in his house broken. He called us about it. Said he was sure it was the Goodman boy. Had he seen him do it? No. Had anyone seen him? No, but the boy had threatened him. Seems he'd cut him off from his scholarship. The professor was on the Scholarship Committee, I gather. Naturally, we said we'd look into it. It wasn't what you'd call a high-priority item, what with there being no proof. But I sent someone down to see Louis a few days later and he reported back that the boy had left town. So maybe he did do it. And that was the end of it. I certainly wasn't going to put out an all-points bulletin over a broken window."

"That's all?"

"Yeah. Oh, then sometime later Louis came to see me about the boy. He had a snapshot of the boy in a long white gown and he was now a member of some crazy group in Arizona. Louis thought they might be a cult like the Moonies or the Hari Krishna and that maybe they brainwashed him and he might be a kind of prisoner. Well, of course, if he was being held against his will, I could notify the Arizona authorities. I *did* make some inquiries. According to the report I got they were supposed to be harmless. Some pot, maybe they even grew it. And, no doubt, some easygoing sex, but nothing the Arizona people were interested in doing anything about. So now he's turned back to his own religion, has he? Well, that's good. Louis and Rose must be happy."

"I'm not sure that they are. Things are not the same with us as with you. Your religion is grounded in faith, and re-turn—some sects use the term 'to be born again' meaning to recover one's faith, to believe once again. But our religion is a matter of obeying specific commandments. One who falls away from his religion doesn't stop obeying all the command-ments—thou shalt not kill, thou shalt not commit adultery, thou shalt not bear false witness—merely some of them. He may stop observing the Sabbath or obeying the dietary laws—or he may continue to obey those because they're apt to be a matter of dietary habit. . . ." The rabbi smiled. "If I con-verted to Christianity tomorrow, I still wouldn't be able to eat a lobster."

"I get it," said Lanigan. "You mean when they fall away and become atheistic they continue to obey the major com-mandments but don't bother with the minor ones."

"Well, in theory we don't distinguish between major com-mandments and minor ones. A commandment is a command-ment. Perhaps you might say the liturgical rather than the moral and ethical ones. But that's pretty much it."

"So when they become a whatdidyoucall it, a ballchew?"

"Baal Tshuvah," the rabbi said with a smile.

"Then he starts observing all the commandments? What sort of thing does he do?"

"Well, he might wear a *kipah*, a skullcap, all the time, and he's apt to stop shaving. 'Thou shalt not trim the corners of your beard.' And he'd be meticulous about reciting his prayers three times a day. He'd make sure to wash his hands and recite the blessings that are called for before eating. Most of all, I suppose he'd spend a good deal of time in study."

"Not in prayer?" asked Amy.

"No, we just recite the prayers that are enjoined on us.

50

There is no merit in repeating them. In fact, it might be considered to be taking the name of the Lord in vain."

"How about girls, women: Do they have to keep away from them?" asked Amy Lanigan.

"Pretty much, in the sense of socializing. But they're expected to marry and have lots of children."

"But if they don't socialize with girls," asked Amy, "how do they get to meet their wives?"

Miriam laughed. "There's always the matchmaker, the *shadchen*."

"And I suppose keeping them apart from women makes the matchmaker's job all the easier," suggested Lanigan. "But tell me, how do they make a living? Does this school train them for any profession? Do they become rabbis?"

"Some of them do, I suppose," said the rabbi. "It's a different kind of job there than it is here, though. It might involve being a clerk in one of the rabbinical courts, or a *mashgiach*, a sort of supervisor of the dietary laws in a hotel or restaurant, or a teacher. Some leave to go into some purely secular activity. Some just stay on."

"So what are you looking for when you go to see young Goodman?"

The rabbi shook his head. "His mother would like to know if he appears well fed and healthy. His father—I don't know. Perhaps whether there is any chance of his coming back. At least that's what I'd want to know if it were my Jonathon."

"You wouldn't want him to become one of those Baal—"

Rabbi Small shook his head vigorously.

"But why not?" asked Amy Lanigan. "It's a religious life, isn't it? I should think you of all people would want him to have a religious life if he could."

The rabbi chuckled. "Not really, not in the sense that you people use the term. I'm not a man of God or the spiritual leader of the congregation in the sense that a priest or a Protestant minister is. My duties are essentially secular. I am authorized to sit in judgment or to arbitrate on disputes, but no one ever comes to me to pass judgment. It has happened to me only once since I've been here. And even as to advising on matters pertaining to the proper way of observing the commandments, I am rarely called upon. The congregation here is not that meticulous in its observance. So I am largely confined to maintaining and teaching our tradition. My sermons are directed to that end, but I'm afraid fewer and fewer of my congregants care. Most of them regard the sermon as a break in the tedium of the service. We have a great respect for learning and study. After all, it's what distinguishes us from the lower animals. But to spend one's life in study in a yeshiva, as in a monastery or convent, is to shirk one's responsibility to the everyday world. We respect the learned, but we expect them to be involved in society and the world's work. Even our great sages of the Talmudic era all had secular jobs of one sort or another, some of them quite menial. You see, the practice of Judaism is essentially an amateur occupation."

"But if he received a call—" Amy urged.

"You mean the way Jonah did? 'Go preach to the people of Nineveh.' No. And if you remember, *he* was unwilling. When he finally did, he found it most unsatisfactory. God didn't destroy the city, which left him disgruntled and embarrassed."

"But you did, didn't you?" Amy persisted.

"Receive a call?" The rabbi smiled broadly. "Only from old Jacob Wasserman, the chairman of the Ritual Committee, at the time."

8

MIRIAM SLID OVER TO OCCUPY THE WINDOW SEAT. THE RABBI folded their coats and laid them out carefully in the luggage compartment above. "Do you want me to put your bag up there, too?" he asked.

"No, I'll keep it on the floor at my feet," said Miriam.

The rabbi took the middle seat, strapped himself in, and then fished in the pocket on the back of the seat in front of him for something to read. There was only the plastic card with the diagram of the plane and instructions on what to do in case of an emergency.

"The stewardess will be around soon with papers and magazines," said Miriam. She fished in her bag. "Or do you want to read my *Ladies' Home Journal?*"

"No. It's all right. I'll wait."

They watched as passengers moved down the aisle, some stopping to check seat numbers, some stopping to load hand luggage and coats into the baggage compartments and then to take their seats beneath. They wondered if it was a full plane, and if someone would take the aisle seat beside them, or if it would be left vacant so they could have an extra seat in which to stretch out.

They were not kept in uncertainty for long. A well-dressed man of medium height stopped at their row, checked the letters of the seats against the notation on his boarding pass, and smiling down at the rabbi, said, "I guess this is it." He placed the topcoat he was carrying over his arm and his carry-on case in the rack overhead and then sat down and buckled himself in. Almost immediately he took out a paperback from his jacket pocket and began to read. But a moment later he unbuckled himself and took off his suit jacket. As he folded it neatly before placing it in the rack overhead, the rabbi noted that his name, James Skinner, was embroidered on the inside breast pocket. Then once again he took his seat, buckled himself in, and opened his paperback.

The rabbi, having no reading matter to occupy him, found himself glancing covertly at his seatmate, wondering about his reason for going to Israel. He was obviously Gentile on the basis of both his appearance and his name. Was he traveling on business, or was he planning to tour the country? Was he, perhaps, a missionary, or a scholar? Perhaps he was an archaeologist who was planning to take part in one of the various digs that were being conducted in various parts of the country.

Miriam turned around to look toward the stewards' station and then asked, "Do you suppose they'll be serving soon, David?"

"On these late-night flights, just as soon as we're airborne, I imagine," said the rabbi.

A steward walked slowly up the aisle, his head turning from side to side, checking to see if everyone was strapped in, his seat back upright.

The rabbi's seatmate looked up from his book, and addressing the steward in Hebrew, he said, "You'll be serving almost immediately, won't you? I'm starved."

"We'll be serving drinks as soon as we're airborne," said the steward, "and dinner immediately after."

When the rabbi translated for Miriam, the stranger said, "Oh, you speak Hebrew?"

"Yes, I'm a rabbi. David Small. And this is my wife, Miriam."

54

"How do you do? I'm James Skinner."

"Yes, I know," said Rabbi Small. "I saw the name on your jacket." He chuckled. "When I saw the name, I assumed you weren't Jewish."

"I'm not."

"But you speak Hebrew."

"I was born in Jerusalem." He smiled. "So was my father, for that matter. We're from Minnesota originally and I still have"—he grinned—"*mishpacha* there."

"It was your grandparents who first came to Israel?" asked Miriam.

"Palestine, then," he corrected her. "But the Holy Land, in any case. That's right, they came because it *was* the Holy Land. It was a pilgrimage of faith. Actually, they were on their honeymoon. That was back in 1906 or '07."

"And they just stayed on?"

"Well, no. But Grandpa saw a chance to do some business there. His people were in the wholesale grocery business, and he had the bright idea of shipping out dried figs under the label 'Fruit from the Holy Land.' See, his family's business covered a good portion of northern Minnesota. That area of the country was pretty religious—still is, I reckon—and he figured anything from the Holy Land would sell."

"And did it?" asked the rabbi.

"It sure did. Not only did it sell well to the firm's regular customers, but it also gave them a toe-in to new territory. Later, Grandpa shipped other stuff—olives and olive oil, dates, almonds, saffron—a whole slew of stuff, nuts and dried fruits. Anything that would travel."

"And your grandfather stayed on?" asked Miriam.

"Oh, he came back to the States now and again, but his home was in Jerusalem. He liked the climate and he liked the area. I guess almost anything is preferable to a Minnesota winter. When I'm in the States I live in Boston, which is bad enough, but not nearly as bad as northern Minnesota. He, Grandpa, stayed in Palestine until his father died, and he went back to Minnesota permanently to handle the family

55

business. And, of course, by that time my father was old enough to take over the operation in Jerusalem. He had bought a house in Abu Tor, and we conducted our business from there. Then things began to get a bit sticky, too close to the Arab section, and we left the house and took an apartment in Rehavia, for safety, you understand."

"So your father opted for the Jewish side?"

Skinner laughed. "Not really. Of course, the Jews were the Chosen People, but on the other hand, they had repudiated the Christ. Then most of his business associates were Arabs. I guess he was inclined to be neutral, except that he did hate the British, and since they seemed to be anti-Jewish at the time, he tended to side with the Jews. You know, the enemy of my enemy is my friend. He was even of some assistance to the Haganah on occasion. My older sister and I had been sent back to the States, where we remained. I went to school in the States, which always was my father's intention. My sister never came back; she met someone and got married. I came back after the Six-Day War.

"Then, with the Old City now in the hands of the State of Israel, my father asked for our house in Abu Tor back. He had the deeds, you see, and there were some powerful people in the government who remembered the help my father had given the Haganah, so they let us have it. Maybe they would have anyway, since we had title, but it certainly didn't hurt to have helped the Haganah."

"And all this time your father carried on his export business?" asked Miriam.

Skinner laughed shortly. "The export business was deteriorating rapidly, and when the State was declared, it practically went down the drain."

"Why was that?" asked Miriam, puzzled.

"Figure it out for yourself. We had been offering the products of the Holy Land. It was unusual. It was exotic. And it was sort of religious. But then your people began exporting, and it was no longer rare or exotic, and since you were trying to establish markets and your farmers were working on a cooperative basis, you were selling the stuff cheaper."

"So what did your father do?"

"Oh, lots of things," said Skinner vaguely. "You see, he had contacts among the Arabs and he was able to put that to good use. For a while he was a sort of unofficial go-between for Israel and Iran. You'd be surprised at the amount of machinery that found its way to Israel from some of the Arab countries. My father had a hand in it. And—oh, lots of things."

"You use the past tense—"

"Yes, Father died a few years ago. I had been working with him for a couple of years, however, so I was able to carry on, since I knew his contacts and they knew me. And, of course, we still do some exporting, mostly honey and olive oil."

"And you live in Jerusalem?" asked Miriam. "I mean, that's your home?"

"No, my home, my official residence, is in Boston. But I do a lot of traveling, so I'm there not more than a few months in the year. This is my third trip to Israel this year. When I'm in the Mideast, then my home is in Jerusalem. I have offices there, and in Haifa, but Jerusalem is home base. From there I might go to Egypt, Jordan, Iran, anywhere in the area. I used to have to go to Crete first, but since the Israel-Egypt Peace Treaty, it's a lot easier. Where are you folks from?"

"We're from the Boston area," said Rabbi Small.

"From Barnard's Crossing," Miriam added.

"Oh, I've visited there. It's a nice town."

"We think so," said Miriam.

"A friend of mine had a boat that was anchored there. Ah, here's our dinner. Although it's kosher, they do you rather well on El Al."

"You would prefer nonkosher food?" asked the rabbi.

"No-o. When I stay in an Israeli hotel, I make a regular pig of myself on the breakfast, except that I like butter with my bread and cream with my coffee, and they can't give it to you if they're serving meat."

"I see." The rabbi tore off a bit of his roll, salted it, and recited the blessing. "Blessed art thou, O Lord . . . who brought forth bread from the earth."

"That's the *motze* you just recited, isn't it?" said Skinner to make conversation as much as to show that he had some knowledge of Jewish practice. "Now, my father would have said grace—"

"But you don't."

"No, I've been away from the Church too long to bother."

"You lose something by it," said the rabbi.

"How d'ya mean?"

"Well, the blessing that we offer, or your recital of grace, makes partaking of food something other than a mere refueling operation. It's one of the things that distinguishes us from the lower animals. We can enjoy our food. They can only satisfy hunger."

Skinner grinned. "Which is why we get fat and they don't, and die of diseases induced by being overweight and they don't."

"Of course," said the rabbi. "There is always a penalty for misusing a gift, for overdoing a virtue."

"I suppose." He nodded in the direction of a young bearded Hasid with earlocks who was sitting across the aisle and was only just now receiving a tray from the steward, one markedly different from those they had received. "That's a glad kosher meal he's getting, isn't it? I understand it's a superkosher meal."

The rabbi laughed. "Not glad. *Glatt.* It's a Yiddish word and means in the context strictly, strictly kosher."

"I should think you would have ordered the same thing, seeing as how you're a rabbi."

"It's because I am a rabbi that I didn't."

"Really?"

"You see," said the rabbi easily as he poured wine from the small bottle that had accompanied his meal into a plastic glass, "kosher refers not only to the species of animal that is permitted, the grazing animal that chews its cud as opposed to meat-eating predators, but it also refers to the condition of the animal and its method of slaughter. The slaughterer, the *shohet,* is an observant and learned man and he performs his work on the animal painlessly. He uses a knife of razor sharpness. If there is a nick on the edge that would impede the movement of the knife ever so little but that might cause pain, the animal is rendered thereby not kosher, *traife*."

"Yes, I knew that."

"But the condition of the animal is also important. After slaughtering, the *shohet* is required to examine the viscera for signs of sickness or disease. Obvious cases he is qualified to judge on his own and either pass as kosher or condemn as *traife*. But if he is uncertain, he submits it to a rabbi, for *him* to judge and make the finding. Well, *glatt* kosher is the meat of an animal that has never been submitted to a rabbi to have its *kashrut*—whether it's kosher—determined."

"There can't be many that are submitted. I mean not in the States, or in any civilized country where there is government inspection."

"True, but as a rabbi, I resent the assumption that an animal that the rabbi has declared kosher is any less kosher than one that was never submitted to him for examination."

"I get your point, but I'm sure not all rabbis agree with you."

"Perhaps not. Do you know many rabbis?"

"Quite a few. Living in Jerusalem, how could I avoid it?"

Shortly after the dinner trays were collected, a stewardess came along with a bunch of earphones on her arm for those who wanted to watch the movie they were about to show.

Miriam shook her head and the rabbi said, "No, thanks. I'm going to try to sleep."

Skinner said, "Yes, I'll have a pair." Then to the rabbi, "And I think I'll go back and find a place in the smoking section. I'm perishing for a cigarette."

The cabin was darkened for the movie, and the rabbi squirmed about in his seat, hoping to find a position that would enable him to sleep. "I wonder if he's planning to come back after his cigarette, or if he'll stay back in the smoking section and watch the movie from there."

"Why?" asked Miriam.

"Because if he's not coming back for a while, I'll lift up the chair arm and stretch out. Maybe I'll be able to sleep."

"Oh, I'm sure he'll stay in back for a while. He took his earphones with him. Maybe he'll find someone to talk to back there and just stay there. He seems a very friendly sort."

"Well, if he does come back, I'll just sit up again."

Skinner did not come back until shortly before landing, after the stewardess had come around to distribute the cards that had to be filled out for the passport authorities and preparations were being made for the descent.

As the plane touched down, there was a burst of applause from the passengers. At the skill of the pilot? That the long journey was at an end? Or to express joy at the arrival? The rabbi was never sure which, but he was curiously touched. As far as he knew, it happened only on the El Al flight to Israel. Simultaneously, the public-address system on the plane burst out in a song of welcome. The plane came to a halt, and the passengers began hauling out their carry-on luggage from overhead compartments. Skinner rose and took out his jacket and bag, then took out the rabbi's and Miriam's coats for them.

"Well, good-bye," Skinner said. "It was nice to have met you. Perhaps we'll see each other in Jerusalem." He stepped into the aisle and was carried forward by the push of the crowd to the exit and the flight of stairs that led to the buses waiting to convey the passengers to the terminal.

In the terminal they had their passports stamped and then proceeded through the barrier to get a cart and go to the carousel on which baggage was already beginning to come through. They did not have long to wait, and the rabbi took it as a good omen that both their valises came through together. Miriam, mindful of the rabbi's bad back, tried to help him lift them off the carousel onto the carrier, but he insisted he could manage, and although he did feel a twinge of pain, he took care not to wince.

There were two gates, one red for those who had something to declare and on which they might have to pay duty, the other green for those who had nothing to declare. They chose the green gate and a moment later found themselves on the sidewalk, facing the crowd awaiting the arrival of the passengers. They searched the sea of faces for Gittel, but it was she who spotted them.

9

"MIRIAM! DAVID! OVER HERE." SHE HUGGED MIRIAM TO HER and then releasing her, she turned to the rabbi, clasped his head in both hands, and kissed him. She was a little older-looking than when they had last seen her, a little more wrinkled, her hair piled on top of her head untidily, a little grayer. But her bearing still carried the note of complete command over any situation she might find herself in.

She demanded to know why Jonathon and Hepsibah had not come with them, and when Miriam told her they were on vacation at summer camp, she asked, "Wouldn't they have a better vacation here in Israel than in camp?"

"But it wouldn't be much of a vacation for us," the rabbi pointed out.

In answer to their inquiries about her son and his family, she said, "Uri is now a banker. He wears a three-piece suit and a kipah. He's religious now, you know. It's one of those little crocheted ones. Not yet a black hat, thank God. Right now he's in the army reserve, in *miluim*. He's a major," she added proudly. "As for his wife, she comes to visit once in a while. I suppose Uri tells her to. She brings the boy when she comes. A real charmer, that boy. He, too, wears a kipah, I'm afraid. Maybe he'll outgrow it."

Then abruptly she led them to the curb and said, "Stand right here, and if anyone tries to park, wave them on. Now, you wait right here and I'll go get the car." She looked mistrustfully at the two heavy bags and added, "It's a small car, but we'll manage. We can put them on the roof. I have a luggage carrier."

Remembering her old rattletrap of a car held together with baling wire and operated by prayer and imprecation, they were pleasantly surprised when a few minutes later she drove up a smart little Renault sedan that seemed almost new.

She parked and got out, and the rabbi said, "Ah, Gittel, a new car."

"Not quite new." Her tone was deprecatory, but she was obviously pleased. "It was only a couple of years old when I got it." A shrug. "The present administration has grandiose ideas for our economy. It used to be that we weren't permitted to buy things like cars and color television sets and new stoves and refrigerators until we could afford them. The present administration has a better idea. They encourage us to buy whatever we want in the hope that we'll eventually be able to afford them. And to encourage us even more, they keep lowering the value of our money so you have to keep buying things so that your money shouldn't become useless before you can spend it. It's quite a system. Look"—she waved at the cars that were lined up along the curb—"not a jalopy among them. Now, let's see: We'll have to hoist those bags onto the roof."

But as the rabbi took the first bag off the luggage carrier, Miriam said, "No, David, I won't let you." And to Gittel she explained, "He has a bad back."

"So I'll get someone to do it," said Gittel. She looked around at a group of cabdrivers who were standing about waiting for fares, and was about to approach them when Skinner, their erstwhile seatmate on the plane, came along and greeted them.

"I see you got through early. My man was supposed to meet me, but I guess he got held up." He noticed the small and cluttered trunk and their two large bags. "Can I give you a hand?"

"We were planning to load our bags on the roof," said Miriam.

"Here, let me help." He picked up one of the bags with a heave and hoisted it onto the roof.

"A regular Samson," said Gittel admiringly. "I've got some rope—"

"Good." And hoisting the other bag on the roof, he took the rope from her and proceeded to thread it through the handles of the bags and then through the supports of the luggage carrier.

"And where are *you* going? Tel Aviv?" Gittel asked.

"No, I'm going to Jerusalem. Maybe I can catch a *sherut,* or take a cab."

"To Jerusalem? But that's where we're going. So come with us."

"I'll be crowding you."

"Not at all. It's a big car. Miriam can sit in front with me, and you two men can sit in back. Women's lib."

The sun had already gone down, and dusk was soon followed by the darkness of night. Although they could see little beyond the roadway, Gittel persisted in pointing out places of interest. "You can't see it now, but that's a kibbutz on the right." And, "If there were light, you could see the armored vehicles that were hit by the Arabs during the War of Independence."

Miriam made noises of interest and appreciation, and Skinner even turned to peer out of the window, which the rabbi thought was very polite of him, since he had no doubt been over that road dozens of times.

As they neared the city Gittel asked, "Where do you go, Mr. Skinner?"

"Please don't bother. You just drive to wherever you're going and I'll take a cab from there. Besides, you'll want me to help you with the bags."

"Oh, I can manage to slide them down, all right," said the rabbi. "It's not like lifting."

"Well, if you're sure you can manage . . . I live in Abu Tor, Rabenu Tam Street."

"Near the American Yeshiva?"

"That's right. Next door, in fact."

"Oh, now I remember where I heard the name. You had some trouble with them," Gittel continued.

"I didn't personally because I wasn't here, but my manager, Ismael, reported some. They wanted to buy our place to expand their operation. It's quieted down now."

"Nevertheless," she insisted, "it was hooliganism. I would apologize to you, Mr. Skinner, for the behavior of these young men of the yeshiva if they were Israelis. But since most of them are American, I think maybe you should apologize, David."

Skinner laughed. "Since I'm an American myself, I'm just as much to blame. Ah, here we are."

Gittel brought the car to a halt, and almost immediately a light appeared above the door. As Skinner got out of the car, an elderly Arab woman came hobbling out.

"Mr. James!" she exclaimed, and making a kind of curtsy, she seized his hand and put it to her lips.

Embarrassed, he explained, "Martha has worked for the family for years." And then as she reached for his bag, he added, "She still thinks of me as the youngster she took care of when she first came."

To cover his obvious embarrassment, Miriam exclaimed, "What a lovely old house!"

"It's an old Arab house," he said. "Would you like to come in and look around? I've remodeled some, but I kept the original floor tiles in the hall and the decorated ceiling." At his side, Martha, still trying to wrest the bag from his hand, continued in voluble Arabic, to which he nodded every now and then.

To his new friends, he explained, "It never fails. Whenever I come back after being away for a while, I'm treated to a litany of disasters that occurred during my absence. There was some emergency up in our Haifa office, and my manager, Ismael, had to run up there. And then he called to say that the car had broken down and that's why he wasn't able to meet me at the airport. And the stove had to be repaired and it still isn't working properly. And there's trouble with the water so that she's had to buy bottled water, and Lord knows what else, but do come in. I'm sure—"

"Never mind," said Gittel. "We must be getting along."

He did not persist. "All right, but you'll come and visit, won't you? Now that you know where I live."

As they drove off, Gittel said, "He seems a resolute man. These yeshiva hooligans better not start with *him*. It was in all the papers. They wanted to buy his place. One report claimed they offered a token, a shekel for the property. It must be worth half a million. But even if they offered a legitimate price—and those religious groups have plenty of money— does that mean he has to sell? And the one they tried to deal with was not the owner, only a caretaker or a manager, an Arab yet, who didn't even have the authority. So they harassed him. They dumped refuse in front of the door. They even started small fires. That brought in the police, of course. And that brought in some of the crazier of the religious groups and that in turn provoked the crazies on the other side. Finally the mayor got involved, and I guess he managed to knock some sense into their heads. The director of the yeshiva was replaced, and things quieted down."

"But what kind of yeshiva is it that would tolerate that kind of thing?" asked Miriam.

"Ask your husband," said Gittel tartly. "That's his department. All I know is that most of the students are Americans. They look like a bunch of bums with their boots and overalls, like farmers in those faded blue jeans. Some wear leather jackets with fringes along the sleeve. They are supposed to be Baalei Tshuvah. They are now presumably concerned only with holy things, and they prove it by throwing stones at anyone who drives by in a car on the Sabbath, even a doctor going to see a patient."

"Is that the yeshiva where the Goodman boy is?" asked Miriam.

"I'm sure it is," her husband answered. "Goodman said it was the American Yeshiva in Abu Tor. I can't believe that there is more than one."

"Oh, dear, it doesn't sound very promising, does it?"

"Oh, I don't know," said the rabbi. "In any organization there are apt to be a few bad apples, at least extremists who lose all sense of proportion in their devotion to an ideal. I find it hard to believe that the yeshiva itself would foster that kind of thing."

"But they changed the head of the yeshiva."

"That doesn't necessarily mean the first one fostered hooliganism—only perhaps that he failed to control it."

Back at the house in Abu Tor, only minutes after Gittel and the Smalls had left, Ismael drove up. He was full of explanations and apologies. He kept dabbing his upper lip and forehead with a large silk handkerchief as he told of the car breaking down and of the difficulty he had had in finding a garage with a mechanic. Then, when he had finally located one, there was the problem of getting the car to the garage. "He kept telling me, Mr. James, tomorrow. He would come for it tomorrow."

He stood over Skinner, his heavyset body leaning forward at an angle, as he then told of accompanying the car to the garage, of the disorder in the shop—"Five minutes, five minutes, Mr. James, he spent looking for a screwdriver. And then he stops in the middle because he must eat. And all the time I am looking at my watch"—he extended his hand to show the watch on his wrist—"I keep telling him I am in a hurry and it is an emergency and he tells me—this, this ignorant, illiterate—I had to write out the bill for him . . ." A high school graduate with even some college courses to his credit, Ismael, who wore polished shoes and a silk shirt and a shiny black suit, had difficulty expressing the indignity he had had to suffer out of loyalty to his employer in dealing with such riffraff as the garage mechanic.

"All right, all right," said Skinner. "You got it fixed, though? No harm done. I got a ride from the airport with some people I met on the plane. Now, tell me what in hell is the matter with the water and what you have done about it."

10

THE RABBI AND MIRIAM AWOKE LATE THE NEXT MORNING and found that Gittel had already gone. There were two keys on the kitchen table, and a note: "A key for each of you. Remember, it is a double throw lock and you have to turn the key twice . . . dairy dishes, blue pattern; meat dishes, red. Plain silver is dairy, the other meat. I shall probably be home around three. . . . If you should need to get in touch with me, this is the phone number . . . if no immediate answer, don't lose patience. Enjoy!"

While the rabbi recited his morning prayers, Miriam busied herself in the kitchen, and when he was through, there were orange juice, toast and eggs, and coffee spread out on the table awaiting him. From long experience, she was able to calculate to the minute how long he would be.

"So much?" he murmured.

"You need a good meal to start the day right, David. All the doctors say so."

"They could be wrong, you know."

"Look, eat what you can. Here's the morning paper," she said, knowing that with print before his eyes, he would go on eating absentmindedly until there was no more left on his plate.

"Aren't you eating? Don't you need a good meal to start the day right?"

"I ate before you got up. And before you start on your paper, let's decide what we'll do today," she suggested.

"Did you have something in mind?" he asked suspiciously.

"It's a fine day, so I thought we'd take a walk, maybe to the Old City."

They took the bus to the Jaffa Gate, and entering, they began to wander down the narrow, tourist-filled passageways, stopping to look at the merchandise displayed or to watch as tourists bargained with the shopkeepers standing or seated on small stools outside their shops.

"It's the same old tourist stuff," said the rabbi. "Let's go to the Western Wall and see what's doing there. I understand they've made a number of changes since we were last there."

"Do you want to pray there?" she asked.

"No, I already recited the *shachris*. I just want to see it."

"All right. And then we can circle by way of the Armenian Quarter and get home for lunch."

They made their way slowly, resisting the blandishments of the shopkeepers who, when Miriam stopped momentarily to look at something on display, offered it at a vastly reduced price because it would be the "first sale of the day" and they were anxious to make a beginning.

"You've got to be careful not to show an interest," the rabbi warned, "or you immediately become involved."

"Oh, it's sort of a game with them," said Miriam. "They don't really expect you to buy just because you stop to look."

"I wonder. They're all selling the same merchandise, so I imagine they interpret any sign of interest as a chance to make a sale. Besides, our own law forbids it on the grounds that it raises the merchant's hopes only to dash them when you turn away."

"But that's if you do it with no intention of buying, isn't it, David? And I might buy something, if only for the fun of haggling. I understand you're supposed to, that they feel disappointed if you don't. Oh, there's something in the window there."

"What?"

"That cross. Isn't that a Jerusalem cross? Isn't that what Amy Lanigan wanted me to get her? I'm going in to ask about it."

He peered in through the window at a display of both crosses and Stars of David.

"The one in the corner," she said.

"Yes, that's a Jerusalem cross. I'll wait out here," he added after looking in and noting that the shop was tiny and, with the two or three other customers and the clerk, already crowded.

In front of the shop directly opposite, two bearded young men in jeans and wearing knitted kipahs were haggling with the shopkeeper over a leather bag. He watched and listened with interest—they were only a few feet away—as the shopkeeper stroked the bag lovingly to show the fineness of the leather and insisted that if he were to accept the price offered, he would be losing money; that he was only asking for the cost, not including his overhead; that he would show them the bills of lading if they doubted him; that it was actually half the normal price, and he held out the little price tag for their inspection; that he was making this sacrifice only because it was the first sale of the day.

Miriam appeared at the door of the jewelry shop, the cross on her open palm, and called to him, "David, what do you think? He wants eight dollars for it."

"I'm hardly an expert. Is it sterling?"

"It's got a stamp."

"Well, if you're overpaying, it can't be by much. Do you have any money with you? Here's ten dollars."

A few minutes later she rejoined the rabbi on the street. "He guarantees it's sterling," she said, "and it has both a pin and a ring so she can wear it on a chain if she wants to."

"And did you haggle with him?" he asked.

"I started to, but he explained that he couldn't on merchandise with price tags. Some ordinance or other. That if he lowered the price he could be fined. Do you think he was telling the truth, David? I noticed that no one else in the store haggled."

"I don't know. You might ask Gittel tonight. It wouldn't surprise me, though. The government has been trying to put something like that in effect for a long time."

At the Western Wall there were only a few people praying, since it was midmorning and hence late for the morning prayers and much too early for the evening prayers. Most of those present were obviously tourists, and most of these were Gentile.

"Are you going to pray, David?" asked Miriam.

"I don't think so."

"Doesn't it do anything for you—the Wall, I mean?"

"Not really. I'm afraid I don't have much feeling for shrines. It's probably a flaw in my character."

"Well, I'm going to."

"Go ahead. I'll wait for you here."

11

GITTEL'S APARTMENT WAS LARGE BY ISRAELI STANDARDS, since it had three bedrooms and even a small dining room in addition to the usual salon and kitchen. For the first two or three days of their occupancy, Gittel did the cooking and the shopping it entailed, but since she also had a job, Miriam insisted on taking over. This arrangement proved to be eminently satisfactory all around, since it not only gave Miriam something to do but also relieved Gittel of the burden of keeping house. She even admitted that the meals were better, since living alone she had gotten used to eating only what she could prepare quickly and easily.

In the morning Miriam would sally forth after doing the breakfast dishes, for her day's marketing. Usually she would take a bus to the supermarket, but if the weather was fine, she would walk. Occasionally she would go to the *shuk*, the open-air market, where she would shop for fruit and vegetables and sometimes even fish and meat, not merely because the prices were much cheaper but also because she felt that everything was fresher. She also enjoyed walking from stall to stall, comparing the merchandise offered for sale, picking, selecting, haggling with the shopkeepers. Then, laden with bundles, she would spend much of what she had saved by taking a cab home. She would prepare lunch for the rabbi and herself—

Gittel usually ate lunch at a commissary connected with her office. Then she would get everything ready for the evening meal, after which she would lie down for a siesta, common in Israel, as it is in most Mediterranean countries. Later in the afternoon she would cook dinner, sometimes dashing out to the nearby *macolet* to buy something she had forgotten.

Three mornings a week, she attended the beginners' class at the *ulpan*. It did not improve her scanty Hebrew much but it gave her a feel for the language, and she was better able to handle the few phrases she needed in her shopping and in her dealings with the neighbors and the *ozzeret* who came once a week to do the heavy cleaning. It also enabled her to make friends with some of the other members of the class, Americans for the most part, with whom she would occasionally spend an hour over coffee.

It was a pleasant life, which occupied her time and yet did not burden her. She felt free to have a sandwich in a restaurant with a classmate from the *ulpan* instead of going home for lunch, certain that the rabbi could fend for himself with a bit of smoked fish and bread and butter, or even a bowl of cereal, for they ate American-style, that is, they had their heavy meal in the evening and only a bite at midday.

In the evening, they watched television, or visited or were visited by Gittel's friends. They would have tea or coffee and cake, and there would be a lot of talk—although, out of deference to her niece's ignorance of the language, Gittel usually would announce, "Tonight, we will talk only English," and though the rest of the company would try manfully to comply, sooner or later they would lapse into Hebrew. Then perhaps someone would notice that Miriam had a blank look on her face and hasten to translate for her. But there were apt to be longish periods of conversation that she did not understand. It did not bother her particularly. The conversation among the female part of the company was likely to be about recipes and where one could buy various things. Even though she did not understand, she enjoyed it, the liveliness of it, the sociability of it, for in Israel, and more particularly in Jerusalem, it was the chief form of entertainment—this coming together and meeting of people.

The men tended to discuss politics, and if the rabbi was at a disadvantage because he did not know the day-to-day political issues or the personalities involved, it was not because of any difficulty with the language. And he was frequently appealed to, to explain American policy and to defend American actions. He found himself constantly defending his country, even when called upon to explain actions of which he himself disapproved. When he thought about it afterward, he sometimes wondered at his own jingoism. As he explained it to Miriam, "It isn't a case of my country right or wrong, it's just that they have no idea of how things work in the States. These people came from Russia and Poland and Germany, and even those who came from England and South Africa have no idea of how things happen with us. With most of them a political party is the embodiment of a set of ideas, and with us it's a little of that and a lot of the personalities involved. When that fellow last night asked, 'Why didn't your president back that bill?' he couldn't understand when I tried to tell him that he didn't because he couldn't. He just wouldn't believe me."

"Yes, I've noticed that," said Miriam, "but they also argue a lot about religious matters. I mean, for people who aren't at all religious—at least they're not observant—and yet they seem to know a lot. Well, those doctors the other night, they were arguing with you about something in the Talmud. That's unusual, certainly."

"Yes, it was. It was a rather involved point about what constituted money for purposes of acquisition of property. I marveled that these secular people, a couple of doctors and an accountant, should be so knowledgeable about this Talmudic discussion. I think it's because all of them came from religious families and so studied Talmud when they were young. That's why they came here, rather than to Canada or South America or the United States—those who would have been able to enter. It was certainly not because life would be easier here, so it must have been because they thought of this as their natural homeland, and that could only have been if they were raised in traditional homes. It makes for an interesting society. Even that cabdriver who took us out to Bayit V'gan last week was as knowledgeable as the average yeshiva student in the States."

"The one who refused to take a tip?"

"Yes, that was refreshing, wasn't it? It was fairly common when we were here years ago, but most uncommon nowadays, I gather."

It was precisely this widespread knowledge of his own general field of interest that made his life in Jerusalem so pleasant. He would get up early and go to one of the several houses of prayer in the vicinity. After a few days he settled on one—not the nearest, but the most congenial—and from then on attended that one exclusively.

The minyan he attended was a pleasant fifteen-minute stroll while the air was still fresh and cool. The service lasted only about fifteen or twenty minutes, a little longer on the days when a portion of the Torah would be read, and afterward, the sun a little higher now and the developing heat of the day already perceptible, he would walk back, arriving sometimes before Miriam and Gittel had left, in which case he would have a full breakfast of eggs and toast and coffee because Miriam felt that a "good" breakfast was important to start the day. On those days when he arrived after she had gone and was left to his own devices, he would heat up the morning's coffee and sip at it as he munched on a roll.

Most of the attendants at the minyan had jobs to go to and hurried off as soon as the service was over, but there were one or two who like the rabbi had no urgent business in hand, and they would stay on for a while engaging in idle talk and then saunter out to a nearby café for coffee and a roll or a piece of pastry before they went their separate ways. There was one, Aharon, who always could be counted on. He was a tall, fine-looking, elderly man who always was very well dressed. In fact, he was something of a dandy, an old-fashioned dandy of several decades back who obviously spent considerable time every morning deciding on his costume, which shirt to wear with this suit, and which tie, and whether the shoes should be black or brown. His manners were formal; when asked if he cared to go to the café, he would click his heels and bow slightly from the waist in acknowledgment and acquiescence. He could easily have been ridiculous, but he had a manner as well as manners and gave the impression of having served in some position where the demeanor was the norm, as in a bank or an embassy. His English was pedantically correct, although he had a faint accent that the rabbi thought might be German or perhaps only the evidence of the Yiddish he had grown up with.

The rabbi liked him. He was quiet, and unlike the others, he never indulged in the heckling, good-natured though it was, of the proprietor and the waiter at the café they frequented. He spoke little, and he nodded gravely when someone made a point. When he did speak, his words carried a note of authority. There was the feeling among the others that he would not guess or theorize, and when he spoke it was because he knew. Certainly, he was rarely challenged.

It was Thursday, so the minyan had finished late because of the Torah reading. A young Bar Mitzvah lad had been present and had been called up for one of the readings. Afterward there was a little celebration of sorts, wine and whiskey, and *kichel* and cakes provided by the father of the boy. There were the usual congratulations to the father, toasts offered to him and to his son. Then someone said, "Oh, it's almost nine o'clock," and all dispersed as though the place had caught fire. On the street, the rabbi and Aharon stood waiting to see if any of the others were interested in going to the café for their usual breakfast. When it was obvious that no one else was coming, Aharon said, "If you have the time, Rabbi, and don't mind walking a little, I should like you to be my guest for breakfast."

From anyone else, the invitation would have been a little ridiculous, since he knew that the rabbi normally had only coffee and a roll, for which the café was completely adequate. But Aharon was different, so the rabbi said gravely, "Thank you very much. I shall be happy to accept your invitation." As they walked along, he asked, "Are you retired, Aharon?" And then with a short laugh, "I never did hear your family name."

"It's Perlmutter. No, I am not retired. For the present, I work afternoons and evenings, which is why I have been free mornings. But that ends tomorrow."

"You mean you're giving up your job?"

"Oh, no. But next week I have to go back on the morning shift. You see, I'm a sort of substitute. I fill in where I'm needed. Ah, here we are."

They had come to the entrance of a hotel, the Excelsior. "You live here?" asked the rabbi.

"No, this is where I work," he said as he steered his guest to the dining room. "I'm on the desk part of the time, and part of the time I'm working in accounting. I am an accountant by profession, you see. I eat most of my meals here. It's one of the perquisites of the job. And there is no objection to my having an occasional guest."

"You are not married?"

"No, my wife . . . I am a widower."

Only one table was occupied, and from the way the half dozen who were seated around it greeted Aharon, the rabbi assumed that they were employees of the hotel, and in reply to his question, Aharon confirmed it.

"Yes, we are open for breakfast from seven to nine, and it is after nine now. As you see, the buffet has been cleared." He steered him to a table. "However, the waiter will get us anything we ask for from the kitchen."

"All I want is coffee and a roll."

"No eggs, no omelet, toast, perhaps smoked fish, herring?"

"Just a roll."

Aharon motioned to a waiter and gave their orders. The rabbi thought it significant that the waiter called him *Mr.* Aharon. As they sipped at their coffee, the rabbi said, "I have noticed in the discussions after the minyan, you appear to have a good knowledge of the Talmud."

"Well, of course, I studied—"

"At a yeshiva? You were perhaps interested in the rabbinate?"

The other laughed. "No. But my folks were comparatively well off. They wanted me to have an education, so I went to a yeshiva, but with no intention of becoming a rabbi." He smiled. "But I got a lovely wife from it."

"Really?"

"You see, I was tall, and considered nice-looking, even handsome. I came of a good family, and my folks, if not really rich, were not poor. But in addition, I was regarded as learned, which boosted my prospects materially. The local rich man, Jacob Grenitz, had a daughter of marriageable age. A *shadchen* came to see my folks, either on his own, or maybe Grenitz himself sent him. In any case, a match was arranged. It was a very good marriage. We loved each other very much."

"That was fortunate," the rabbi observed.

Aharon regarded him quizzically. "You think so? You are young, Rabbi, and grew up on the romantic assumption that a marriage should result only through the free choice of the principals. And yet I dare say that your grandparents, if not your parents, had their marriage arranged by a *shadchen*. And all your ancestors before them. Do you think that none of them knew marital happiness? Believe me, Rabbi, as long as the ages and backgrounds of two people are not too dissimilar, a happy marriage is likely. And the *shadchen* ensures that. It's his basic function, to match equals."

"I suppose that's true," the rabbi said thoughtfully. "I know my grandparents had a very good marriage and as you say, the match was arranged."

"Even in my day," Aharon admitted, "romantic notions were current. But my in-laws were very conservative people, and their daughter was guided by them."

He sighed. "For almost ten years we were very happy together. My father-in-law owned a glass factory. He manu-

78

factured pharmaceutical bottles. I went to work in the office, and after a short while I became the accountant for the company. But we had no children.

"Nowadays one can do something about it. It can be determined whether the fault is with the husband or the wife, and in either case, measures can be taken. But in those days, the husband's parents automatically assumed that it was the fault of the wife, and the wife's parents that it was the fault of the husband. My own folks, anxious for grandchildren, even hinted that I should get a divorce, God forgive them. If my father-in-law had any such thoughts about me, he never betrayed it for a moment. He was very fond of me, and we got along very well together. And then after ten years, my wife became pregnant."

"And?"

"My wife died in giving birth."

"And the child?"

"Was stillborn."

"Oh, how awful."

Aharon nodded. "Yes. I gave up our house and moved into my father-in-law's house for the year of mourning. We supported each other in our grief, and in any case, I could not go on living in our house; everything reminded me of her. And then my father-in-law sent me on a mission."

"What sort of mission?"

"He had been negotiating for some machinery in Switzerland, and almost at the last minute, he decided that I should go in his place. Perhaps he thought it would be good for me to get away. He came down to the railroad station to see me off, and that was the last I ever saw of him."

"What happened?"

"Germany invaded Poland and—" .

"But that was around 1940."

"September first, 1939."

The rabbi made rapid mental calculations and exclaimed, "Then you must be in your seventies."

"Seventy-five," said Aharon.

79

"I thought you at least ten years younger."

"Troubles age some, and for others it seems to halt the process. I obviously could not go back through the German lines. And then Russia thrust into Poland from the east. Subsequently, they made a treaty dividing the country between them. Ironically, the line of demarcation ran through our town; you see, my father-in-law's name, Grenitz, means boundary. Years later, after the war, when I was able to return, I found no trace of the family. They had all been killed off."

The people at the other table had left and they were the only diners in the room. The waiters were moving about preparing the tables for lunch, changing tablecloths, setting out napkins and silver. The rabbi looked about and said, "I think I had better be going."

"Yes, I think the waiters want to clear this table." He got up and with a little formal bow said, "I will not see you at *shachris* for a while. Maybe at *mincha, maariv.* I was informed yesterday that I would be going on mornings for a while. At seventy-five, you understand, one doesn't have much choice in these matters. I have to get here a little before seven to check those who come down to breakfast against my list. I do that until nine and then go on to the front desk. Obviously I can't go to the minyan. I'll have to recite the morning prayers at home."

"And when do you get through?"

He shrugged. "Probably at three, but in a hotel one never knows. Perhaps I can arrange for you, and your wife, of course, to have dinner with me here some evening. We have an excellent chef."

"I should like that very much, Aharon," said the rabbi and held out his hand.

12

SINCE THE ENVELOPE WAS MARKED "PERSONAL," MRS. MILLS brought it to Professor El Dhamouri unopened. He glanced at the envelope, saw that it was on the stationery of the Olympia Hotel, Athens, and noted that it bore a U.S. postal stamp and had been mailed in New York. It was from Grenish, of course. The first sentence told him what he had already surmised.

"Dear Hassan: A chance acquaintance here at the hotel told me he was flying back to the States tomorrow morning. So I am taking the occasion to write you so that he can mail it when he lands in New York. I understand that if I were to use the Greek mails, there would be a good chance that I would arrive home before it reached you.

"The flight over was not at all tedious except for an inquisitive bore who dropped into the seat beside me—the plane was only half full and there was a lot of moving around as a consequence. He told me that he was going back to the 'Old Country' from which he had come when he was a 'little kid.'

"And what was I going to Greece for? And did I know anyone there? And was I planning to stay for a while, or would I be moving on to other countries? Did I have a hotel in Athens? When I mentioned the Olympia, he was all but overcome by the coincidence, since he, too, was staying there.

And that would be a great break for me, since his cousins would be seeking him out, and they would show us—note the plural pronoun—around the town.

"I finally got rid of him by closing my eyes and murmuring sleepily that I was drowsy because of the heavy dinner we had been given—which wasn't bad, by the way. And after a while I did indeed doze off. When I awoke, he was gone, and needless to say I did not go looking for him.

"At Athens Airport I was a little surprised—and pleased—that he did not board the bus with me. He had evidently been met by one of his cousins, because I saw him in a private car that passed our bus. I assumed he would arrive before me, and I half expected he might be waiting for me in the lobby, but when I arrived, the coast was clear.

"I left the hotel shortly after checking in, to walk the streets for a while and to avoid my erstwhile seatmate. My first impression was surprise at the hustle and bustle of the city. I had not thought it would be as modern and so busy."

He went on to write of the friendliness of the Greek shopkeepers and wondered if this was merely the face they presented to customers—*"Timeo Danaos et dona ferentes,* although I expect I'll have to pay for anything I get"—the clarity of the air, the heat. He ended by saying he was planning to go up to Olympus on the morrow and then later in the week perhaps to one of the islands.

The professor folded the letter and carefully put it back in its envelope. Then he reached for the telephone and called Albert Houseman at the Holiday Inn.

Houseman, in jeans and sneakers, came over as soon as he was sure that Mrs. Mills would have left for the day. He read the letter El Dhamouri tossed to him.

"What's this *timeo* business?" he asked.

"Oh, that's a Latin quotation. It means, I fear the Greeks even though they come bearing gifts. Abe Grenish is something of a pedant. He frequently uses a Latin tag when he can pull it in."

"He doesn't mention the guy's name."

"You mean his Greek friend? No, he doesn't. Maybe he didn't catch it, or maybe the other didn't give it. What do you think?"

"It's probably just a guy wanting to talk and finding someone to listen. Transatlantic flights can be pretty boring after a while. Still . . ." His fingers drummed the desk as he took thought.

"You think he might—"

"I think we shouldn't take any chances. I'll alert one of our people in Athens. This other guy, the one who mailed the letter, he doesn't mention *his* name, either. Now *he* knows he's in touch with you because your name was on the envelope."

"But he's here in the States now—"

"Sure, but he could have tipped off someone before he left Athens. Let's see that envelope." He focused his attention on the back of the envelope.

"What are you looking for?" asked El Dhamouri.

"To see if it's been steamed open and resealed." He tossed it back. "If it has been, I can't tell. All right, I'll get on to Athens as soon as I get back to the hotel."

In the studio apartment Avram watched as Gavriel threw darts at a cork target affixed to the wall. Gavriel squinted and tossed his last dart. "Bull's-eye!" he exclaimed.

"Pure luck," said Avram. "You jerk it. You'll never get accuracy that way. You've got to follow through."

The telephone rang, and Gavriel picked it up from the floor. He listened and said, "Uh-huh. All right, I'll get back to you." To Avram he said, "El Dhamouri was visited by an Albert Houseman, the second or third time, always in the afternoon after the secretary has gone."

"Is that so?"

"You know him? Who is he?"

"Oh, you never served on the West Coast. He used to be Ibn Hosni, Abdul Ibn Hosni. He changed his name, officially, which is interesting. Used to be years ago, anyone coming to

America, first thing they did was to Americanize their name. Sometimes it was done for them at Immigration. So Hans became Henry and Jorge became George, and Yitzchak became Isaac or Isadore or Irving or Irwin."

"It's no different in Israel," said Gavriel. "There Irwin or Irving becomes Yitzchak and Greenberg becomes Ben Gurion and Scholnick becomes Eshkol."

Avram nodded. "Sure, but not nowadays here. At least, not so much. You notice El Dhamouri is still El Dhamouri. Nowadays here people tend to keep their original names. Heinrich remains Heinrich, and Ian and Ivan aren't changed to John. As for our people, we now have Moshe instead of Moses or Morris, and Yaacov instead of Jacob. Notice that the older one is Isaac Stern, but the younger one is Yitzchak Perlman."

"So?"

"So it's funny in a way that Abdul Ibn Hosni should become Albert Houseman."

"You think it's to cover up his Arab origin?"

"No-o, not in the sense that he might try to deny it. Maybe he just finds it easier. Chances are that if he went to a hotel and registered as Abdul Ibn Hosni, the clerk would automatically signal to the hotel detective, but as Albert Houseman, even though he looks Arab, probably not."

"You know him well?"

"Well enough. He's one of Ibrahim's bully boys."

"Dangerous?"

Avram shrugged. "He's a long way from home."

"He's staying at the Holiday Inn in Cambridge."

"Is that so? He's Druse, you know, like Ibrahim."

"So is El Dhamouri."

"So it might be just a social call. Still, it might be something else. It might be interesting to know what else he does besides visit El Dhamouri. I don't mean to follow him around, but just kind of keep an eye peeled for him."

"Okay. Are you going to pass it on?"

"Naturally. Fortunately, we don't have to evaluate information, just gather it."

13

AS A CONSERVATIVE RABBI, DAVID SMALL HAD NO STANDING, certainly not as a rabbi, with the Orthodox establishment that controlled religion in Israel. At best, his title was there only a courtesy title, like a Kentucky Colonel, carrying no authority—which was why he did not look forward to going to see Louis Goodman's son at the American Yeshiva, since from all accounts its orientation was ultra-Orthodox.

Although he was particularly adept at forgetting to do unpleasant things, or things he did not want to do, he knew that this duty he could not avoid since he had given his word. So on a bright, sunny day, after the minyan, and after he had breakfasted leisurely, he took a bus to Abu Tor.

The yeshiva was housed in what had formerly been the home of a wealthy Arab. It was built of blocks of the pinkish-beige Jerusalem stone. There was an arched doorway outlined in blue tiles, guarded on either side by a smallish cement lion, one of which was missing a paw while the other had had a portion of its muzzle chipped away. In front of the house, the bit of land that had at one time probably been elaborately landscaped and carefully tended was now a mass of overgrown bushes. The iron fence that encircled the grounds was badly rusted with here and there a gap where the iron pickets had been wrenched out.

The rabbi looked about him curiously and then walked

slowly up a flagstone path to a pair of large wooden doors with heavy ornate brass handles. There was a brass knocker in the shape of a lion's head, but he looked about for a more discreet bell button. At the point on the door jamb where the push button might originally have been, a slot had been cut out, and a mezuza inserted. The rabbi automatically touched it with his fingertips and then touched them to his lips as he wondered idly if the bell had been purposely removed lest someone absentmindedly push it on the Sabbath, thereby presumably desecrating the holy day of rest by performing work. As he stood there, a tall, blond young man came striding up the path. He was bearded, and perched on top of his long hair he wore a small crocheted kipah. He was dressed in faded blue jeans tucked into leather boots, and a sweat shirt, the arms of which had been cut off. He looked questioningly at the rabbi and then pulled open the door and held it in invitation for the rabbi to enter.

The rabbi stepped into a large, empty foyer of black and white marble tiles, to face a broad staircase with a wide mahogany balustrade. The young man left him there and mounted the staircase two steps at a time. The rabbi looked about uncertainly and noticed a hallway to the right, along which were several doors that presumably led to rooms or offices. Near the entrance was what appeared to be a receptionist's window—at least it had a round hole cut out of the glass. The rabbi walked over and saw a small office with a desk and numerous file cabinets. Seated at the desk, working at a ledger, was a man with a straggly black beard. He was wearing a black alpaca coat over a white shirt open at the neck. On his head, but pushed back from his forehead, he wore a narrow-brimmed black felt hat.

The rabbi cleared his throat and coughed apologetically, but the other did not raise his head from his work. The rabbi waited a minute and then tapped on the pane. This time the other looked up, obviously annoyed. His eyes were set deep in bony sockets and glittered like a man with a fever. The rabbi judged him to be in his forties.

"I'm looking for Jordan Goodman," said Rabbi Small.

"Goodman? Goodman? We have no Goodman here."

"I believe he now calls himself Ish-Tov."

"Ah, yes. Ish-Tov. And what do you want with him?"

"I should like to talk to him."

"And you are?"

"David Small. I am the rabbi of his hometown in the States."

With a sigh, the other got to his feet, and opening the door beside the window, gestured the rabbi inside. He did not introduce himself, but Rabbi Small saw that the brass nameplate on the desk bore the name Joseph Kahn.

There were a number of ledgers on the only visitor's chair in the room, so Rabbi Small remained standing. For a moment or two Kahn surveyed him, his gray flannels and seersucker jacket, his linen cap, the fact that he was beardless, and then said patronizingly, almost insolently, "Ah, a Reform rabbi."

"No, Conservative."

"Same thing." Kahn sat down and pulled the ledger he had been working on toward him, as though in dismissal. Then he turned his head to Rabbi Small and said, "I don't think Ish-Tov would be particularly interested in talking to you."

"Not even if I bring greetings from his parents?"

"They are well?"

"Yes, but—"

"Then I will convey it to him."

The angry retort that came to mind, Rabbi Small suppressed. He even managed to achieve a smile. "It seems curious," he said, "that here in a yeshiva you would want to prevent one of your students from performing a mitzvah."

Kahn glared. "And what mitzvah is that?"

"Honor your mother and father."

Kahn drummed nervously on his desktop as he took thought. Then he rose swiftly to his feet and said, "Perhaps you had better talk to Rabbi Karpis, our director," and circling the desk, left the room. He was back after a minute or two and nodded for Rabbi Small to follow him. He led him down the corridor to a door marked "Director." He knocked, opened the door, and stood aside for Rabbi Small to enter. Then he withdrew and closed the door behind him.

The director was a large, fleshy man with a square gray beard. He sat behind an ornate teakwood desk that was clear except for a chessboard with a few pieces in place, which he had evidently been studying and which he pushed aside just as his visitor entered.

Rabbi Small glanced at the board and immediately recognized the position of the pieces as a problem that had appeared in the newspaper a few days before.

Rabbi Karpis caught the glance and asked, "You play chess? It's a problem. White to move and mate in three. I'll admit I'm baffled by it." He spoke in English with a trace of a British accent.

"Yes, I saw it in the newspaper. You move the knight."

"Why move the knight?"

"Just to get it out of the way and clear the file."

"But then black takes the queen."

"Let him. You move your other knight to bishop eight, which cuts off the black king from—"

"Ah, yes, I see. Of course. How stupid of me!" And then, "How long did it take you?"

"A couple of days," Rabbi Small lied. "And then it was mostly a matter of luck."

"Hm." Rabbi Karpis sat back and surveyed his visitor suspiciously from under lidded eyes. Then he said, "My colleague tells me you are a Conservative rabbi."

"Yes, and he seemed to disapprove."

Rabbi Karpis smiled. "Mr. Kahn is"—he fished for a word and settled on—"young. Young men have strong convictions. While I am myself opposed to these experiments—Conservatism, Reform, Reconstructionism—with God's commandments, nevertheless from time to time we have received support, financial support, for our work here from Jews of those persuasions."

"Indeed!" said Rabbi Small politely.

"Does it surprise you, Rabbi? Consider. Why do our students come to us? Because they wish to return to the beliefs and practices of their fathers. And why? Because while some of them have led perfectly normal, commonplace lives and found them unsatisfactory, others have experimented with strange religions, with drugs, with exotic life-styles. Some of them have even gotten in trouble with the secular authorities. And how do their parents feel about their coming to us, about their return? Grateful, Rabbi. They feel grateful."

"And they send you a check in acknowledgment."

The director nodded, beaming.

"It's only fair to tell you," said Rabbi Small, "that there is little of that sort of thing to hope for from Goodman—er, Ish-Tov. His folks are in very modest circumstances, which is why they have not come over to see him. They just couldn't afford it. When they heard I was coming over, they asked me to look him up and see if he's all right."

"Oh, you mustn't think we are interested only in those whose parents might make a contribution," said the director reproachfully. "We need money, as every organization needs money, but we have not forgotten our original purpose."

"And what is that?"

Rabbi Karpis looked in surprise. "Why, to bring Jews back to their faith, to their heritage. They were all worldly and for the most part unhappy when they came to us. We teach them what they should know as Jews. We reorient them, and they are—"

"Born again?" asked Rabbi Small innocently.

Rabbi Karpis waggled an admonishing forefinger at him. "Ah, you're chaffing, of course." Then primly, "We are all born again every morning when we wake up." He leaned forward and rested his arms on the desk. "Are you suggesting we seduce these young men? Brainwash them? That we are a cult like those that have arisen in such profusion recently in your country?"

"I rather wondered when your colleague at the front desk said that Goodman wouldn't want to see me, when he had not bothered to ask him. And then when I persisted, brought me to you, instead of merely notifying Goodman that someone had arrived with a message from his parents."

"Ah, well, Mr. Kahn is somewhat peremptory, even short-tempered. He is not only our secretary, but is also charged with maintaining the discipline of study and ritual observance. For our purposes it is good to have a man like that in charge of discipline. They came to us, many of them, because they realized that the lives they had been leading were unsatisfactory, ineffective, counterproductive. They were slaves of their emotions and did things on the spur of the moment. Do you know how your friend Goodman—Ish-Tov—happened to come to us, to Israel? He was in California and was planning to go to South America when he met someone named Good who had the return portion of a round-trip ticket from Israel to America. It was about to run out, so he was able to buy it for a few dollars, and it was easy to change the name on the ticket from Good to Goodman. So he came to Israel, just like that." He snapped his fingers.

"Now, if one of these young men wants to go to Eilat for a weekend, or even to a movie one night, there is Mr. Kahn to tell him he can't. If he should insist, do you think we would hold him here by force? No, he would walk out, but he would not be permitted to return. Discipline, Rabbi Small, discipline! Once study and ritual observance have become a matter of habit, in other words, once he has achieved self-discipline, ours is no longer necessary, and he is free to come and go as he pleases.

"Now, Mr. Kahn has an acute understanding of the needs and the special weaknesses of each of our young men. Why didn't he want Ish-Tov to see you? Perhaps because he felt that at this moment in time, Ish-Tov's study should not be interrupted. Or that at this particular time, it would be unwise for Ish-Tov to have his attention diverted from his studies to his former life in the States. Or"—he smiled broadly—"Kahn may have had a headache."

"A headache?"

"Yes." Rabbi Karpis folded his hands and nodded. And then shook his head slowly in commiseration. "The poor man is subject to severe migraine headaches, and sometimes he is apt to be short-tempered as a result."

"I see. And when your young men throw stones at passing cars on the Sabbath, or pile trash on your neighbor's garden, is that because of Mr. Kahn's headaches, or is it a part of the discipline?"

The older man leaned forward and said earnestly, "Believe me, Rabbi Small, I never approved of that. And it has not happened since I took over." He raised his shoulders and then dropped them in an elaborate shrug. "In our organization, in any organization, there are differences of opinion as to the best way of achieving its goals. These differences crystallize into factions. Even among the *tannaim,* there was the School of Hillel and the School of Shammai. My predecessor is a man of vast learning and great probity. He is part of what might be called the activist faction. Then the"—he fished for a word—"shall we say, the climate, yes, the climate shifted and our—er—strategy for—of a number of things—changed."

"I see. Well, in the light of this shift in climate, can I speak to Mr. Ish-Tov? I have no intention of interfering with your discipline or—"

"My dear Rabbi Small, of course." He reached for the telephone on his desk, pressed a button, and said, "Yossi? Would you have Ish-Tov come down to my office immediately?"

He listened, nodding, and then hung up. "I'm terribly sorry, Rabbi. I had quite forgotten. Ish-Tov went up to Haifa today with our truck. We have some new desks coming. He won't be back until quite late. But you can see him tomorrow, or whenever it is convenient for you. If you give me your phone number, I can call you and arrange for an appointment, but I'm quite sure that anytime tomorrow will be all right." He smiled. "And if you have time, perhaps we can play a game of chess afterward."

14

As he was making his way to the bus stop, Rabbi Small heard his name called. He stopped and looked about him uncertainly, and then he saw James Skinner waving to him from a second-floor window. He waved back and was about to proceed, but the other signaled to him frantically, so he waited, assuming that Skinner wanted to speak to him. In a moment Skinner came running out of his front door and shouted, "Come and have a coffee, Rabbi!"

The rabbi looked about curiously as Skinner led him up the path to the front door. On either side of the path there were little circles of stones in which various flowers grew. Radiating from the circles were small oblong plots, also set off by rows of stones in which various forms of cactus were set out. On the side that adjoined the yeshiva land, there was a row of tall cypress trees that effectively cut off the view of the building.

"We can't maintain grass," Skinner explained. "Too dry, I guess. I have a gardener who comes around once a week or so. He tried because I insisted, but when I found he wasn't able to manage, I gave him his head and let him do what he wanted. As long as he keeps it fairly neat, I don't mind. Nevertheless, I didn't appreciate it when our friends over there"—a nod toward the yeshiva—"decided to add to the decor."

"I spoke to the director, and I gathered that you are not likely to be troubled that way again."

"Yeah, so I understand."

The rabbi was not altogether surprised to find when he entered the door that the layout was similar to that of the yeshiva. There was the same broad staircase leading up to the second floor and the same arrangement of large black and white tiles on the floor of the foyer. On the right, however, was a large room with double doors, one of which was partly open. The rabbi glanced in.

"The salon," said Skinner. "I don't use it much. It gives me the willies." He opened it, however, perhaps to prove his point.

It was a large room with oriental rugs scattered about, and full of massive furniture inlaid with mother-of-pearl. There were all kinds of brass lamps on teakwood tables. The walls were almost covered with tapestries or small, finely woven oriental rugs.

"It's like a room in a museum," Skinner went on. "My grandfather collected most of it, although my father added to it as well. I suppose some of the things are worth something these days. I'd be inclined to get rid of all of it and make a modern room out of it, but Martha would be horrified and probably would never forgive me. She dusts and polishes in here as though it were a shrine. Actually, I have occasionally entertained some of my Arab customers here, because they're apt to be impressed by that sort of thing. Let's go upstairs to my office. We'll be more comfortable there."

The room was as much a living room as it was an office. Most of the space was taken up by a large sofa, upholstered chairs, and a coffee table. However, to be sure, on one side was a large, old-fashioned rolltop desk, its top covered by a mass of papers, old letters, bills, receipts, the corners of those that protruded from the bottom of the pile yellow with age. All the pigeonholes were stuffed with business cards and folded-up papers. Jammed against it was an old swivel chair covered with worn and in places torn black leather. Beside the desk was a modern metal file cabinet. And on the other side was a modern metal flat-topped desk at which a youngish Arab was working. He immediately jumped to his feet when they entered.

"Get us some coffee, Ismael. And some of those cookies that Martha bakes," said Skinner.

"Yes, Mr. James. Regular or Turkish?"

Skinner looked inquiringly at the rabbi, who said, "Regular for me. Black."

"I'll have the same, Ismael. And we'll have it here."

"Yes, Mr. James."

"Martha is always annoyed when I serve coffee to a guest here in my office," Skinner remarked. "She thinks it highly improper. But she's not in today because it's Sunday. It's her day off. She's Christian."

"And Ismael?"

"Oh, he's Muslim."

"So his day off is Friday?"

Skinner chuckled. "No, he doesn't get a day off. Not as such. You see, he lives here and . . ."

He broke off as Ismael entered with the coffee. He had a pot and two cups and saucers and a plate of cookies on a tray. He placed a cup on the little semicircle of bare space on the rolltop desk for Skinner, and the other with the cookies on the coffee table in front of the sofa, on which the rabbi was sitting.

"Is there anything else, Mr. James?" he asked.

"No, Ismael. This is fine. Oh, and take all telephone calls, will you?"

"Yes, Mr. James." Ismael bowed and left the room, closing the door softly behind him.

"You see," said Skinner, "Ismael is my manager. He's in charge all the time I'm away. So he can take off anytime he wants to—when I'm not here, that is. Who's to know? So when I'm here, he's with me all the time."

"He appears to have other duties besides attending to your business affairs," remarked the rabbi.

"Yeah." Skinner chuckled again. "He does just about everything. He's my chauffeur. I don't drive. And he does the cooking Sundays when Martha is off. I guess I can count on him for practically everything."

"You're lucky to have him."

"And he's lucky to have me. He sort of attached himself to my father eight or nine years ago, and he's been with us ever since. He had no family, no money, and now he lives well. He has a fine home, eats well, dresses well, and has status in the Arab community."

They talked of general matters for a while, and then, when the rabbi said he had to be going, Skinner offered to have Ismael drive him.

"Oh, I wouldn't think of troubling him. I can take the bus."

"Nonsense, Rabbi. You might have to wait fifteen or twenty minutes in the hot sun at the bus stop. And when one comes along, it might be jammed to the doors. It's no trouble for Ismael to take you. I'll tell him to bring the car around."

He walked to the door with the rabbi when Ismael drew up in the car. "Oh, you might have to direct him, Rabbi," he said. And at the rabbi's look of surprise, he explained, "He never goes to Rehavia. Neither do I. We just have no occasion to. All our business is in East Jerusalem or the Old City. . . . Were there any phone calls, Ismael?"

"Only one from the plumber to say he could be here Thursday."

"Thursday? Did you argue with him?"

"I asked if he couldn't come sooner, but he said Thursday was the earliest."

"Okay. We'll just have to be patient, I guess."

15

THE NEXT DAY RABBI SMALL WAITED IN THE VISITORS' ROOM at the yeshiva, a small, bare room containing a sofa, a round mahogany table, and a few armchairs. Even though the shabby chairs and sofa were spruced up with crocheted antimacassars, there was a feeling that the room was rarely used. On the table there was a bowl of artificial flowers. When he came in, Jordan Goodman, now Yehoshua Ish-Tov, looked about curiously, suggesting that he, too, might be seeing the room for the first time.

He looked vaguely familiar, and the rabbi assumed he must have seen him on the streets of Barnard's Crossing—clean-shaven, of course—or perhaps in his father's store. Then he decided it was merely that he resembled his father.

Ish-Tov nodded shortly and sat down in one of the armchairs. "You're Rabbi Small, and you have a message from my parents?" He was a large young man who carried himself awkwardly. His manner was one of complete disinterest and studied boredom. He slouched in his chair as though it were for him the normal posture that he slid into automatically. He was dressed in blue jeans and a white shirt open at the throat. He wore sandals on his bare feet.

"I have no special message from your parents, only greetings. They asked me to see you—"

"To see me, so that you could report to them how I look? My mother, I suppose, wanted to know if I had lost weight? And my father—let's see, he'd want to know if I was properly dressed when you came to see me, was I wearing a tie and were my shoes polished."

The rabbi smiled tolerantly.

Ish-Tov got up, and with arms spread, turned around as though modeling his clothes and then resumed his slouch in the chair. "All right, you can tell my mother I'm in good health. I've even gained a few pounds. I should probably get more exercise."

The rabbi smiled. "If that's what they were interested in, they didn't stress it. I supposed they meant for me to talk with you and see if you were, er—happy in your new life and what your plans for the future were."

"And being a rabbi, you could report to them on whether or not I was sincere in my return, or if I had just got caught up in another cult and been brainwashed."

"I suppose that was their principal concern," said the rabbi good-naturedly.

"Yeah, they would," said the young man contemptuously. "Well, I don't go baring my soul to your kind of rabbi."

"And what kind of rabbi is that?"

"The kind that buys crosses," said Ish-Tov venomously.

Then it came to Rabbi Small that he must have been one of the young men who had been bargaining for the leather bag in the Old City and that was why he had seemed familiar. He shrugged. "A Christian friend of mine asked me to buy it for him."

"Well, the kind of rabbis I know wouldn't do it."

"No? And you wouldn't do it either because you are a Baal Tshuvah, one who has returned, one who has repented."

"That's right."

"Tell me, what is it you repent of? What did you fail to do formerly that you do now?"

Ish-Tov looked at him in surprise. "The commandments, the *mitzvoth*. Formerly I did not obey them, and now I do."

"Which *mitzvoth*? There are six hundred and thirteen of them—"

"Oh, come on. You know, the daily prayers, putting on the phylacteries, *tfillin*, wearing *tsitsis*, observing the *kashrut* regulations, the Sabbath—"

"And the major ones?"

"What do you mean by the major ones?"

"Well, *tfillin*, *tsitsis*, the *kashrut* regulations—these are ritualistic. The *tfillin* and the *tsitsis* are reminders. The *kashrut* regulations about not mixing meat and dairy products and keeping separate dishes for the two are an elaborate rabbinical device for adhering to the biblical law that one must not seethe the flesh of the kid in the milk of its mother because the idea is essentially repugnant and shows a complete disregard for life as manifest in the lower animals.

"But how about the ten commandments? Thou shalt not murder, thou shalt not steal, thou shalt not bear false witness. Did you do those formerly? Thou shalt not covet—"

The young man grinned. "Well, maybe I did a bit of coveting."

"And now you don't? How about the injunction to honor your father and mother? There's not supposed to be any scale of comparative values on importance in the mitzvoth, and one is supposed to be as important as another, but I think most people would agree that honoring one's parents probably rates a little higher than wearing *tsitsis* or observing *kashrut*. There is also the commandment about not creating and worshiping idols. If someone fashions a bit of metal in the shape of a cross, you may regard it as making an idol. Knowledgeable Christians deny it and say that even when it includes the figure of Jesus and they appear to be worshiping it, praying to it, it is not the thing of wood or metal that they are worshiping, but that they are merely using it to focus and direct their thoughts to the being it represents, somewhat as we use *tfillin* for a somewhat similar purpose. But"—and he held up an admonishing finger—"when you fear this bit of metal because of its shape, and think that its shape confers on it a special power, whether for good or for evil, then you have made an idol of it, and you are worshiping it by the very act of disdaining it."

The young man remained silent, his fingers drumming on the arm of his chair, his eyes focused on a point beyond the rabbi's shoulder. The rabbi realized that if Ish-Tov appeared to be listening, he was not really hearing. He was reminded of Jonathon when he was younger and had done something naughty, and he had tried "to reason" with him. There was the same apparent attention while the boy probably thought only whether he would be punished or not, and what the punishment might be. To be sure, he had silenced the young man, but what credit could he derive from that? And the Goodmans had come to him not to ask him to reprimand their son but to try to understand him.

He decided to try a different tack. "What are you studying?" he asked brusquely.

"I study Hebrew. Right now, it's mostly practice in reading. I learned how when I went to Hebrew School as a kid, but I kind of had to spell it out. We use the *siddur,* the prayer book, and since we say the prayers so often, we practically memorize them. Of course, we also learn what they mean— I mean, we translate them. Then we also get practice in conversational Hebrew and grammar and vocabulary. Things like that. And the Books of Moses. And," he ended up proudly, "I've already started Talmud."

"Talmud! Indeed! And what are you studying in the Talmud?"

"It's about damages. How you'd assess damages, say you were a judge, in different situations. We don't get very far, day to day. Maybe a couple of lines in a session on account of we argue about it a lot. We do it in English."

"And you enjoy it?"

"Oh, sure, the discussions and all . . ." But in talking about his studies he had lost some of his unconcern. He leaned forward, and tapping on the table with his forefinger, he said, "Look, Rabbi, get one thing clear, and you can pass it on to my folks: I now have certainty. I know who I am, where I came from, and what I have to do. And that's all I've got to say." He rose abruptly to indicate that as far as he was concerned, the interview was at an end.

"Just a minute," the rabbi halted him. He tore a page from his notebook and wrote on it. "Just in case you want to get in touch with me, here's my phone number."

Ish-Tov thrust the scrap of paper into his pocket and then with a nod left the room.

16

SKINNER SAW THE PANEL TRUCK FROM HIS OFFICE WINDOW
on the second floor. There was a sign on the side that read
Shimon the Plumber. He ran down the stairs and out the
front door to meet the man who got out from behind the
wheel. "You're Gerber."

"That's right. Shimon Gerber, master plumber. You got
trouble?" He was a short, stocky man with grizzled hair and
beard and heavy features.

"There is almost no pressure, just a trickle, and the water
is actually dirty. I called the Water Department and they
checked the main. They said the trouble was on my side of the
meter and wouldn't do a thing." He led the way into the
house and into the kitchen.

Shimon turned the faucet and watched the resultant trickle.
"It's either a clogged or a broken pipe, probably broken."

"How would it get broken?"

Shimon shrugged his shoulders and spread his hands in
elaborate refusal to hazard a guess about the mystery. "Look,
pipes break. If pipes didn't break and have to be replaced,
how would I make a living? It could be from like old age, or
from rust. It could be from a little earth tremor. We had one
about a week ago. Nothing serious, the pictures on my wall
jiggled."

"So what do I do?"

"You don't do nothing. I send a couple of men over and they dig up the pipe. Then I replace it with a new one, galvanized, which this one maybe wasn't if it was put in some years ago, and then we shovel back the dirt, and everything is fine again."

"How soon will—"

"This morning I'll come down with a couple of men with picks and shovels. In a couple of hours, if we're lucky, we'll find the pipe—"

"What do you mean, if you're lucky?"

"The pipe is in the ground. Who knows if it's straight from the meter to the house? The tank is in back, so it could be it curves around"—he made a broad curving motion with his hand. "You've got maybe the original plans, blueprints?"

Skinner shook his head. "But why wouldn't it go directly to the tank?"

"Because sometimes when you're laying pipe, you find there's a big rock in the way. So do you blast it out with dynamite? Sometimes you do, and sometimes you decide to go around, or over. If we find it first shot, it takes a couple of hours. The ground is hard, and Arab workers—it's not that they're lazy, but they like to work easy. Maybe it's just one length of pipe. Whatever it is, I come down and take a look at it, get my supplies, replace it. The men shovel back the dirt, and it's as good as new."

"How far down will they have to go?"

Again the contractor shrugged. A quick glance over the terrain, and he said, "Maybe four, five, six feet. You not only got to go down to the pipe, but under a little, so we can have some work room."

"Well, all right," said Skinner. "I'm in your hands."

The contractor smiled broadly. "And I'm in God's hands. Don't worry, this time of year, I'm a busy man. Right now, I've got half a dozen different jobs I'm working on. I start a job, I got to finish as quick as I can."

Sure enough, Shimon came with a couple of Arab workmen. From his office Skinner could hear him giving orders in Arabic with an occasional Hebrew phrase interspersed. Although they were within feet of each other, they spoke in loud voices as though they were calling across a field.

Skinner immediately left his office and went to the back door to see what they were about. Shimon with wide arm motions was showing his men the direction in which he wanted them to dig, and the two Arabs, now resting, nodded every now and then to show that they understood. Shimon saw him standing in the doorway and waved to him but made no move to come over. The men started to work, and the contractor watched them for a few minutes, shouting instructions. Then he went back to his truck parked on the side of the road, got in, and drove away.

The two Arabs had been digging assiduously while their boss was present, but now that he was gone, they slowed down. Then one, the older one, stopped altogether, sat down on the ground, and lit a cigarette while his comrade continued to dig. Then *he* stopped and lit a cigarette, while his older colleague went to work with a shovel, piling up the earth he had loosened. They continued that way, the one with the shovel idling while the one with the pick worked, and when the shoveler worked, the one with the pick rested.

Skinner watched them through the window. Once he went out and came over to see how far they had progressed. They grinned and nodded to him. He remarked that the day was warm, and the younger one said something about the ground being very hard. Skinner did not stay long, having learned from past experience that the innate politeness of the Arab worker made it unthinkable for him to talk and work at the same time.

He went back indoors and went about his business. Later he looked out and saw that they were sitting on the ground, eating their lunch. And that afterward, instead of returning to work, they had both stretched out in the sun and appeared to be enjoying a siesta. This struck him as too much, and he went out to remonstrate against them. They jumped to their feet when they saw him and grinned and motioned to the trench.

They pointed to the rusty pipe they had unearthed. It had involved their digging a trench almost five feet deep, six feet long, and three feet wide.

Skinner nodded in appreciation and asked in Arabic, "So now what?"

"We wait for Shimon to get back."

It was almost four o'clock before the bearded Shimon pulled up in his truck. Skinner came out to greet him. He waved in greeting and explained, "I was tied up in another job."

Then he jumped into the trench and examined the exposed pipe. He called out to Skinner above him, "There's a crack underneath that I can feel with my fingers. But the connectors look good at both ends. You're in luck. It was this piece, and we don't have to continue digging to the meter. I'll probably be able to unscrew this length of pipe and fit another one in using the same connectors." He held up both arms to the workers and they grasped him by the wrists and helped him out.

"How soon will you be able to finish?" asked Skinner.

"I have to get the pipe length from the shop to replace this one. I have to thread the ends. Then I have to remove this one, which involves cutting it. Then I have to fit the new one in."

"So how long will it take?"

Shimon looked at him reproachfully. "The day is already gone."

"There's still plenty of time before sunset."

"I got to take the men over to another job, an emergency. Look, Mr. Skinner, tomorrow without fail. I'll be back and finish the job."

"But—but you mean you're going to leave an open trench—"

"So what? It's the back of the house. Who comes here? I'll leave the picks and shovels because I may have to go a little deeper to have room to work. It's just overnight. Believe me, it will be all right."

"But I have no water to wash with. My housekeeper has no water to cook with—"

"It's only one day." He smiled broadly. "So give her a day off, and you take a vacation and go to a hotel for the night."

17

THE NEXT DAY SKINNER SAW SHIMON'S TRUCK DRIVE UP AND park in front of the house. He was about to go down to tell him that he could drive around to the parallel street in back and he would open the fence gate for them, but Shimon and his two Arab workers were already unloading their equipment, and a moment later began carrying it up the path and around the house to the rear, so he did not bother. It was now after ten and he had rather expected them to come the first thing in the morning, and perhaps be done by now, but he knew there was little use in expostulating, that Shimon would have an excuse, and in the ensuing argument, he would be sure to lose. In the Mideast it was necessary to cultivate patience.

As he worked at his desk, he could hear, faintly, occasional orders issued by Shimon to his workers from the back of the house. Finally, around noon, there was a banging at the back door, and when Martha opened it, Skinner heard voices in the kitchen and shouts, presumably to Shimon at the trench. Skinner went down to see what was happening, and when he appeared in the kitchen, there were the two Arabs, who grinned at him and pointed to the sink where the water was pouring out of the faucet.

He went outside and saw that Shimon was in the trench, feeling under first one connection and then under the other to see if there was any leakage. He saw Skinner and said, "So is the water running all right? Pressure look good to you?"

"It looks fine. Now if you'll fill in the trench—"

"Ah, filling in the trench, that presents a problem. See that? I had them dig a little farther so I could work at the connector a little easier. And they uncovered that."

"What, that rock? So what? What's it got to do with the pipe?"

"It's not just a rock. You can see that it extends in both directions, maybe for quite a distance."

"So it's a ledge, but the pipe misses it."

"No, it's not a ledge, either. Maybe you can't see from up there, but if you get down in the trench and take a good look at it, you'll see that it is hewn stone. There's no mistake about it."

"So what?"

"So that means it's an artifact. Archaeology. Don't you understand?"

"All right, so it's an archaeological artifact. You mean there's maybe some broken old pots down there. Frankly, I'm not interested."

"There's no telling what might be there. Maybe statues, maybe coins, maybe who knows what."

"I'm still not interested. I'll pass it up. Just have your men fill in the trench and—"

"It has to be reported. It may not be important to you, but it can be of great importance to the State. It's your duty to report it."

"And if I don't?"

"Then you're liable to a heavy fine."

"Oh, come on."

"Oh, yes."

"But who's going to know about it? If I don't report it, I mean."

"I know about it. My two Arab helpers, they know about it. And when they talk about it, pretty soon everybody will know about it."

"All right. So what happens if I report it?"

"You report it to the Department of Antiquities. They're part of the Ministry of Education and Culture. They send a man down to evaluate it, archaeologically, you understand. If they don't think it's important, they notify you, and they let you fill in the trench. If they consider it important, worth investigating, they send a crew out who start digging—"

"They could be at it for months!"

Shimon shrugged his shoulders expressively.

"Look, I'm sure if I gave your two Arabs, say, five dollars each—"

"And how much would you give me?" asked Shimon coldly. "No, no, Mr. Skinner, it is your duty to the State to report this. It could bring out important information about the past. The chances are they won't even be interested, because this part of Jerusalem they know all about. But you will have done your duty. And then again, it could turn out to be an important find and your name will be mentioned in textbooks."

Skinner gave him a searching look and then said, "All right, I'll phone them." He beckoned with his head and Shimon followed him into the house.

It was not easy to reach the Department of Antiquities. For that matter, it was not easy to get the telephone answered by the Ministry of Education and Culture, of which they were a part. Skinner let the phone ring and ring—fifteen times, twenty times. After all, someone must be there. When the connection was finally made and he asked to be connected with the Department of Antiquities, he was told, "Ahuva is not at her desk."

"Who's Ahuva?"

"The secretary, of course," came the answer in a scornful tone, as if to say, Don't you even know that?

"So let me talk to someone else."

"Just a minute." (He imagined her stretching to look through an annex door.) "I'm sorry. Gedaliah isn't at his desk. He won't be back until late this afternoon."

"Well, can you take my number and have him call me when he gets in?"

108

"Of course."

Shimon counseled, "Look, secretaries, especially in government offices, you can't rely on them. If she wrote it down at all, she'll put it away and forget about it. You call this Gedaliah later in the afternoon."

Later in the afternoon, around three o'clock, he tried again. When he asked for Ahuva, he was told, "Oh, she's gone home. Her little boy was sick."

"All right. Let me talk to Gedaliah."

To his great surprise, he was put through immediately. He gave his name and address and told what had been unearthed and explained the circumstances of the find. Gedaliah was obviously interested. In fact, he said so again and again. As Skinner talked, Gedaliah kept saying, "That's interesting," much the same way someone else might say "Uh-huh."

"This trench that you dug, is it visible from the street?"

"Not really," said Skinner. "It's in the back of the house and there're trees and bushes that conceal it from the road."

"Ah, good. Now, Mr. Skinner, will you please be careful not to talk about it. Don't tell your friends about it."

"Why not?"

"Because this is a country of amateur archaeologists. Any apartment you go into has a collection of potsherds, old coins, and bits of ancient glass that they've found at a construction site or at the beach in Caesarea, or wherever. If word should get out that there is an artifact there, you'll have dozens of people snooping around, digging, spoiling things. And you won't have a quiet moment from then on. So please, keep it quiet. I'll have Asher, who is our inspector for that area, come out and evaluate it. If it is of interest to us, we'll take care of security from then on."

"When will he come out?"

"Oh, within a few days."

"A few days? Look, Mr.—er, Gedaliah, I can't have an open trench, maybe five or six feet deep, right at my back door for several days. It's a hazard. Someone could fall in and—"

"You say it's in back of the house, so who could fall in?

Look, Mr. Skinner, it's Friday afternoon. The Sabbath will begin soon. And tomorrow is Saturday, the Sabbath, you understand? And Asher, who covers that area, is in *miluim* and won't be back until Sunday—"

"Sure, and then you'll call me, if you remember," said Skinner bitterly. "And I'll have to get hold of my plumber, who will be busy with a whole bunch of emergency jobs and—"

"Is the plumber there? Let me talk to him."

Skinner surrendered the phone to Shimon, who talked in Hebrew for a few minutes and then handed the instrument to Skinner once again.

Gedaliah's tone was soothing. "Mr. Skinner, there is no chance that we can get to the site before Monday. But I have arranged with Shimon to call him before we go out so that he can meet us there with his workers. Asher makes his evaluation, and if there is nothing there that interests us, he gives the word and Shimon and his men fill in the trench immediately. If for any reason Shimon can't make it, when Asher makes his inspection, Asher and his assistant will fill it in. Shimon says it's only a half hour's work for two men. He'll leave his shovels there. That's the best I can do."

"Monday, you say?"

"Monday, possible. We'll do our best."

"And in the meantime? How about the hazard of an open trench in the meantime?"

"Look, Mr. Skinner," said Shimon soothingly, "I'll spread a tarpaulin with a couple of boards across it and I'll put a barrier at either end. It will be all right, I guarantee."

"Well . . ."

18

THE TOUR GUIDE BRACED HIMSELF AGAINST THE CHROME handrail in front of the bus. He tapped his microphone to make sure it was in working order and said, "Welcome to Jerusalem, the holy city. The Excelsior Hotel where we will be staying and where we will be arriving in a few minutes now is a four-star hotel, noted for its comfort, service, and convenience. As you know, the Jewish Sabbath starts at sunset today, and in Jerusalem, they really keep it. All stores and restaurants in the modern portion of the city will be closed until sunset tomorrow." He glanced at his watch, and seeing that it was after two, he said, "As a matter of fact, everything is closed down right now. And there are no buses running, either. You can get cabs, however, but they're not too plentiful during the Sabbath, and if you order one, you may have to wait a while. In the Old City, behind the Wall, and in East Jerusalem stores and restaurants are open. That's because these sections are Arab. Fortunately, the Excelsior is within walking distance of the Old City. I suggest, however, that you wait until tomorrow morning before exploring the Old City. There will be a guided walking tour at eleven, and the bus will take you to Jaffa Gate, where it will begin. Dinner tonight in the luxurious hotel dining room will be a typical Sabbath dinner. Ah, here we are."

The bus swung off the street into the hotel driveway and came to a stop just beyond the door. The driver and tour guide descended and stood by the bus door to help the older passengers alight. From the hotel, half a dozen porters hurried out. Two of them wheeled forward a kind of platform that was as high as the bus, while two others climbed onto the roof of the bus to fold back the tarpaulin and to pass the luggage that was loaded on the roof to those manning the platform, who passed it to others to bring into the lobby of the hotel.

As they alighted, the passengers yawned and stretched, and then with dangling cameras and handbags shuffled into the lobby to stand about and gape at the decor and watch as the floor in front of the elevators gradually filled up with their valises and suitcases. While some stood in little groups, making plans, gossiping about other members of the tour, recalling incidents that had occurred and sites they had visited, some began drifting toward the reception desk, where the tour guide was checking names against a list and distributing room keys. There was none of the anxiety about luggage and room choices that had characterized the beginning of the tour. They were old hands now and knew that when they went up to their rooms their bags would be there on the little folding stands against the wall, or at the foot of the bed.

A few minutes later a cab drew up to the hotel entrance and Professor Abraham Grenish got out. The cabdriver opened his trunk and took out his passenger's bags and deposited them on the sidewalk. Grenish looked around for a porter as he drew his wallet out of his pocket, but they were all involved with the bags from the tour bus.

As he looked about uncertainly, the cabdriver said, "I take for you." Seizing the two bags, he marched into the hotel and deposited them in front of the desk. It occurred to Grenish that it was something that a cabbie in Boston or New York would be most unlikely to do, so he added a generous tip to the fare, and was in turn rewarded by an expression of obvious gratitude.

To the clerk who offered him a registration form on which

he printed his name, his address, and his passport number, he said, "The reservation was made by my travel agent. Is there a letter waiting for me?"

The clerk checked a list and said, "Yes, we have your registration. It's for six nights. Correct?" He glanced at the mail slot behind him, and added, "No letters."

"I might want to stay a little longer."

"No trouble. But let us know as soon as possible. Room seven-thirteen. It faces the Wall. Enjoy your stay." He nodded to a porter and handed him the room key. He waited until Grenish and the porter entered the elevator and it began to rise. Then with a quick glance to see that the other clerks at the desk were occupied, he picked up the telephone and dialed a number. When the connection was made, he said, "He has just checked in. Room seven-thirteen."

In his room Grenish unzipped his bags and hung up suits and jackets to minimize wrinkling, fished out pajamas and bed slippers and shaving materials, and then rezipped the bags. Shirts and underwear he preferred to draw on from his bags rather than lay them out in the available drawers. He then drew back the curtains on the window and looked out at the Wall and the valley in front of it, in which he could see a number of goats grazing.

He had come from Tel Aviv. It had been a long ride, and he wanted to stretch his legs. Normally he would have headed for the business section of the new part of the city—to look at the store windows, to get a feel of the place, to stop at a bookstore. But he realized that by now all the stores would be closed and the streets deserted. It occurred to him, however, that he could go to the Old City. There, since it was Arab, all shops would be open. Furthermore, it might be a good idea to locate Mideast Trading. Then when El Dhamouri's letter arrived he would be able to go there directly. He might also get a chance to make the acquaintance of El Dhamouri's cousin. From his window the Old City did not seem too far away. He would walk over, wander around, locate the Mid-

113

east, perhaps talk with the proprietor, and then look around for a restaurant. Afterward he would either walk back, or if he was tired by that time, he was sure he would be able to get a cab to take him back. The alternative was to hang around the hotel until dinner, which he would have to take in the hotel dining room, since all other restaurants were closed, and after several weeks in the country, he had no hankering for the usual Sabbath meal in an Israeli hotel, the fatty chicken soup, the chopped liver, the roast chicken and gravy.

He went down to the lobby and spoke to one of the desk clerks. "How would I get to the Old City?" he asked.

"You can take a cab—"

"No, I want to walk if I can. Is it within walking distance?"

"Oh, yes. About fifteen or twenty minutes. It's down the hill. Take the first street on your right when you leave the hotel. That will take you to Mamilla Street. You follow that until you get to the Wall. If you follow it to the right, you'll come to the Jaffa Gate."

The streets were largely deserted. The occasional pedestrian obviously hurrying along, frequently clutching a bunch of flowers, to prepare for the Sabbath. But as Grenish approached the Jaffa Gate of the Wall, he saw there were a number of people, obviously tourists with cameras dangling from their shoulders. He approached a policeman. "The Mideast Trading Corporation, can you tell me where it is?"

"Ah, Mideast Trading. *Français?*" And when Grenish shook his head, the policeman pointed and made a motion with his hand to indicate that he was to descend. Then he held up two fingers and curved his hand to the right and then pointed.

"I go down this street and at the second street to the right—"

To make sure he understood, the policeman held up one finger, then turned his hand to the right and shook his head violently. Then he held up two fingers and again curved his hand to the right and nodded and smiled.

Grenish interpreted this to mean that he must not go

114

down the first street but rather down the second. He smiled back to show he understood and said, "Thank you, thank you." He walked away thinking how unnecessary knowledge of other languages was for traveling.

The narrow street with shops on either side, most of them with displays of merchandise in front of the shop, sloped sharply down, amply justifying the policeman's initial motion that he was to descend. Here and there it was broken by little flights of two or three shallow steps, presumably to make progress in the other direction easier. He walked slowly, looking from side to side at the displays of wool rugs and brass pots and olive wood carvings and sheepskin vests and leather handbags and mother-of-pearl jewelry and, and . . . Once he had to crowd over to one side to let through a youngster who was wheeling a large cart loaded with pitas down the incline, leaning back on the handbar so it should not get away from him. And no sooner had he passed when again he had to press to one side as a porter came up the incline, bearing a large chest on his back, supported by straps over his shoulders and one across his forehead.

At the first intersection another youngster with a stick maneuvered a couple of donkeys, each laden with an arch of wooden boxes as they minced down the incline with delicate little steps. When he reached the second intersection, he saw his goal. There was a sign in English and Arabic on the corner announcing "Mideast Trading Corporation. Wholesale and Retail." It was just beyond the corner. But the store was dark, and a steel grille was drawn across the windows and padlocked in place. There was no sign on the door or in the window to the effect that it was closed temporarily, or that the proprietor would be back at some future day or hour. Did it mean that his mission was canceled, and ought he write to El Dhamouri so that he could make other arrangements?

He saw a policeman and went over to him. He pointed. "That store near the corner, can you tell me why it is closed?"

The policeman nodded and smiled.

The policeman obviously was Arab, and like the other,

probably spoke French. He tried to recall his college French. What was the word for store? Finally he pointed and said, *"Fermé Pourquois?"*

The policeman nodded and burst into rapid-fire, explosive French. Grenish did not understand a word, but the man was so eager and willing that he felt it would be ungracious to indicate that he had not understood. So he smiled and turned away.

"Can I help you?" It was Skinner. "You seem to be having some trouble."

"No trouble. I just wondered why that store was closed. I asked the policeman, but I'm afraid my French wasn't up to understanding what he said."

"Oh, well, that's easy. This store is closed because the proprietor is Muslim and it's Friday. By law, all stores have to be closed one day a week. Jewish stores are closed on Saturday, Christian stores on Sunday, and Muslim stores on Friday."

"And all these other stores—"

"Are Christian. In this section most of the proprietors are Christian."

They had been strolling along as Skinner explained. Grenish said, "You seem to be quite knowledgeable."

"Yes, I know the Old City well."

"Then perhaps you can direct me to a decent restaurant."

"Oh, there are lots of them. There's one down this street that I occasionally eat in."

19

AT A QUARTER TO SEVEN ON SUNDAY MORNING, AHARON
Perlmutter, having received the guest list from the front desk,
took up his station at a small table in front of the entrance to
the dining room.

A waiter came over. "A cup of coffee, Mr. Aharon?"

"That would be very nice."

"And some toast?"

"If you please."

As he ate his toast and drank his coffee, he ran a practiced
eye over the guest list. He noted that there was a French
group that had been put on the third and fourth floors, and
an American group on the fifth floor. Tour groups were
always put in consecutive rooms so that the constant traffic
between rooms (with the resultant banging of doors) and
their frequent loud hilarity in the corridors did not disturb
other guests.

The other guests, those not attached to tours, were assigned rooms on the sixth and seventh floors, which offered
better views of the city. There were many nationalities rep-
resented: German, French, English, Spanish, and a Japanese
couple. These names he studied, pronouncing them to himself so that he would recognize them when they were said to
him. He noticed the name Grenish in Room seven-thirteen,

117

and as he said it to himself, he wondered if it might not be an Americanization of his wife's family name, Grenitz. Of course, even it were, it did not necessarily mean a connection with his in-laws. The word meant "border," and when Jews were required to assume surnames, no doubt many who lived along a border—perhaps between Russia and Poland—had taken or been assigned that name. Still, his father-in-law had once mentioned a relative—a cousin or an uncle—who had immigrated to America. He wondered how he would broach the matter. If he were to ask outright, "Was your name formerly Grenitz?" the man might take offense and regard it as an impertinence. He worried about it and finally decided that when the man pronounced his name, he would reiterate it and then as he pretended to search through the list, he would add that he knew someone by that name, "Granish or maybe Grenitz." If the man had indeed changed his name from Grenitz, he might say so. Then he, Aharon, could identify himself, and perhaps the other might have some information about his in-laws in Poland. Maybe one or two had managed to escape and had made contact with him at the same time. He looked forward eagerly to the arrival of Grenish for breakfast.

The early arrivals were all tour people. There was no mistaking them. They had cameras and field glasses and maps and travel books. They wore badges for easy identification by the tour guide. Many of them wore *timbals*, the little white duck hats that tour managements often distributed as protection against the sun. They always breakfasted early, for they were scheduled to board the large buses for a day's touring of Jerusalem and its environs.

By eight o'clock the tour people were all gone, and guests from the upper floors began to make their appearances. But it was not until a quarter to nine that Grenish appeared. He had no sooner given his name and room number when the hotel manager came hurrying over and said, "Oh, Aharon, you speak Polish, don't you?"

"Yes, of course."

"Then would you please go to the front desk. There's

someone there who seems to be able to speak only Polish, or maybe it's Russian—"

"I know both."

"Fine. Go and interpret for the desk clerk, will you? I'll cover for you here."

With a lingering look at Grenish, who was helping himself at the buffet table, Aharon left the dining room. He was kept at the front desk until well after nine. When he was at last free, he returned to the dining room in the hope that Grenish might still be there, but the room was clear of guests and the waiters were busy changing the tablecloths.

He went back to the front desk and asked one of the clerks, "Grenish, seven-thirteen. How long is he staying?"

The clerk checked his list. "He's here for the week, Aharon." It occurred to Aharon that he certainly ought to be able to make contact in the next few days.

At the minyan there was always a hiatus of a few minutes between the conclusion of *mincha*, the afternoon service, and the beginning of *maariv*, the evening service. While occasionally someone used the opportunity to expound some interesting argument he had come across, more often it was merely a recess during which the men sat about and just talked. Perlmutter had arrived just as the service was about to begin, but now that the *mincha* service was over, Rabbi Small went over to him and asked how he liked his new job.

"Oh, it's not really new. I've done it before. It's a bit of a rush for me. Of course, I get through earlier, but—"

"But you'd rather sleep a little later in the morning," said the rabbi.

"Very true." He grinned ruefully. "But at my age, I can't be too particular. Strictly speaking, the whole business is pretty silly. We have very few guests who are not entitled to the breakfast, and the few who aren't, don't usually come down to the dining room for breakfast. The last time I had this duty, some months ago, there was only one in the two weeks that I was on the job that we had to charge for a breakfast. My

119

salary for those two and a half hours is a lot more than the occasional breakfast that we might fail to charge for, but we are part of a chain, and the rules are issued by the head office."

"And it's only for a couple of weeks?"

"Maybe only a week this time." He brightened. "And you meet so many people, if only for a moment. A whole world. This morning, for instance, in going over my list, I see the name Grenish."

"And this Grenish, you knew him?"

"No, but my wife's family name, I think I told you, was Grenitz. So it occurred to me that maybe that had been his name, and he had changed it, you know, Americanized it. So I'd ask him. No harm in asking, is there?"

"And?"

"Ah. He came. He gave me his name. But just then the manager asked me to go to the front desk. When I got back, Grenish was gone. So I'll ask him tomorrow. At the desk, they told me he was staying for a week. So I'm hoping."

20

ISH-TOV'S CLOSEST FRIEND AT THE YESHIVA WAS YITZCHAK (formerly Irving) Cohen of Amarillo, Texas. Cohen was a year or two older, had been at the yeshiva more than a year before Ish-Tov's arrival. Thin, intense, nervy, Cohen was meticulous in his observance of the commandments to the point that Ish-Tov considered superstitious. He once remarked on it jokingly, and Cohen had replied, "When you've led the kind of life I have, and a couple of times come to the verge—well, never mind, and then you find something that seems to work, you don't go fooling around and experimenting with the formula. Understand?"

Ish-Tov nodded, but he did not really understand, since he knew little or nothing of Cohen's earlier life. Cohen was curious and prying. He had ferreted out all kinds of secrets from his fellow students and his teachers, and these he did not mind passing on, but about his own affairs he was careful to tell nothing.

He not only knew a great deal about the members of the yeshiva, faculty and students, he also had an intimate knowledge of the building itself. He knew where everything was kept, how you could get in and out of the building without going through the front door, just where to stand in their dormitory so you could hear what was being said in Kahn's office a floor below. It was from him that Ish-Tov learned of the sanctuary on the roof.

Sunday afternoon, when they found themselves momentarily alone in the dormitory they shared with four others, Cohen took out a half-empty box of cigarettes and shook loose a couple of misshapen and obviously hand-rolled cigarettes. Ish-Tov's eyes opened wide.

"Pot? Where'd you get them?" he asked.

"In the Old City. When we finished dickering with that Arab over the bag, you walked on ahead. Remember? I hung back and bought a few."

"From the same guy? How did you know he—"

"I knew. That's why I took you there to dicker about the bag. How about it?"

"Okay. You go first and I'll be along in a couple of minutes."

Yitzchak nodded agreement and sauntered out of the room. After a quick look around, he walked to the end of the corridor to a door, which he eased open, then up a flight of dusty steps and pushed open another door, which opened onto the roof.

He sat down on the cement roof and rested his back against the shed, which also provided shade against the hot sun. After a couple of minutes he was joined by Ish-Tov, who sat down beside him.

"What kept you?" he asked.

Ish-Tov drew out of his pocket a pair of small, prismatic binoculars. "I wanted to dig these out."

"What for? To look for birds?"

Ish-Tov grinned lewdly. "Yeah, that's right, for birds. Once I looked right into a bedroom and saw a bird undressing."

"Hey, boy, you know what that kind of talk around here gets you? A *shadchen*. He comes around, and in a week you're married. And then it's a kid every year for the next ten or twelve years. You're twenty-five? Twenty-six? They'll be arranging a marriage for you pretty soon, anyway. No need to hurry it, though."

"How come they haven't got you?"

Yitzchak smiled in great satisfaction. "They can't. I'm married."

"Yeah? Hey, where—"

"Back in the States. Gentile girl. We're getting a divorce." He laughed coarsely. "That is, if and when the guy she's living with now decides to marry her."

"Then you'd let the matchmaker arrange a marriage for you?"

"Sure. Why not? He couldn't do any worse than I did for myself. In college, the dean picks a roommate for you, and usually it works out all right. Same kind of thing when the *shadchen* picks a wife for you. It's like a business contract, and usually both parties are satisfied. When you marry for love, though, it's a different kind of thing altogether. You think she's the only one in the world and she thinks the same about you. Then after a while the spark isn't there and you begin to wonder if maybe it's because she's focusing in another direction, on someone else. Look at Kahn."

"You mean our Kahn, the secretary? What about him?"

"Married five years or more and no kids. The older men tell him he should get a divorce, but he won't think of it. He's in love with her. You know where he is right now?"

"He wasn't at the desk in the front office. Yossi was there. I figured he was sick, or maybe making the arrangements for the trip to Safed tomorrow."

"He's not sick, and he may not even go on the Safed *teeyul*. He's home watching his wife, that's where he is and that's what he's doing."

"How do you know?"

"Because I heard Rabbi Brodny talking with Rabbi Ellsberg. They were joking about it. Their wives—at least Brodny's—socialize with Mrs. Kahn. She got a letter from some guy in America, an old boyfriend, saying he was coming to Jerusalem and would call Sunday—today. Being an American, I suppose he figured it was part of the weekend. So Kahn takes the day off to be home and make sure there's no hanky-panky. That's what marrying for love does for you."

"How come you hear so much, Yitzchak?"

"Because I like to know what's going on. The teachers here, when they don't want us to know what they're saying, talk in Hebrew. They figure none of us know much of the language beyond what we've learned here. But I went to a Hebrew day school when I was a kid. And when I came here I went to an *ulpan* for six months where you lived in and were not allowed to talk anything but Hebrew, and when we weren't talking we were listening to radio and television. So I'm pretty fluent."

"You're pretty sharp, Yitzchak. Don't you ever worry about cutting yourself?" Ish-Tov took a last drag on his roach and then tossed it on the concrete and rose to his feet.

"Hey, shred it," said Yitzchak. "If someone comes up here, I don't want him to know we've been using the place to smoke pot."

Obediently, Ish-Tov stepped on the stub and ground it to dust. Then he strolled over to the parapet that encircled the roof. "Boy, what a view," he exclaimed.

"You'd better stand back," said Yitzchak. "Someone might see you."

"So what?"

"I don't think we're supposed to be up here. Besides, if it got known, you'd have guys up here all the time, and then where would we go to puff a joint?"

"Right." Ish-Tov stepped back a pace or two but continued circling the shed now and then, raising the binoculars that dangled from his neck.

"See any birds?" asked Yitzchak.

"Just the kind that live in trees." He continued to circle, and when he faced the Skinner house, he called out, "Hey, Yitzchak, come and take a look at this."

Yitzchak joined him and looked in the direction in which he was pointing. "That hole in the ground?"

"Yeah. Looks like a grave."

"That's no grave. I'll bet that's what Kahn was all worked

up about last night. He was hotfooting it down the corridor like his pants were on fire. So naturally when he went in and closed the door, I stopped to listen—"

"Naturally."

"Look, buster, in any institution or organization, you last longer if you cover your ass. Which means it's a good idea to know what's going on. I figure that when Kahn goes hurrying to see the director and barges in without even knocking, it must be something important."

"So you stayed outside and listened? Did you bend down to look through the keyhole?"

"And maybe be seen by somebody? Nah." He grinned. "I went to the door just beyond the director's and slid in there. That's kind of a storage closet with pails and mops and a little sink, and it's separated from the director's office by just a thin plywood partition. I could hear as plain—as plain as I hear you now."

"So what did you hear?"

"Listen. Kahn had got a call from a former student who works in the Ministry of Education and Culture. The guy next door, Skinner, had phoned the Department of Antiquities— they're part of the Ministry, you know—that he'd discovered an archaeological artifact, and they said they'd come down and look at it in a couple of days."

"So what's the excitement? They discovered an arti-fact—"

"Don't you understand? They could start a dig and it could spread to here, the yeshiva land. There's a theory that there must be a tunnel under the wall of the Old City—"

"That's silly."

"Why is it silly? If you're in a walled city, surrounded by the enemy, and you want to send a messenger to your allies who are holed up in Ramallah, say, how would you do it? Or if you wanted to make a sortie and attack the besieging force from the rear, wouldn't you need a tunnel? But that's not all. Kahn was telling the director that the same thing happened here a few years back. They found an artifact and someone reported it to the Department of Antiquities, and Rabbi Moshe Stern, who was director before Karpis, and who was an activist, ordered the hole to be filled up."

"And what happened?"

"Nothing. Absolutely nothing. The investigator for the department came and reported back that there was nothing of consequence here. See, he didn't want to get into a hassle with the religious establishment. But Karpis wouldn't do anything like that. He's the kind who would cooperate with the authorities."

"Well, he's running the show, isn't he?"

"Maybe," said Yitzchak cryptically. "Here, let me see those glasses for a minute."

He peered at the trench, and then handing the binoculars back to Ish-Tov, said, "They left a couple of shovels there. Take a look. That shows they are planning on doing some more digging. Tell you what. How about we go down there after dark and fill up that trench."

"Why should we do it? What's in it for us?"

"Because it would be a good joke on this guy Skinner—"

"But he could get in trouble."

"All the better. And after a while, when things quiet down, we let it be known that we did it and we'll be bloody heroes here, especially with Kahn, and that could be useful."

"But there's a big mound on either side of the trench—"

"A half hour's work."

"And how about Skinner? Won't he see or hear us?"

"He's not home. There's never anybody there Sundays. That's the housekeeper's day off. She's Christian. And Skinner and that Arab usually go off. Usually they don't get home until after eleven, and make a bloody racket when they do. Look, soon as it's dark, I'll show you how to sneak out the back, and you'll go over there and start shoveling the dirt back. Then I'll join you a little while later."

"Why should I go first? It's your idea."

"Because it might be a grave site, maybe an ancient cemetery."

"So?"

"So I'm a Kohane, a descendant of Aaron. I'm not supposed to be in the presence of a dead body, not even of the bones after centuries. Maybe that's what they found there—bones. That could be why Kahn was so excited. He's a Kohane, too. We are polluted by it for a whole year after a single contact. For a whole year we cannot perform a priestly function."

To Ish-Tov, Yitzchak's religiosity, at such curious variance with his general attitude, was always a source of surprise.

"And it means so much to you?" he asked.

"A special privilege," said Yitzchak gravely, "carries with it special responsibilities. Once you cover the bottom with a layer of earth and cover any traces of bone, if there are any, I can then come over and help you fill in the rest."

21

EARLY MONDAY MORNING, AS HE DID EVERY WEEKDAY morning, Joseph Kahn descended from the bus and walked to the yeshiva, getting there just in time to join the group in the *shachris* service, after which he had his breakfast in the dining hall, sitting at the head table with the rest of the faculty. This morning, however, breakfast was somewhat hurried, for the big air-conditioned bus that was to take them all on the *teeyul*, a holiday trip to Safed, had already pulled up to the door while they were still engaged in their morning prayers. By half past eight they had boarded and were singing, laughing, joking, and waving at passing cars on the road. It did not often happen, perhaps a couple times a year, but it was, of course, all the more enjoyable for that reason. This outing was through the generosity of one of the wealthy backers of the organization, and the occasion was the completion by the advanced class of the section of the Talmud they had been studying since the beginning of the year.

The trip was a long one, but they would spend the whole day in Safed entertained and fed by members of the organization in Safed and would return late at night tired, exhausted. It was a break from their routine, from the study and the discipline, and they would savor it and talk about it for weeks to come.

* * *

At ten o'clock Monday morning, the chambermaid on the seventh floor of the Hotel Excelsior knocked on the door of Room seven-thirteen, waited a moment, knocked again, and then put her ear to the door to hear if there was any sound of movement within. Hearing nothing, she inserted her master key in the lock and opened the door. Noting that the bed was made, the bedcover neat and smooth as she had left it the day before, she went into the bathroom. There, too, all was in order, the towels neatly folded, the soap she had left, dry and untouched. She considered for a moment and then went to the telephone on the night table and phoned the housekeeper.

The housekeeper said, "The room was not occupied? The bed was not slept in? You're sure? All right, lock the door and go on to the next room. And, Yael, don't mention it to anyone."

The housekeeper notified the manager, who came out of his office and motioned the tall, burly security guard to come to him. "Go up to seven-thirteen, Avi, and have a look around. The room was not occupied last night."

When Avi returned ten minutes later, he said, "I double-locked the door so his key won't work. He'll have to go to the desk, and I'll open the door for him. His stuff is all there, so he didn't skip out to avoid paying his bill. Shall I call the Shin Bet?"

The manager, who had but recently been transferred from the Tel Aviv unit of the hotel chain, said, "Shin Bet? Why not the police? In Tel Aviv we always call the police."

"Security is a little tighter here in Jerusalem. If we were to call the police, they'd just call Shin Bet."

"All right. Call them."

In the office of the Shin Bet, Israel's national security bureau, Uri Adoumi, chief of the Jerusalem section, sat at his desk, thumbing through the stack of files before him. He would pick up a folder, take a swig of coffee, which his secretary had brought in as soon as he had entered the office,

129

then lean back in his swivel chair, his right foot braced against the open deep drawer against the pressure of the spring. Occasionally he would sit up straight to make a note, in which case he would take a gulp of the coffee before again resuming his recumbent position. He was a blocky, bulky man with grizzled, red hair, what there was left of it, that was rapidly turning a yellowish-white.

An aide, a young man in jeans and T-shirt, opened the door.

Adoumi sat up and said irascibly, "Don't you know you're supposed to knock?"

"Bourgeois formalities. If I knocked, you'd tell me to come in. If you didn't answer, I'd think something was the matter, so I'd come in to take a look. Either way, I'd be in. So why should I knock?"

"In the kibbutz, you never knocked?"

"If the door was locked, you knocked so they should come and open the door, but if it wasn't locked—"

"Suppose Shoshana was in here and we were fooling around?"

"Aw, you wouldn't fool around with Shoshana. Besides, she's sitting at her desk."

"All right, what do you want?" asked Adoumi wearily.

"We got a call from the Hotel Excelsior, from the security guard. One of their guests is missing."

"Missing? Since when?"

"Since yesterday, I guess. He didn't come down for breakfast, and his bed hadn't been slept in."

"The call came from the police, or direct from the security guard?"

"From the security guard. He went up and looked at the room. His clothes were still there, so they called us. You want me to run up there and take a look?"

Adoumi surveyed his assistant, the sweat-stained T-shirt, the worn jeans, the heavy scuffed boots. The Hotel Excelsior was not the most posh hotel, but it was four-star. The guests, probably on a chartered tour, would be respectable middle-class people from whatever country they came from. And the staff would wear clean uniforms, properly pressed. He temporized. "They give you a name?"

"Yeah. An American. A Professor Grenish."

"Professor Grenish? Seems to me I've come across that name, Grenish. Look, run it through the computer. Maybe I saw it on one of our lists."

While his assistant was in another office, operating the computer, Adoumi sat upright, his hand drumming the top of the desk as he concentrated, trying to remember where he had seen the name Grenish.

A minute or two later, the assistant returned and said somewhat sheepishly for not having checked on his own, "It's on one of the Mossad lists. Nothing special, except that he's Jewish and is very friendly with some high muckamuck Arab. He arrived in the country by boat from Greece, stayed in Haifa. He was there for almost a week and then went to Tel Aviv. He stayed at the Oceanview for a couple of days and then came up to Jerusalem Friday."

"Uh-huh. Maybe I'd better go to the Excelsior myself."

22

THE MANAGER OF THE EXCELSIOR, HIS RECORDS SPREAD OUT on the desk before him, said, "You understand, for some of our guests, staying in a hotel is a comparatively new experience. They register, stay a few days, and then perhaps they go to visit a relative in Tel Aviv or Haifa or Netanya. They are persuaded to stay over, or they miss the last bus, or whatever. Or sometimes they go on a trip and are gone a few days. Sometimes they assume that as long as they haven't spent the night here, they are not responsible for the price of the room for that day. Some of them are quite indignant that we should charge them for those days." He smiled sadly.

"You always charge them?"

"Of course. The room is occupied. We can't rent it to someone else, can we? What do we gain if the guest is absent for a night? A few minutes of the chambermaid's time? That room she doesn't have to make up the next morning, so we save the day's linen and towels. And we save a breakfast."

"So if he comes for a week or two, let's say," suggested Adoumi, "and in the middle of it he wants to take a trip for a couple of days—say, down to Eilat—he'd have to pay here and in Eilat?"

"Not if he checks out here first. He can check out, pay his bill, and we'll even store his things at no charge. Then when he comes back, he registers again. If it's not during the busy season, he probably would get his old room again."

"And if it is the busy season?"

"Ah, then he takes his chances. We will tell him that we cannot guarantee him his room when he returns. We may even tell him that we can't guarantee him any room."

"I see. Now, in the case of this Grenish?"

"Let's see." He surveyed the top of the desk and picked up a registration card. "Here we are. Professor Abraham Grenish. He arrived on Friday afternoon at five after two in the afternoon." He picked up a sheaf of papers and thumbed through them rapidly. "He did not have dinner with us that evening. In fact, he didn't have either lunch or dinner in our dining room at all. That's not too unusual. I should say the great majority of our guests don't unless they come in a bus and it's included in the price of the tour."

"And breakfasts?"

"Ah, that's usually included in the cost of the room, so practically all our guests have breakfast with us, even though some of them have no more than a cup of coffee and a bun. But not all. Some arrange for just the room. They save a little." He picked up another sheaf of papers and held them out to the Shin Bet officer. "See, these are lists of the guests and their room numbers. There's a separate column for each day. As the guest comes to the dining room, we have someone sitting at the entrance with this checklist. The guest gives his name and room number, and it is checked off. Now, our Mr. Grenish, or rather Professor Grenish, had breakfast on Saturday and on Sunday."

"All right, so he was here from Friday afternoon until Sunday morning, at least. Is there someone here who can give us a description of him?"

"Our Arab staff that we use for the Sabbath comes in Friday at half past one. So you can ask the Arab desk clerks. The one who registered him might remember him, but I doubt it. A tour bus came in just about then and they were probably pretty busy. Maybe the porter who took his bag up might remember him if he gave him an especially big tip. But I doubt it. Likewise, the *maître d'* who was on duty for breakfast. It's pretty busy at breakfast time, and most of them, they don't even look at the guest."

"The chambermaid?"

The manager shook his head. "No. They tend to stay out of the way of the guests. They do their work while the guest is out of his room. You could try.

"The porters and the chambermaids you can interview now. They work here full time. The Arab desk clerks, some are here only for the two days of the Sabbath. They're on from Friday half past one until nightfall Saturday. They won't be here until Friday. I can give you their addresses, though. The picture on his passport—"

"Ah, you have it?"

"No, but it may be up in his room."

"Didn't your security guard search the room?"

"Of course, but I'm sure it was only a cursory search. You know, just to see if what was left was worthwhile leaving to avoid a hotel bill. But if you made a thorough search—"

"Don't you believe it. He must have it on him. If he didn't take it with him, he wouldn't hide it. It would be on the bureau or in a drawer, and your man would have found it. If he was afraid of losing it or having it stolen, he wouldn't hide it in his room, he'd leave it in one of your safe-deposit boxes. He didn't, did he?"

The manager pulled open a drawer, took out a sheet of paper, studied it for a moment, and then shook his head.

"I'll go up and take a look at the room now."

"I'll have Avi, our security guard, take you up and open the door for you."

In the room, Adoumi went directly to the bathroom. Avi followed him and stood in the doorway.

"Clean-shaven. No beard or moustache," said Adoumi.

"How can you be sure? Lots of people shave but have a little beard or a moustache."

"There's no scissors. If he had any kind of beard or even a

moustache, he'd be sure to have a pair of scissors to trim it with."

He picked up the comb and brush. "Short hair," he remarked. "If you had longish hair, you wouldn't use a fine-tooth comb like this. You'd pull out too much of it, especially after you'd showered. Ah, yes, here we have some specimens. Brownish, wouldn't you say? And graying. Give me one of those hotel envelopes in the desk there. That would make him probably anywhere from forty to, say, fifty-five. His own teeth. See that dental floss? And look at the brush and toothpaste. People with false teeth use a special toothbrush and a special toothpaste when they don't use one of those tablets you dissolve in a glass. All right, let's see what he's got in his bag, and in the closet."

From the floor of the closet, he picked up a pair of black shoes. "Eight and a half C. I've got to check that with a table of equivalent clothing sizes, but I think it's about a forty-one." He made a note on the envelope in which he had placed the hair samples. Then standing on one leg, he matched one of the shoes to his own, sole to sole. "He's shorter than I am." He reached in and took one of the suits off the rod and held it up in front of him and looked in the full-length mirror. "Yeah, maybe one sixty-seven centimeters." Then he took the jacket off its hanger, and after quickly divesting himself of his own jacket, he tried to put it on. "He's a lot thinner than I am. Maybe sixty-four or sixty-five kilos." He made another note on the envelope.

"You've gone through the pockets?"

"Uh-huh. There was nothing in any of them."

Nevertheless, Adoumi searched each of the pockets in each of the suits. "You can never tell," he said half apologetically. "Okay, let's look at the bags."

"He didn't put any of his stuff, his underwear, his shirts in the drawers," remarked Avi, and he proceeded to pull open each of the drawers of the bureau to demonstrate.

"That's a little unusual, isn't it?"

"Oh, I don't know. A lot of guests do it. They just take out suits and trousers—you know, so they won't crease—and maybe their shoes and a pair of pajamas. The rest they're apt to leave in the suitcases so they shouldn't have to pack them again."

"But that's because they stay only two or three days. But our friend was planning to stay for a whole week."

Adoumi opened a suitcase and from it drew a long strip of cloth backed by sponge rubber about eight inches wide and a yard or more long. "Our friend occasionally wears a belly-band. That means he's probably developing a potbelly. I'll just change that estimate of his weight to seventy kilos." He made a note on the envelope.

"Some people wear them because they got back trouble," said Avi.

"Yes, but look at these shirts. Size sixteen, whatever that means. About forty-one, I'd say. But do you notice the way that top buttonhole is pulled? Those shirts were getting tight on him. Ah, and here's one that looks newer than the others and it's sixteen and a half—say, size forty-three."

He scratched his head and then picked up the suitcase and dumped the contents on the bed. He felt the lining and inner pockets. Then he replaced each item, squeezing, bending, feeling each in turn. Then he did the same with the other suitcase. "No passport," he announced as he straightened up.

"He probably has it with him," said Avi. "Most of them do, as identification in case they want to use credit cards."

"I suppose, but it's better to make sure. Now, I want you to pack up all his things, the suits, the shoes, the toilet articles, everything, just as he would if he were leaving. Then I want you to store them where no one can get at them. Or do I have to have someone come from my office to put them under seal?"

"No, I can store them all right. But what if he comes back?"

"Then you'll call my office, and I or someone will come right down. By the way, did he turn in his key?"

"No."

23

ADOUMI SAT WITH YAACOV LURIA, POLICE CHIEF OF THE Jerusalem district, a thin, cold, precise man who sat with his back straight, with hands folded on the completely cleared surface of his mahogany desk, his eyes fixed unwavering and unblinking through small oval pince-nez.

"He had breakfast at the hotel, and that was the last that was seen of him," said Adoumi.

Luria unfolded his hands and opened a drawer of his desk to take out a pad of paper. From his breast pocket, he produced a mechanical pencil. "Description?"

"I gave it already to your lieutenant. There isn't much. Around fifty years old, brown hair beginning to gray, weighs around seventy kilos, maybe one sixty-seven tall, probably beginning to develop a potbelly, wears an eight and a half C shoe—say, a forty-one—and his shirt collar is sixteen or sixteen and a half—say, forty-three."

Luria's eyebrows went up, causing a series of ridges on his forehead as his eyes opened wide. "This is a description? What color eyes? What's the shape of his nose? Of his mouth? The person who gave you this description knew what size shoe he wore, and his collar size?"

Adoumi opened his hands in resignation. "That's what I was able to gather when I examined his effects. No one saw

137

him, or at least no one remembers him. It's a hotel. He came in with a group of about a hundred people—"

"Then the people in the group—"

"No, no, he was not one of them. He merely came in the same time they did. I questioned the porter, the chambermaid, the clerks. Avi, the security guard, remembers a letter came for him and that he claimed it, but he didn't really look at him. Someone said, "Seven-thirteen . . . Grenish," and he took it out of the slot and handed it to him. The clerks were busy Sunday morning registering a new group."

"Do you realize how many hundreds, thousands of people would fit this description?"

"I know, I know."

"All right, so we can't actually go looking for him. If he turns up, maybe this will help to identify him. The lieutenant has this information, you say, so what do you want from me?" He put the pad back in the drawer, returned the pencil to his pocket, and looked expectantly at Adoumi, his hands once again folded primly on the desktop.

"Well, it isn't just a police matter. His name was on a list we got from Mossad."

"Dangerous?"

"I don't think so. I don't know. From what I was able to get from them, he may be perfectly innocent. He's Jewish but is a good friend of an important Arab in the States whom they keep an eye on."

"I see. So?"

"So if you do run across him, I want the word passed that he is not to be questioned, just held, until I get a chance to question him."

"All right." Luria nodded in token of agreement—and dismissal.

It was after four Monday before Dr. Asher Gur, the Department of Antiquities expert for the Old Jerusalem area, was able to clear up the work that had accumulated during his absence in the army reserves. To Moshe, his young blond giant of an assistant, he said, "I think I'll call it a day. You might as well run along now, too."

"How about that find reported by"—he glanced at a note on their bulletin board—"James Skinner?"

"Tomorrow," said Gur wearily.

"Skinner. Say, isn't that the guy who had all that trouble with the yeshiva thugs?"

"As I remember it, he wasn't here at the time. There was an Arab manager or caretaker. So?"

"So don't you think we kind of owe him? I mean, he was treated pretty shabbily—"

"But not by us, not by the department."

"I know, but here he has this trench right in his yard—"

"It's in back—"

"Yes, but he's afraid someone might stumble into it. And Gedaliah told him he had to leave it like that until we inspected it."

"Yes, and Gedaliah also told him he'd contact the plumber to fill it in once we decided, and we'd do it if we couldn't get the plumber—"

"I could have Ahuva call him and tell him we're going over there and to meet us—"

"All right, all right, we'll take a look at it. I'm sure there's nothing there for us. I know that section well. You'll find it's a stone that he took from the rubble of another building and that it's part of an old cistern or a cesspool that was constructed maybe fifty, sixty years ago. Let's go."

Twenty minutes later, Gur brought his dusty little Peugeot to a halt in front of the Skinner house. Moshe got out and went up to the front door and knocked. He waited, and knocked again. Then he saw the bell button, and pressed that. He could hear it ring inside, but no one came to the door.

"There's nobody home," he called out to Gur.

The other got out of the car and joined him. "Well, we don't need an audience. Let's go around back and have a look."

They circled the house and then stopped to stare at the

mound of soft earth where the trench had obviously been. "Our Mr. Skinner appears to have taken matters in his own hands," said Gur.

"So what do we do now?"

"What we do is notify the department that Mr. Skinner, acting against implicit instructions and against the law, covered up his find, and after some wrangling, your Mr. Skinner finds himself subject to a sizable fine. Too bad, because I'm sure there's nothing there worthwhile."

"Couldn't you—"

"Couldn't I what?"

"I mean, where you're sure there's nothing there—" Moshe was obviously distressed.

"I could report," Gur conceded, "that we inspected, and finding nothing, we filled in the trench ourselves, since the plumber didn't arrive—assuming, of course, that Ahuva was able to reach him, or even tried. Is that what you'd like me to do?"

"Well, if you're absolutely sure there's nothing there. Gedaliah thinks—"

"Gedaliah thinks it might be a lead to the tunnel he's been hoping to find for the past ten years."

"Look, Asher," said Moshe earnestly, "how about if I dig it up—not the whole trench, just the part nearest the back door where they said they found the stone. The earth is soft, freshly dug. It wouldn't take me more than ten or fifteen minutes."

Gur shrugged. "If you want to sweat—"

"I need the exercise. I was in the office all day."

"All right. I'll unlock the trunk and get the spade."

"No need to. I'll use one of these." Seizing one of the shovels, he set to work. Asher watched for a minute or two and then went back to the car, looking over every now and then as the figure of his assistant sank lower into the ground. Then he got some papers out of the glove compartment and soon was absorbed in them.

Suddenly he was aroused by a cry from his assistant. "Asher, come quickly! I've found a shoe!"

Gur leaped out of his car and came running. "A shoe? You mean a sandal. Roman?"

Moshe looked up from the pit in which he was standing and said quietly, "No, a modern shoe. And there's a foot in it."

Adoumi had left his office and was already home when he got the call. "Uri? Yaacov. We've found someone who might be your man. Forty, graying brown hair, about seventy kilos."

"Your men haven't questioned him?"

"No, my men haven't questioned him."

"Swell! I'll be right over. Where is he?"

"In the morgue."

Adoumi could just see the stretching of the thin lips to display even teeth that passed for a smile with Yaacov Luria. "Your sense of humor, Yaacov, comes out at strange times. You're at your office? I'll come right over."

Adoumi slouched in the visitor's chair as Luria, sitting up straight with hands folded on the desktop, recounted the events that had led to the discovery of the body. "Curiously, it was the shoe"—his lips stretched to show his teeth—"eight and a half C, that was the first bit of evidence. The young man who was digging passed it up to his boss, who told him to climb out and stand guard while he went to call the police. Fortunately, I was around and able to arrange to keep it quiet. So far nothing has been given to the newspapers, but I don't know how long we'll be able to keep it out of the papers."

"There was no identification on the body? No letters, no wallet, no—"

"Nothing, except labels on the clothing, which were all from American establishments."

"How about the autopsy?"

"Dr. Shatz is on leave and we have a not-too-experienced young man doing it. He was hesitant about giving us the time of death. You see, not only was the body buried, but also he was lying beside a cold-water pipe, which would affect the normal processes. He thinks he'll be able to give us something when he examines stomach contents."

141

"What condition was the face in? Would someone who knew him be able to recognize him?"

"Well, I think so." But he sounded doubtful.

"Look here, that artist you've got, the one who does portrait sketches from witnesses' descriptions—do you suppose he could work up a drawing?"

"I think we can do better than that, Uri. We can have the face made up and photographed. Maybe touch up the photograph."

"That's fine. And when could I have copies?"

"Sometime tomorrow. Maybe I can reach my man and he could come in tonight. In that case I could have copies sent over first thing in the morning—to your house, if you'd like."

"I'd like. I could take them down to the hotel first thing in the morning before I go to the office."

"And if no one at the hotel can identify him?"

"Ah, then things become difficult. I—or rather you, my friend—notify the American consul, who notifies the State Department, who search their files for the duplicate of the passport picture. It could take weeks."

"Or you could notify the Mossad," suggested Luria, "who through their contacts in the State Department might get it done in days."

"True, but I would prefer not to ask Mossad."

Luria smiled, knowing of the petty rivalry between the two branches. "I understand."

24

ALTHOUGH YAACOV LURIA WAS PREPARED TO ACCEPT THE
authority of the Shin Bet in matters of national security, he
was not prepared to accept the word of Uri Adoumi on just
what constituted a matter of the security of the State and what
was a straight police matter. As he explained it to his lieutenant, Yishayah Gross, "How do we know the man we uncovered is this Professor Grenish? Because he wears the same
size shoe? Ridiculous!" He glanced at his assistant, mentally
gauging his size and weight. "Chances are you wear the same
size shoe."

"So what are you planning to do?"

"Here we have a man who has been murdered—"

Yishayah coughed discreetly. "We don't know that yet."

"He didn't bury himself. Well, that's something we're
supposed to investigate. Now, that trench was not visible
from the street. So who knew about it?"

"Well, the ones who dug it. The plumber fellow, Shimon,
for one. And the two Arabs who actually did the work."

"Who else?"

"I suppose the Department of Antiquities people, they
must have known about it even though they may not have
seen it. This Shimon spoke to them—and, oh yes, the man on
whose ground it was dug, and anyone in his household."

"I think we can forget about the Department of Antiquities people. They didn't see the place until Monday evening. And the owner of the property, what's his name, Skinner, if he knocked someone off, he wouldn't be apt to bury him on his own property. If he killed him for some reason, some personal vendetta, you know what he'd do? He'd put him in his car and then ride out somewhere late at night and dump the body out on the road. No, we can forget about Skinner. Unthinkable, especially where he knew that the Department of Antiquities people were coming to examine something found in the trench. Which brings us back to Shimon, the plumber, and his two Arabs."

"So?"

"So let's think about it. The man came in Friday afternoon. He didn't eat at the hotel, which means he had to have eaten in the Old City or East Jerusalem, because there's no other place to eat on the Sabbath. And we have some confirmation that he was in the Old City. It was Officer Kassim who recognized the photo—"

"*Thought* he recognized the photo," Yishayah amended.

"All right, *thought* he recognized the photo as that of a man who stopped to question him about one of the Muslim stores that was closed."

"He *thought* that's what he was asking, but he couldn't be sure because he didn't know the language."

Luria was a little annoyed with his subordinate. "All right, that's what he *thought* he was asking. I'm just considering possibilities. Now, we know that our man did not dine or lunch at his hotel the next day, although he did have his breakfast there. So the likelihood is that he had lunch and dinner in the Old City. That means he was there all day. Now, what was he doing there? He may just have been wandering around, looking at sights. Or he may have had some business there."

"What kind of business?"

Luria shrugged elaborately. "I don't know. Maybe he was trying to buy some archaeology junk, some old manuscript,

144

perhaps, like the stuff that was found in the Qumran caves. After all, the guy was a professor."

"Or maybe he was just trying to get hold of some hashish," suggested the lieutenant.

"Could be," Luria agreed. "Let's see, Kassim was stationed where?"

"Corner Lohamin and David."

"That's across from—what's that store on the corner?"

"Mideast Trading Corporation."

"Mideast, eh. Seems to me we kept an eye on that a couple of years back."

"That and maybe a couple of dozen others. But we never found anything."

"Still, it's a possible starting point. If we could find some connection with someone in one of the stores in the area with one of that plumber's two Arabs—"

"What's the connection with the two Arabs?"

"Because they knew of the trench. Moreover, they could be suspects on their own. Look, the man is found with no wallet, no passport—what's an American passport worth in criminal circles?"

"I've heard anywhere from five thousand to as much as ten thousand dollars."

"Right. So it's worth killing for. Now, if there is a death resulting from a robbery, the body is taken out in a car and dumped out on a dark road somewhere. And it makes no difference to the thieves if the body is found the next day. But if it is a passport that was stolen, especially if it might be used in the next few days, then it's important that the body not be found, and if there's a trench where he can be dropped and then covered over—"

"Yes, but in that case, it seems even more important that the Shin Bet or Mossad handle the matter," said the lieutenant.

"But we don't know, do we? We'll keep Shin Bet informed, of course. But there's no harm in our doing a little investigating on our own."

There was a knock on the door, and a subordinate stuck his head in and said, "There's a Mr. Skinner here who insists on seeing you, Chief."

"Skinner? Show him in."

Skinner came striding in. "Chief Luria?"

"That's right, Mr. Skinner. Sit down."

Reluctantly, and obviously annoyed, Skinner took the chair indicated and pulled it up to the desk. "Look here," he said, "I was told that the matter was in your hands."

"And what matter is that, Mr. Skinner?"

"The matter of the trench in back of my house. This plumber who dug the ditch to replace a broken pipe saw what he thought was an archaeological artifact, so he wanted me to notify the Department of Antiquities."

"Very proper," murmured the lieutenant.

"You think so? Well, maybe from your point of view, but I was left with a trench in my backyard. And because it was Friday afternoon, they couldn't send someone down to look at it right then and there. And of course not the next day because of the Sabbath. And probably not the next day because their man was on reserve duty. And then what was I going to do about having the trench filled in? Call the plumber? And who knows when he'd come. So they finally said they'd get hold of the plumber, and if they couldn't, or if he couldn't come down right away, they'd fill it in themselves."

"What were you afraid of, Mr. Skinner?" asked Luria.

"What was I afraid of? With a trench four or five feet deep right next to my back door? My housekeeper might fall in. Or I might forget and fall in. Or some tradesman coming in the back door."

"All right, I understand."

"So I had to go up to Haifa Sunday, and I was gone all day and didn't get back until late. Actually, I had to go on to Hebron, where I was going to spend the night, but I thought I'd stop off at the house first. All right. I come home and find the trench has been filled in. Fine. But I notice the plumber's things are still there, a pickax and a couple of shovels. So I assumed it was the Department of Antiquities people who had filled it in, because if it had been the plumber, wouldn't he have taken his stuff with him? So we go to Hebron—"

"We?"

"Yes, my manager, Ismael Hakem, and I. We were in Hebron all day yesterday and spent the night there. This morning I come back and find I've got a trench again. The pickax and shovels are gone, so I call the plumber. I spent half the morning trying to get hold of him. Finally I called the Department of Antiquities. They told me to see you."

"And the archaeological artifact?" asked the lieutenant.

"Oh, that. That turned out to be nothing. Part of an old cistern that had been constructed when the house was built about fifty or sixty years ago, and then filled in when the water system was installed."

"So you'd like to know our concern in the matter?" said Luria. "But first"—he opened the top drawer of his desk, and taking out a photograph, handed it to Skinner—"do you know this man? Have you ever seen him?"

"Looks familiar," said Skinner. "Yeah, it's the man I spoke to in the Old City a few days ago. Tourist, isn't he? What's he done? And what's he got to do with it?"

"Do you remember just where you spoke to him, and what you said?"

"It was somewhere along David Street. He was jabbering away at a cop, who didn't understand a word he was saying. He wanted to know why some of the stores were closed. So I explained to him that all stores had to be closed one day a week, and that Friday was the day for Muslim stores to be and this one was closed because it was presumably Muslim."

"Which store was that?"

"Mideast Trading Corporation, the one on the corner."

"All right. And then what did you do?"

"Nothing. We walked together for a little way, and then I branched off. He continued on, I suppose to the Western Wall. At least, he had asked me how to get to it."

"Did he tell you his name, or where he was staying?"

Mystified, Skinner shook his head.

"All right. You can go ahead and fill in your trench."

"But—but aren't you going to tell me what happened? But I—"

"State security, Mr. Skinner. It's a matter of State security."

"Oh, well. . . ." He rose to go.

"One moment, Mr. Skinner. Your account of your movements, what you've just told me, might be needed as evidence in the event of a trial, yours and Mr. Hakem's."

"I understand. Naturally, I'll cooperate. You have only to let me know, and I'll be there. And I'll see to it that Hakem is there, too."

25

As his secretary waited expectantly, the manager said to Adoumi, "You'll have coffee?"

"No-no. Oh, all right. Black."

"And something with it, perhaps? A roll? A piece of cake?"

"No, nothing. Just coffee."

"And I'll have one, too," said the manager, and nodded in dismissal to the girl. "And now, what can I do for you?"

Adoumi handed him a black-and-white photograph. "You ever see this man? Here, in your hotel, I mean?"

The manager smiled. "Right this moment, there are seven hundred and eighteen guests in the hotel. By noon, three hundred and forty-two will have left. Actually, by ten o'clock. This afternoon, three hundred and eighty-six are scheduled to arrive."

"I suppose," said Adoumi gloomily. "And you're in the office here most of the day, I assume."

"That's right."

The secretary brought in a coffeepot and two cups and saucers on a tray. She set the tray on the desk to one side so as not to cover the photograph, glanced curiously at it, and then left. The manager poured the coffee and offered a cup to Adoumi. Then as his guest lit a cigarette, he slid over an ashtray. Adoumi sipped at his coffee, puffed his cigarette as he considered. Then he said, "But your security guard hangs around the lobby and circulates—the dining room, the bar."

"That's right."

"A clerk at the desk registered him. A porter brought his bags up to the room. Perhaps the chambermaid on that floor—"

"Let's see. He arrived around two, so the chambermaid would have made up the room several hours earlier. She'd probably be at the end of the corridor by that time, around the corner—no, two corners. But it's possible." He got up and went to a file cabinet and got a registration card. "Ah, it was Hassan who registered him. It was the beginning of the Sabbath, you understand, and the Arab staff take over the desk. But he's working now, working in our bookkeeping department."

"How do you know it was Hassan who signed him in?"

"Oh, we have them initial the card. I'll call him."

"I see. But don't tell him who we think it is. Just show him the photo."

"As you wish."

"You tell him this is a photo of Professor Grenish, whom you registered last Friday, and, of course, he'll say he recognizes it," Adoumi explained. "I'll question him, if you don't mind."

"Whatever you say."

Since he was working in the bookkeeping office, Hassan was wearing blue jeans and a sweater rather than the formal black trousers and gray jacket with gold buttons that he wore when he was at the front desk. He was nervous, and there were beads of perspiration on his forehead. The manager tried to put him at ease. "Nothing serious, Hassan. This gentleman wants to ask you a few questions. That's all."

Adoumi showed him the photograph. "Have you seen this man? Here in the hotel, I mean."

Hassan took the photograph from Adoumi and held it in front of him with both hands, and then away, at arm's length. Then he asked, "Is it one of the guests?"

"Just tell us if you've seen him," said Adoumi.

He smiled apologetically. "I see so many people."

"This would be last Friday," Adoumi suggested.

"Just when you came on duty," the manager added. "You registered him."

"I may have seen him, but I do not remember. I see so many. There was a tour group that came in then. Maybe Youssef, the porter—"

"Why Youssef?" asked Adoumi. "You've got a whole gang of porters, haven't you?"

"All right, Hassan. You may go." To Adoumi he explained, "We had a tour bus come in at that time—a couple of them, in fact. When a group comes in, the porters work like a team. There is baggage on the roof of the bus under a tarpaulin, as well as in the regular storage compartment. They unload the bags and pass them hand to hand into the lobby. Youssef is a little—er—nervous and is apt to get confused. So he doesn't participate. We use him for other errands required at the time. If someone came in alone, as Grenish did, he'd be the one to take his bags up."

He called the front desk, and presently Youssef appeared. He was grinning ingratiatingly. In response to Adoumi's question, he nodded eagerly. "Of course, he is my patron, my benefactor."

"What do you mean, your benefactor?" asked the manager.

"He gave a tip of a hundred shekels."

"He gave you a hundred-shekel tip? When was this?"

"Ah—two, no, three weeks ago. I was out sick. I come back, and the first day, I'm still weak. This man have a little bag. So big." He held his hands a foot apart to indicate the size. "I take it to his room and he give me a hundred shekels. I say, this is a hundred shekels. And he say, I deserve. So I—"

"You say this was two or three weeks ago?"

"Well, maybe a month."

"All right, Youssef. You can go back to your station now."

He smiled at Adoumi. "You're not having much luck, I'm afraid."

"I'm not surprised. Let's try the chambermaid."

The manager reached for the phone and dialed the house-keeper. "Who was the chambermaid who found the bed unslept in last week, Mrs. Burns? . . . Yael . . . Send her down to my office, will you?"

When the girl came, Adoumi thrust the photograph in front of her and demanded, "Do you know this man?"

She looked from one to the other, frightened, and then buried her face in her hands and began to wail, rocking back and forth.

"She thinks you're accusing her of something improper," said the manager. To the girl he said, "No, no, Yael. It's nothing bad, it's nothing wrong. We only want to know if you have ever seen this man—in the corridor, perhaps."

She peered between her fingers, and then, seemingly re-assured, lowered her hands and looked at the photo once again. Then she shook her head no.

"There's still Avi, the security guard," the manager offered.

"Yes, but he knows who it is we're trying to identify."

"So what? He's not like the others. He's had some training in this kind of thing, so I don't think he'd say he recognized him if he hadn't actually seen him."

"All right. Have him up."

When Adoumi showed him the photo, he asked, "Gren-ish?"

"That's what we want to find out," said Adoumi. "Ever see him?"

He shook his head. "I don't make him at all." He chuckled self-consciously. "And yet, you know, I saw him."

"What do you mean? You saw him but you don't remem-ber what he looks like?"

"Sunday, right after breakfast, maybe ten o'clock, Shoshana asks me to move the typewriter for her. So I'm behind the desk unplugging the cord and somebody says, 'I think there's something for me, Room seven-thirteen.' So I look up, and sure enough, there's a letter in the seven-thirteen pigeonhole. I glance at it, and I say, 'Grenish?' and he says, 'That's right.' So I give it to him. I didn't look at him—maybe his back as he turned away."

The manager turned to Adoumi. "The desk clerk, the chambermaid, the porter, and Avi here. That's about the lot. They're the only ones who might have seen Grenish—"

"How about Perlmutter?" asked the security guard.

"What about him?"

"He had the dining-room trick at breakfast Sunday morning. He checked him in. He might remember."

"It's worth a try," said the manager.

The security guard glanced at his watch. "He's just getting through. I'll get him."

But Perlmutter only shook his head when he was shown the photograph.

"You checked him in for breakfast," the manager urged.

Perlmutter shrugged. "And three hundred or three hundred and fifty others," he said. "It's a very ordinary face. There's nothing outstanding about it. Why should I be apt to remember him? And if he came in at the same time as several others, I probably didn't even look up at him. They give their names and room numbers and I check them off."

Later, alone again with Adoumi, the manager refilled their coffee cups, and lighting a cigarette, leaned back in his chair. "Can't you get a copy of his passport photo from the American authorities?" he asked.

"Sure, but it takes time. I was hoping—here, let me see his registration card."

The manager tossed it over to him. "You think maybe his fingerprints might be on it?"

"We-el . . ."

The manager looked up at the ceiling as he pictured in his mind's eye the behavior of someone registering. He shook his head. "The registration cards are held in a sort of leather frame, so only the edge of his writing hand is apt to touch the card itself. There are probably half a dozen clerks who might handle it after that."

But Adoumi was reading aloud. "Abraham Grenish, Fourteen Newhall Street, Barnard's Crossing, Massachusetts, U.S.A. Barnard's Crossing." He repeated the name of the town, sampling it on his tongue, his forehead wrinkled in thought. "Barnard's Crossing? Barnard's Crossing? Now, where have I heard that name before?" Then it came to him. Of course—Gittel's niece and her husband, the young rabbi. And only yesterday his wife had said something about their being in town. Was it a coincidence, or was the rabbi leading some sort of tour? He smiled, and to the manager said, "Let me have the telephone, will you. How do I get an outside line?"

"Dial nine."

He dialed and then said, "Sarah? Uri. You were telling me that your friend Gittel had some visitors, her niece and her husband. That's the young rabbi we met some years ago? . . . And she wanted us to come over for tea one evening? Then make it for tonight."

He smiled at the manager. "You've been very helpful."

26

GITTEL HAD KNOWN THE ADOUMIS FOR YEARS AND WAS PARticularly friendly with Sarah Adoumi, who had been a colleague in the Social Service office when they were both living in Tel Aviv. Now that they were both living in Jerusalem, Gittel would occasionally have lunch with her. When her niece and her niece's husband arrived, she naturally invited Sarah and her husband to spend an evening and renew their acquaintance with her relatives. So far it had not been convenient.

"You know how it is, Gittel. Uri has no regular hours, and for the past week or so, he's been busy most evenings. Sometimes I don't see him until midnight. But as soon as his work allows . . ."

Evidently, Tuesday it allowed, and Sarah phoned Gittel. "If you people are free this evening, we can come for coffee. Uri would like to see your niece's husband—and your niece, too, of course, and—"

"Lovely, Sarah. Miriam baked today. And I bought a dress I'd like to try on for you. Miriam thinks it doesn't hang right."

"So you'll try it on and I'll pin it for you."

They came at half past eight, and after the usual greetings, they sat around the dining-room table, where Gittel and Miriam had set out cheese and crackers, fruit, and the cake

Miriam had baked, reminiscing, joking as they nibbled and sipped their coffee. The conversation was largely in English for Miriam's benefit, lapsing into Hebrew every now and then because Sarah's English was limited.

Later, when the two older women went into the bedroom so that Gittel could try on the dress she had bought, Adoumi was alone with the Smalls. By this time, of course, he knew that the rabbi was not leading a group from Barnard's Crossing. He slid the photograph he had been given by Luria out of his pocket and placed it on the table in front of them. "Do you know him?" he asked casually.

The rabbi looked at Miriam, and when she shook her head, he asked, "Does he say that he knows us?"

Instead of answering the question, Adoumi urged, "It might not be a characteristic expression on the face, and you might not actually know him, but he's from your town in the States. You might, perhaps, have seen him on the street, at a bus stop, or in a store."

Again the rabbi shook his head, as did Miriam.

"That's funny," said Adoumi. "I mean, yours is a small town, isn't it? I should think you would have seen almost everyone living in your town at one time or another."

"The population of Barnard's Crossing is around twenty thousand," said Miriam.

"Twenty thousand, and you call it a town?"

"In our area, it's a matter of how the local government is set up," the rabbi explained. "If it has a mayor, then it's a city. If it has a Board of Selectmen, as we have, then it's a town."

"Oh, I see." It was evident that Adoumi was acutely disappointed.

"You mean, he says he's from Barnard's Crossing, and you don't believe him?" asked Miriam. "Did he say he knew us?"

The rabbi smiled. "No, Miriam, if this man were available, I'm sure Mr. Adoumi would not have shown us a photograph, and he would already have asked him if he knew us. If he had, he wouldn't have been so disappointed when we failed to recognize him."

156

Adoumi grinned. "Then what would I have done, Rabbi?"

"If it were someone who claimed to be from our town, and you were in doubt, I think you would arrange for us to meet him and talk with him, to ask him questions about people and places and customs of the town to see if he really had lived in the town. Who is he, anyhow?"

Adoumi nodded slowly. He sighed. Finally, speaking very slowly, he said, "A man is missing. He was staying at the Excelsior. He had breakfast Sunday morning. Monday, the chambermaid reported that his bed had not been slept in. The security guard checked the room. Sometimes it is a case of someone trying to skip out without paying his hotel bill. You find a worthless old suitcase full of rags and weighted down with a couple of stones, perhaps. Then they call the police. But when all his effects are there, they call us. All we know about this man is that he registered as Professor Grenish of Barnard's Crossing."

"You mean, if he's just absent one night?" asked Miriam. "He could have met relatives who insisted he stay over, or—"

"Yes, quite possible," said Adoumi. "But Grenish has been gone since Sunday."

"But you have a photograph, and it doesn't look like a copy of his passport photo. These usually give just head and shoulders—and they have the State Department seal impressed over the picture."

Adoumi nodded approvingly. "That's right. This is the photo of a body that turned up with no identification. We thought it was just possible that it was the same man. Of course, we could televise it to the States, to the police department of your town. Or we could ask them to see if they could send us a picture of Grenish, by going to his house, perhaps. But that would take a lot of time. I thought if you people knew him, or even if you remembered having seen him occasionally, that would not be positive identification, of course, but it would be enough for us to go on. If I thought there were others in the country from Barnard's Crossing—"

"But there are," said Miriam. "The Levinsons. They called us. They rented a car and are touring, but they said they might drop in on us tomorrow night, perhaps. And next week there'll be a whole busload on a tour, you know."

"Ah, Levinson, you say?" Adoumi got out his notebook. "And where are they staying?"

"They didn't say. I asked, but Sheila—I spoke to the wife—was rather vague, so I gathered they might be staying with friends. They are not very good friends of ours, so perhaps she didn't want us calling if they couldn't make it. It was a duty call she was making, you understand."

"Since they rented the car, I imagine you would be able to trace it and locate them," suggested the rabbi.

"Of course," Adoumi agreed, "but it might take several days. I'll tell you what. Suppose I leave this photograph with you, and if they call, you can show it to them. Then, if they recognize the man, you can let me know. It's curious. The man is a professor. I would think a professor in a town the size of yours would be well known."

The rabbi smiled. "We are about a half hour by car from both Boston and Cambridge. In Cambridge are both Harvard and MIT. In Boston there are a number of colleges—Boston University, Boston College, Northeastern, Suffolk. Both cities are full of students, and that makes a quiet place like Barnard's Crossing highly desirable as a place to live for their teachers."

"I suppose so," said Adoumi, his face showing obvious disappointment. "I don't know where Grenish teaches—"

"Grenish? His name is Grenish, is it?" The rabbi smiled broadly. "Then I can tell you how you can identify him. A friend of mine, someone I see at the minyan I attend, works at the Hotel Excelsior. Was it from there he was missing?"

"And he spoke to him?" Adoumi made no effort to conceal his interest and excitement.

"Well, I don't know that he spoke to him. I think he said that he was about to when the manager called him to the front desk. But you see, my friend's wife's family name was Grenitz, and he thought Grenish might be an Americanization of the name, so—"

"And your friend's name is. . . ?"

"Perlmutter, Aharon Perlmutter."

But Adoumi had been fingering his notebook. "Yes, here it is. Breakfast checker at the dining room." He shook his head. "He saw the photograph. He was unable to identify him."

"Then it's not the man," said the rabbi.

Adoumi smiled wanly. "Or, more likely, he didn't get a good look at him." He closed his notebook and put it back in his pocket.

He was so obviously disappointed that Miriam was led to suggest, "How about the Goodman boy, David?"

The rabbi shook his head. "No, he left Barnard's Crossing some years ago, and he was only in town for a short while before that. His folks are from Salem, you remember."

"And this Goodman, who is he?" asked Adoumi.

"He's a student at the American Yeshiva in Abu Tor," said Miriam. "His folks asked David to look him up."

"The American Yeshiva in Abu Tor, eh? That's very interesting. I'll go and see him."

27

THERE WAS NO QUESTION THAT IT WAS MERELY A COURTESY call. Indeed, Sheila Levinson had demurred. "Do we have to? We're only going to be in the city a few days—"

"Yeah, but how can I go to a foreign country six thousand miles away and there's a guy from my hometown living practically next door to my hotel and I shouldn't give him a call and drop in on him for a cup of tea, especially where the country in question is Israel and the guy is the rabbi of my temple back home? I mean," Ira Levinson went on, "how will it look when we get home and we tell people how we were so many days in Tel Aviv and so many days in Jerusalem, and they ask did we see the rabbi, and we say we didn't get around to it?"

"So all right, call him, but I don't see why we should have to waste an evening and go and see him."

"I tell you what. I'll call him, and if he asks to see us, I'll say okay, and then later I can call and say something has come up and we won't be able to make it."

He had called while they were still in Tel Aviv, and in response to Miriam's invitation to drop in Wednesday night, the day after they reached Jerusalem, he had readily agreed. Then according to plan, around six o'clock in the evening,

Sheila had called and said, "Oh, Miriam, Sheila Levinson. About tonight . . ."

"Yes, we're expecting you."

"Well, something has come up, and I don't think we can make it."

"Oh, can't you possibly? If only for a few minutes? There's something we want to show you."

"What is it?"

"Oh, I don't think I can tell you over the phone, but it's quite important."

Torn by curiosity, Sheila Levinson agreed, but hedged by saying that they might be able to stay only a few minutes, and was strangely disappointed when Miriam said, "Oh, that's all right. We'll expect you around eight."

"What do you suppose it is?" she asked her husband, who had been at her elbow as she phoned.

"I don't know. It could be they bought something for the temple. Maybe a crown or a breastplate for one of the scrolls. And they're worried that the Board might kick about buying it from them. So maybe they want to get some backing from us. And maybe it's a big-ticket item, they hope the Sisterhood might undertake to spring for it if the Board doesn't."

"You know, Ira, I think you're right. So let's be cool about it when they show it to us. I mean, we can say it's nice without getting all enthused, if you know what I mean."

And because they were determined to be cool about it and wanted to avoid any suspicion of great interest, they did not inquire about what it was the rabbi had to show them, but talked of their trip, of the sights they had seen, and about the impressions they had formed.

As they sipped tea and nibbled on cookies, they asked the Smalls about their own manner of living in Jerusalem. "I suppose you go to the Wall for morning prayers every day, Rabbi," suggested Ira Levinson.

"No, it's a bit far."

"He probably goes to that big place, you know, the Great Synagogue, what do they call it?" Sheila offered.

"The Hechel Shlomo," the rabbi supplied. "No, I don't go there, either. It's also a little distance from here. There are a dozen places where they have a minyan within a stone's throw. I go to one of those."

It was obvious to all that they were merely making talk and that the two couples had no interest in each other. Finally Ira Levinson said, "There was something you wanted to show us, Rabbi?"

"Oh, yes." From his pocket, the rabbi drew the photograph Adoumi had left with him and put it down on the table before them.

Mystified, the Levinsons looked at the photograph and then at each other and then at the rabbi. "That's it?"

"M-hm."

"I don't get it."

"Do you know him? Have you ever seen him?"

A slow shaking of heads. "We haven't been in the country very long. And in hotels most of the time—"

"No, someone from Barnard's Crossing," said the rabbi.

They both studied the photograph again. "It looks a little like Fred Stromberg," suggested Sheila.

"No, Fred is a lot thinner, and he's got this long nose." He looked at the rabbi inquiringly.

The rabbi felt it necessary to explain. "A friend of Gittel's"—he nodded in her direction—"is a high official in the security—"

"David! These are matters one does not talk about," said Gittel sharply. Except for acknowledgment of the original introduction, she had been silent until now. The Levinsons had assumed she did not speak English.

The rabbi nodded. "All right. Let's say a man who claimed to be from Barnard's Crossing is missing. It is thought it might be this man. Under the impression that Barnard's Crossing is a small village where everyone would know everyone else, Gittel's friend brought this photo to us."

"Village? Over twenty thousand," said Ira.

"Precisely. It's the name, I suppose. People are apt to

confuse it with 'crossroads' and assume it's just a village for that reason."

"Yeah, I've known people in the States to make the same mistake."

"You don't have to know the man," the rabbi urged, "just remember having seen him back in Barnard's Crossing."

"It could be—" Sheila began.

"No, it couldn't," said her husband decisively. "Sorry we can't help you out, Rabbi, or your friend. We'll have to be running along now." At the door, he said, "It occurs to me Louis Goodman's boy is in a yeshiva here. We were planning to drop in on him. Louis and Rose asked us to. He might recognize your man."

"Yes," said the rabbi. "I thought of him. I mentioned him to Gittel's friend."

Once outside, Sheila said to her husband, "Why did you cut me off when I was going to suggest—"

"Because I didn't want for us to get involved. That's why. The rabbi began to talk about a high official in security who was a friend of the old lady's. And she cut him off; told him these matters he was not supposed to talk about. So that means it was some sort of police matter, or maybe even something the Israeli secret service is involved in. For all we know, that guy whose picture he showed us might be a spy. We could be kept here—who knows, an extra week or even two while agents would grill us. Maybe even whisked around the country from place to place to look at this guy or his pals through a peephole or one of those one-way mirrors. And if he is a spy, and it got out that we identified him, how about his Arab or Russian pals or whoever? You want to avoid grief, you keep your nose clean."

Back in the apartment, as Miriam removed the tea things from the table, Gittel said, "These people, David, they don't like you. I could see that almost from the minute they came in."

The rabbi nodded. "No, I don't think they do."

28

To Uri Adoumi's request to see Jordan Goodman, Joseph Kahn interposed no impediment. Instead, having seen his credentials, he escorted him to the visitors' room and said he would send the young man down immediately.

On being informed that there was a policeman waiting to see him, Ish-Tov was understandably nervous. Someone must have seen him filling in the trench. What else could it be? And even before he entered the room, he had already begun to plan his defense. His friend who was a Kohane had a terrible fear that an ancient cemetery had been dug up, and out of consideration for him . . .

Although he could see that the young man was nervous by the way he crossed and uncrossed his legs and the way he fumbled with a wrinkled package of cigarettes, Adoumi did not take this as a sign of guilt. People were always nervous when the police came to question them. He tried to put him at ease. He offered him a light, lit his own cigarette, and then said, "You are from Barnard's Crossing in Massachusetts?"

"Yes—well, sort of. I mean, I haven't been there for some time." Perhaps it was his airline ticket they were concerned about. "My folks live there, but I was living out West mostly the past few years. I mean, how do you know I come from Barnard's Crossing?"

"A Rabbi David Small told me."

"Oh. Yeah, he was here the other day to see me."

Adoumi drew the photograph from his pocket and slid it across the table. "Do you know this man? Have you ever seen him in Barnard's Crossing?"

The young man's face relaxed in a slow grin. "It looks like an old prof of mine, name of Grenish."

"Prof? Ah, professor. You mean he was your teacher? And where was that?"

"Northhaven. It's a small college not far from Barnard's Crossing, about twenty miles north."

"And you knew him, you knew him to talk to?"

"Yeah, I knew him, all right. Hey, what's this all about?"

"We need to establish his identity—"

"And he says he's somebody else?"

"He doesn't say. He's dead."

"Dead? You mean here in Jerusalem? What was he doing here?"

"His presence here surprises you?"

"Yeah, kind of. See, he was Jewish, but you know, like pro-Arab. Unless he came to see some—"

"Some of his Arab friends?" Adoumi suggested.

"Well . . ."

Adoumi smiled. "Something tells me you didn't like him."

Ish-Tov, now relaxed, said, "Well, I wouldn't call him one of my favorite people. In fact, I had a little run-in with him. See, I was on a scholarship and he was chairman of the Scholarship Committee. He took away my scholarship and I had to leave school. I think it was because I was Jewish."

"I see. Well, if you'll come down to police headquarters at the Russian Compound tomorrow—"

"What for?"

"You'll be taken to the morgue to identify this Professor Grenish."

"Oh, no, you don't. I'm not going looking at dead bodies."

"Mr. Goodman," said Adoumi firmly, "the State requires it." His tone softened. "There's nothing frightening about it. The body is covered with a sheet. The top will be lifted. You will look, and then say if it is or is not Professor Grenish. That's all there is to it."

"Well, if you say it's important . . ."

"I assure you it's most important. So tomorrow you will present yourself to police headquarters at nine. If I am not there, ask for Captain Luria. Oh, and bring your passport."

"Why do I have to bring my passport?"

"To prove that you're you, of course."

"What did he want?" Yitzchak whispered. "Was it about filling in the trench?"

They were standing at a small pulpitlike table with the large volume of the Talmud they were sharing. There were more than a dozen such pairs at similar tables in the room, swaying back and forth, gyrating as they read the text aloud.

"Naw, he just wanted me to identify some guy from my hometown. He showed me a picture—you know, a photograph of the guy. I got to go to police headquarters tomorrow to make like a formal statement. Hey, Yossi is looking at us."

"So what? He can't hear what we're saying with all these guys yammering away."

"You're wrong. He's like an orchestra conductor who can tell just which violin is playing flat."

"Okay, so later."

Later, in response to his friend's question, he said, "They had me look at the body. I guess, for official purposes, you can't just look at a photograph."

"Gee, wasn't it scary? What did he look like?"

"Like—like he was asleep. He was covered, see? So they just pulled this sheet off his face and asked me if I recognized him. And I said yes, that it was Professor Grenish, and then they covered him again."

"Gee, I wouldn't have, if it had been me. I wouldn't even have gone into the room where he was on account of I'm a Kohane and I'm not supposed to be in the presence of a dead body."

"They could make you."

"Oh, yeah? If they tried it, every rabbi in the country and all the religious, too, would be up in arms. That kind of thing could overthrow the government."

"Sure, and maybe they'd make you prime minister. Anyway, they asked me a lot of questions, and then they typed it up and asked me to sign it."

"Was it this same Adoumi guy?"

"No, it was a cop in a uniform. Then they took my passport—"

"They took your passport? What did they do that for? What's your passport got to do with identifying somebody?"

"Oh, he said they'd send it along in a day or two. And kind of jokingly, that they might need to ask some more questions, and they wanted to make sure I didn't decide on taking a trip to America just then."

"You know, Yehoshua, I don't like it. Without a passport, you're nothing. If you should want to leave the country—say, you want to go home—"

"I'm not planning to leave the country."

"Yes, but even if you were to go to Tel Aviv or Haifa and wanted to stay over, you might have trouble getting a room in a hotel. This guy Adoumi, how'd he get on to you in the first place? How'd he know you were from Barnard's Crossing and could identify this guy?"

"Oh, he said this Rabbi Small who came to see me told him."

"So how did he get on to *him*? How did he know he was from Barnard's Crossing?"

"I don't know. I sort of gathered that he knew him."

"You know what I'd do if I were you, Yehoshua? I'd call this Rabbi Small and I'd ask him what gives."

"Yeah, maybe I will."

*   *   *

"... So he said I had to look at the body itself, that identifying the photo was not enough."

"That's reasonable," said the rabbi. "And it was Professor Grenish?"

"Oh, it was him, all right. See, I had this fight with him—"

"Yes, I heard about that from your father."

"Oh, yeah? Well, anyway, so I signed something that said he was Professor Grenish and that I recognized him. But then they took my passport."

"Your passport? Why did you bring your passport?"

"On account of your friend Adoumi told me to. He said I had to have it to show I was me."

"I see. Well, I suppose that's a kind of legalism that's required. In the court, everything has to be proved every step of the way."

"Yeah, but they didn't give me back my passport."

"Did you ask for it when you were leaving? It could have been a simple oversight—"

"Oh, I asked for it, all right, and they said they'd send it on in a day or two."

"Hm. I suppose they want to check it."

"Sure, but how long does it take to check a passport? I mean, what's involved?"

"It could mean nothing more than that the person who does the checking was away from his desk at the time."

"Yeah, but my friend Yitzchak here who knows his way around, he says you're nothing without a passport. I mean, where I'm a foreigner—"

"There is something in that—"

"Like, suppose I want to leave tomorrow."

"I understand. Were you thinking of it?"

"No, but even if I wanted to go up to Galilee, say, and stay in a hotel for a couple of days—"

"I see what you mean."

168

"So I thought you could ask your friend Adoumi. He is your friend, isn't he?"

"I know him," said the rabbi cautiously.

"So I thought you could ask him what gives."

"All right, I'll try to see him and let you know what he says."

29

WHEN THE LEVINSONS CAME TO THE YESHIVA AND ASKED TO see Goodman, it was a subdued Joseph Kahn who asked, "And you are?"

"We are from his hometown, friends of his parents. The name is Levinson."

No further questioning, no arguments, no objections, merely a polite "Just a minute" and he was gone, to return a moment later with, "If you will follow me. Our director, Rabbi Karpis, will see you."

Rabbi Karpis did not rise but very graciously waved them to chairs. They were charmed by him, by his majestic presence, his patriarchal beard, his benevolent smile, his British accent.

"You are friends of Ish-Tov, Mr. Goodman?"

"Well, we know his parents," said Mr. Levinson.

His wife amplified. "We don't really *know* him, but I trade with his folks." She strove to make it plain that they were not friends in the social sense. "I drop in to their store several times a week, for a loaf of bread, or a can of something that I need for a recipe. And while waiting to be served, you know, one talks and becomes friendly."

"I see. And they asked you to look him up and extend their greetings?"

"That's right," said Ira Levinson. "And talk to him and see if he's, you know, comfortable, happy."

"To inspect his sleeping quarters, perhaps, and to look over some sample menus?"

"Oh, no," said Levinson quickly. "We had no idea of er—snooping. We just want to see him so that we can tell his parents that—er—er, we did, if you see what I mean."

"Of course, Mr. Levinson, I understand. Unfortunately, the young man is not with us right now."

"You mean he's left? He's gone somewhere else?"

"In a manner of speaking. He's been taken into custody by the police."

"Good Lord! When? What for?"

"Quite early this morning. And I'm afraid it's in connection with a homicide."

"You mean he killed someone? Someone here? A fellow student? Oh, his poor mother!"

Rabbi Karpis shook his head slowly. "No one here, Mrs. Levinson. I don't know the details, but it appears to have been a tourist, someone from your own town in the States, from Barnard's Crossing. A Rabbi Small—do you know him?—who was here to see the young man, notified the police—"

"You mean that Small fingered him?" demanded Ira Levinson.

"Fingered? Oh, I see what you mean. As I understand, he told them that young Ish-Tov was from Barnard's Crossing."

"Have you—are you going to notify his parents?"

"I wouldn't without the express permission of Ish-Tov, and only at his request. He's of age, you know. Of course, you can do as you like, or think best. When are you planning to return, by the way?"

"Tomorrow."

"Ah, that's unfortunate."

"Why is it unfortunate?"

"Because I have notified our attorney, who will be seeing the young man in a day or two. We should then have more information as to what took place and the degree of the young

171

man's involvement. It may be that he is being held only as a material witness."

"Well, that's a fine how do you do," said Ira when they were out on the street. "Do we tell Rose and Louis?"

"We've got to. If our Jay were in the same trouble, wouldn't you want to know?"

"Yeah. We'll have to. Or maybe I'll call Small. Let him tell them. He's a rabbi. That's his job."

"But the Smalls won't be coming back for quite a while."

"So he can phone them. After all, he fingered him."

"He probably just told that friend of his that Goodman was from Barnard's Crossing and was at the yeshiva. You mentioned it yourself when he showed us that photo," she pointed out.

"Sure, but I wasn't talking to the police. And he was. I knew there was something fishy about that photo. If I hadn't stopped you, and you had gone on to say the face looked familiar, we'd be sitting in the pokey right now, waiting for the high muckamuck in charge of corpses to arrange for us to view the body. I'm calling the rabbi. The phone is probably in the name of that old lady they're living with. Do you remember her name?"

"Schlossberg. Gittel Schlossberg."

"I'll have the people at the hotel switchboard look it up."

"Oh, I have the number."

"I must say you're taking this rather coolly, Rabbi," said Levinson.

"Well, it doesn't come as a complete surprise," said the rabbi.

"You knew there was something in the works when you fingered him?"

"Fingered him? That's a strange expression, Mr. Levinson. I gave the authorities Goodman's name as someone who was from Barnard's Crossing. I gave them your name as well, and Mrs. Small mentioned that in a few days there would be a busload of people from our town in Jerusalem."

"So you gave them my name as well. I don't suppose you bothered to mention how many Israel Bonds I've bought, or that Sheila is secretary of the North Shore Friends of Israel?"

"I didn't think they were interested, Mr. Levinson."

"And you're not surprised that they arrested Goodman?"

"No, because he called me yesterday to say that they had retained his passport. His arrest doesn't have the same significance that it would have in the States. Here it is a normal part of the investigative procedure. But I'll inquire and see what I can find out, and let you know."

"We're leaving tomorrow morning early."

"Oh, well—"

"And I'll have to tell the Goodmans. I promised them that I'd look up their son. So they'll ask me, and I'll have to tell them."

"I suppose you will. I hope you won't alarm them unduly."

"I can only tell them what I know, Rabbi."

To Miriam's inquiry later, he said, "I think the Levinsons are planning to be troublesome."

30

IT WAS NOT EASY FOR RABBI SMALL TO REACH URI ADOUMI, and when he finally did make contact with him, Adoumi seemed reluctant to meet with him. Seemingly he was busy all during the day, and to the rabbi's suggestion that he come to his house in the evening, he explained, "I have one unbreakable rule, Rabbi. I see no one on business at my house. Sarah is very nervous, and it would upset her."

"Then how about coming here to Gittel's?"

"No, I don't think I'd care for that. Gittel would be there and—look, I'll tell you what. I'm meeting someone at the King David Hotel. I'll be through in an hour. Suppose I meet you in Liberty Bell Park, near the entrance at one. That's not far from where you are. Or better still, I'll walk down King David Street. I'll start out from the hotel, and I'll stay on that side of the street. Then we can go into the park and sit on a bench and talk."

"I'll be there."

Rabbi Small was there a quarter of an hour early, and was impatient and worried until he saw Adoumi approaching—on time. They met as though by chance and then wandered about in the park until Adoumi found a bench to his liking. "So what can I do for you?" asked Adoumi abruptly.

"You saw young Ish-Tov, and he identified the photo you

showed him. Then you had him come to the police headquarters to make a formal statement to that effect. You also had him look at the body." He canted his head to one side as he thought about it. "All right, I can understand that that might be part of your normal procedure. But you also took his passport—and kept it."

Adoumi shook his head impatiently. "None of that is my doing, Rabbi. It's a police matter."

"I don't understand. It was you who went to see him."

"Sure, because at the time it *was* my concern. The name—Professor Grenish—I had on a list."

"A list?"

"Sure, we have all kinds of lists: lists of people whom we watch closely, or whom we keep an eye on every now and then, or whom we watch if they go to certain places. The security group in every country does the same. Not lists of people who are criminal, or even suspect, you understand, but of possibles, or of people who are connected with someone who might do something. You understand? Your FBI is no different. So where the person is on one of our lists and is unaccountably missing from his hotel—that's enough for me to handle it myself."

"Why was he on a list?"

"His name was given to us by Mossad. We work closely with Mossad the way your FBI works with your CIA. Mossad was interested in him because, although Jewish, he was a member of the radical Arab Friendship League. Also, he was friendly with an important Arab—a professor at Harvard—back in the States—whom they were also keeping an eye on."

"All right. I understand. So what made it a police matter rather than one for your department?"

"You did, Rabbi." Adoumi laughed coarsely.

Rabbi Small stared at him in astonishment.

"Uh-huh. You gave me Goodman's name, and I went to see him. He not only recognized the photo, but admitted that he knew him well, and that it was due to him that he had had to leave school. This Grenish was chairman of the Scholarship Committee and—"

"Yes, I heard something about that back home."

"Did you now? Well, next to the yeshiva there is a house occupied by—"

"James Skinner," said the rabbi promptly, and was gratified to see that Adoumi's face showed astonishment.

"You know him?"

"He sat beside me on the plane coming over. We gave him a lift to Jerusalem. We drove him right to his house."

"I see. Well, that's where Grenish's body was found, on Skinner's land, next door to the yeshiva."

"You mean Skinner found the body and reported it to the police?"

"No, the body had been buried, and it was unearthed by agents of the Department of Antiquities. They reported it to the police." He smiled at the rabbi's bewilderment and proceeded to explain about the trench in Skinner's backyard and how the Department of Antiquities became interested in it. "So here we have the body of a dead man who turns out to be Professor Grenish, who is the mortal enemy of young Goodman who lives right next door. As I talked with the young man, it occurred to me that this might be an ordinary homicide—a police matter in other words. So I told him to report to police headquarters at the Russian Compound. They took his fingerprints and—"

"He didn't mention that they took his fingerprints," said the rabbi.

Adoumi smiled. "Oh, they didn't use an inked pad. I imagine Chief Luria gave him a glass of water, or had him pick up a piece of paper that slid off his desk, or maybe passed his cigarette case across the desk and offered him a cigarette. Something like this." He drew a silver cigarette case from his pocket. "Cigarette?"

"No, thanks," said the rabbi.

Adoumi smiled and took one himself.

"They matched the prints on the cigarette case or what-

176

ever with those on one of the shovels, and that did it. No Arab involvement, no international intrigue. Just a case of two people who had quarreled, meeting by accident, renewing the quarrel, and one of them ends up dead. So the police proceed to make inquiries. They hold his passport so that he's not likely to run away. Then this morning I was told they picked him up. They took him before a court and got a remand of fifteen days, a secret remand, because there still might be some national security involvement, while they continue their inquiries."

"Does he admit he did it?"

"So far, no. Claims he didn't even know Grenish was in the country."

"But that's awful. You arrest a young man for murder on the basis of—of a wild guess on your part. If he had met him and quarreled with him, would he have admitted that he'd had trouble with him? Would he even have admitted knowing him?"

"You forget there are the prints on the shovel."

"So what? He might have picked it up once."

"I didn't say he murdered him, only that he buried him, and it is a logical assumption that if he buried him he must have had something to do with his death. When we examined the body, we found no bullet wound, no stab wound, no sign of a blow on the head with a heavy instrument. When we did an autopsy, we found that he had an aneurysm of the abdominal aorta. That's the tube that goes from the heart down to the extremities. You might call it the main artery. It had ballooned up from a normal of about two centimeters to five centimeters. A sharp blow to the belly could very easily have caused it to rupture. Or it could even have ruptured of its own accord. Death would follow almost immediately. I'm not suggesting that Ish-Tov necessarily struck Grenish, or tried to kill him, or even to injure him. I suspect what happened was that the meeting was accidental, that they recognized each other and started to argue or quarrel. Then there may have been some pushing. Suddenly Grenish falls to the ground. Ish-Tov,

177

frightened, doesn't call anyone or notify the police. He remembers a trench and dumps him in there and fills it in. He doesn't know anything about the Department of Antiquities being concerned. He just assumes that the trench was left there because the workmen hadn't gotten around to filling it yet. Happens all the time in Israel, jobs are left unfinished. We had trouble with our gas stove. We called the gas company and they sent a mechanic over who took it apart and then walked out, presumably to go to lunch, and didn't come back for two days."

"Does Ish-Tov admit to any of this?"

"No, not yet. But let me tell you something about criminal investigation, Rabbi. You almost never have a perfect case, with every 'i' dotted and every 't' crossed. And even when you do, the perpetrator will frequently deny it regardless of how damning the evidence is. But when you have an obvious explanation, it's usually the right one. I can dream up a scenario that could cover the facts. I could think of a dozen ways that Ish-Tov could have gotten his prints on the shovel. Maybe something like what Luria used to get his prints on his cigarette case. A man is working, filling in a trench. He's wearing work gloves, naturally. He sees someone, Ish-Tov walking along the street on his way to the yeshiva and he calls him over and then tosses the shovel to him and says, 'Here, look at this.'

"But that's so farfetched as to be ridiculous. What do we have? Here's a tourist who comes to Jerusalem. He knows no one here, and no one knows him. He comes from Barnard's Crossing, a town that I'll bet no one outside your state ever heard of. And he ends up dead and buried next door to a yeshiva where there is a student who also comes from Barnard's Crossing. That's quite a coincidence. It isn't as though they both came from New York. They're from Barnard's Crossing, a town of twenty thousand, you said. Then it turns out that they had quarreled; that Ish-Tov claims he had to leave college on Grenish's account; that his life was changed. Then to top it off, we find the prints of Ish-Tov on the shovel that was used to bury Grenish. Now, that's a *prima facie* case if ever I saw one. Keep in mind the basic principle: The obvious is the likely."

The rabbi nodded. He sat silent for a moment and then said, "Can I see him?"

Adoumi pursed his lips as he considered. "Where it's a secret remand, I doubt it. You planning to do a little investigating on your own?" he asked with a smile.

The rabbi shook his head dolefully. "I don't know what I'll do, but I am the rabbi of the Jewish community in Barnard's Crossing, and it was I who sent you to Ish-Tov. I feel—"

"Responsible?"

"No, but I feel I should do something, at least try."

Adoumi rose. "I had better be getting along. My office will be wondering what happened to me. Look, Rabbi, I remember our little business a few years back. So if you come up with anything, I promise to listen."

"I don't know what I can do. But I've got to do something," said the rabbi doggedly. "Maybe I shall hold you to that promise."

31

THE CHESSBOARD WAS ON THE DESK IN FRONT OF HIM WHEN
Rabbi Small went to see Karpis again. "Have you solved this
one yet, Rabbi Small? It was in yesterday's paper. It's a three-
mover."

"No, I haven't had a chance to." He studied the board for
a moment and then said, "You might try pushing the pawn."

Rabbi Karpis looked at him in surprise. "Why the pawn?"

"Because it's the least likely move. These aren't actual end
games. They're puzzles that people think up. So I suppose the
trick is to make the first move one that no one would ever
think of making if he were actually playing a game."

"Perhaps you're right. I shall have to try it." He pushed
the board aside regretfully. "But I don't want to encroach on
your time with my personal interests. You want to talk about
Ish-Tov."

"That's right. I feel a sense of responsibility."

"Why, Rabbi Small? Because it was through you that the
police were led to him?"

Rabbi Small considered for a moment and then said,
"Someone from Shin Bet came to see me, someone I had met
years ago here in Jerusalem. He came because he remembered that I was from Barnard's Crossing, which he thought
was a little village. He showed me a photograph of someone

who was also supposed to be from Barnard's Crossing, hoping I would be able to recognize the man. But our town has some twenty thousand people. And he was very disappointed that I could not make the identification. So I suggested Ish-Tov as also coming from Barnard's Crossing, and also some people whom I expected would be visiting me in a day or two—"

"The Levinsons?"

"That's right. And he left the photo with me so I could show it to them. I knew nothing of the matter, you understand, except that I presumed since my friend was Shin Bet, it was the security of the State that was involved."

Rabbi Karpis shrugged. "Then I can't see how you are in any way responsible."

"I'm not." He smiled ruefully. "But nevertheless I feel responsible, somehow."

Rabbi Karpis nodded sympathetically.

"His folks are not members of my congregation," he went on. "They go to a synagogue in Salem, a nearby town, where they lived for a number of years before moving to Barnard's Crossing. Still, they are members of the Jewish community of our town, and I am the only rabbi in the town."

"Shepherd of the flock?" suggested Rabbi Karpis.

"No," said Rabbi Small sharply. "But I have a sense of jurisdiction."

"Then wouldn't I have a greater claim as far as Ish-Tov is concerned?"

"Ye-es, but I think his being here might have had something to do with it."

Rabbi Karpis pursed his lips. "You mean because he was living here, next door to where the incident occurred?" He studied his visitor. "Or do you mean something else? You do not approve of our operation here?"

"No, I don't." It was pure reflex, and the words were out before he realized he had said them. He laughed shortly. "I have a cousin whom we call Simcha the Apikoros. He is not an atheist or an agnostic. He's a religious man and observant. But he has some curious ideas. One is, for example, that one may eat dairy products after chicken on the grounds that a chicken does not give milk so that the injunction not to seethe the flesh of the kid in the milk of the mother does not apply."

Rabbi Karpis nodded. "I have heard of whole communities who take the same view."

"Really? Well, his part of the family runs to businessmen and merchants, whereas my side has a number of rabbis. He is apt to be disparaging, even scornful of my side. Professional Jews, he calls us. Says our profession, especially in America, is just being Jewish. He insists that being a Jew is an amateur occupation."

"What does he mean by that?"

"That we Jews are supposed to participate, we don't withdraw from life. 'In the sweat of thy face shalt thou eat bread' and confirmed in the commandment 'Six days shalt thou labor.' Simcha is no ignoramus. He is a learned man, and he studied, but his main concern is his work. Here you have a group of young men whose sole interest is study. It's like a monastery, except that instead of prayer, they are engaged in study. Some few may eventually become rabbis, I suppose, so in that sense their study is preparatory for the work they intend to do, but the majority, I imagine, study for themselves. They are not engaged in research that would benefit others, but study only for themselves. The intention of our religion is to make men whole rather than holy."

"You don't believe in repentance? In the Baal Tshuvah?"

Rabbi Small shook his head. "He's too much like the born-again Christian. Baal Tshuvah, Master of Repentance. It's like a degree or a title, like the Moslem Haji. If someone has led a sinful life and wishes to repent, he should go to those whom he has injured and make it up to them and beg their forgiveness. That's our way, rather than an ostentatious display of his religiosity. There is a certain rationale for the born-again Christian. After all, his religion calls for him to try to become as one with his God, but we have no such justification."

Rabbi Karpis sighed and then smiled. "I'm sure you realize, Rabbi Small, that I have heard these arguments before. I won't try to refute them now, but sometime, perhaps in a social evening, after a game or two of chess I might discuss it with you. Right now, what do you want of me?"

"I want to see Ish-Tov. I want to speak to him."

"What has that to do with me? How can I help you?"

"The Shin Bet man whom I mentioned earlier tells me that it is more or less out of his hands and is a police matter now. There is probably no question of State security. It has to do with something that happened back in Barnard's Crossing. It seems that the two services, the police and the Shin Bet, are very touchy about their prerogatives. According to him, the police would not take kindly to a request from him to let me see their prisoner."

"So?"

"The attorney for your organization, I understand, is looking into this matter. Only the prisoner's attorney is permitted to see him. I am sure that if you asked him, he would consent to letting me join him as an associate—to take notes, perhaps—when he goes to see him."

"Ah, I see. I think I can manage that. Shiah Greenberg is not only our attorney but also a friend of mine. He, too, is a chess player. If you will give me your telephone number, I'll have him call you."

"Is he a member of your organization? Does he think as you do?"

"Shiah? Shiah is a pagan, an agnostic. Now, *there* is an apikoros.

"And yet you retain him?"

Rabbis Karpis smiled broadly. "We fight fire with fire, Rabbi."

32

BETWEEN THEM THEY SPOKE ENGLISH, RABBI SMALL AND
Shiah Greenberg, the attorney, dropping into Hebrew momentarily only when it offered *le mot juste*. Greenberg, forty-
five, short, balding, and fattish, had left the States fifteen
years before, but not long enough to have softened his
Brooklyn accent. And he still retained his street-smart cyni-
cism. As they made their way to the police station where
Ish-Tov was being held, he said, "What you've got to understand, Rabbi, is that punks are punks whether in New York or
Jerusalem, Arab or Jewish. And it doesn't make any difference how pious they are. When I was with Legal Aid in New
York years ago, many a time I found myself defending a Hasidic
punk—theft, armed robbery, once even murder. They wore
the black hat and the dark clothes and had the *tsitsis* showing.
I remember once I was seeing my client in the jail, and he
asks me which way is east so he can face that way and *daven
shachris* while I wait. And he was guilty of armed robbery,
guilty as hell. Maybe he thought seeing him *daven* I'd be
more apt to think he was innocent. Or maybe it was just a
habit with him that he couldn't break or he'd feel like he
forgot something all day.

"And they lie. They all lie. It used to bother me, but then

I decided, what the hell, maybe he's just trying to convince himself. And what difference did it make, anyway? I wasn't going to put him on the stand. Take this kid Ish-Tov. There's a *tsatske!* He tells me not only he didn't do it, but he never even knew the guy was in Jerusalem and never even saw him. And his fingerprints are on the shovel the guy was buried with, clear as day. That's where our client had some real bad luck."

"Bad luck?"

"Yeah. See, when the police told me about the prints, I figured they were planning to pull a fast one, that they'd get a fingerprint expert to testify that some smudge had so many points of identification with his prints that he was sure it was his. See, these shovels, the Arabs who had dug the trench originally, their prints were on them. And then the Department of Antiquities people who dug up the corpse, they had used those same shovels. So there had to be prints on prints. But our guy was just plain unlucky. It seems that the Arabs were wearing these cotton work gloves, so *they* didn't leave any prints. And then the Antiquities guys, there were two of them, but only one did the digging, and he used the other shovel. Now, that was bad luck. You know, when you pick up a shovelful of dirt, you hold the handle with one hand—no prints there because it's rough wood—but with the other hand, you grasp the metal shank of the shovel. And because the Arabs wore gloves, that shank was nice and shiny. And our client left a perfect set of prints on it."

"I see."

"So there's no chance of befuddling a fingerprint expert. But with the autopsy report, we get a little break. Death was the result of an aneurysm that had ruptured, an aneurysm of the abdominal aorta." He ran a finger up his belly. "That's the main artery that runs down from the heart and bifurcates down both legs. According to his doctor, his aneurysm was just under five centimeters in diameter. Do you know how much five centimeters is?" He tucked his briefcase under his arm and held up both hands with the forefingers extended.

"That much. About two inches. And normal is about three quarters of an inch. So I talked to a doctor friend of mine, an internist. And he tells me that five centimeters is usually the cutoff point. Less than that, they watch it. But at five centimeters or more, they operate. The results are about ninety-five percent good. They just cut it out—that section, I mean—and replace it with a Dacron pipe. Marvelous what they can do nowadays.

"But if the thing ruptures, or springs a leak, then unless he can get to a surgeon right away, and one who knows what's wrong, then he's a goner. And even if he does, the chances of saving him drop to about fifty percent. So I imagine he was seeing his doctor every three months or so and having it measured with an ultrasound picture. He probably saw him just before he left the States—"

"But could he travel? Wasn't he in pain?"

"No symptoms, none at all—until it ruptures or leaks. Then you get a terrible bellyache or backache. That's when you've got to get to a surgeon. Now, what could trigger that rupture? Would a blow to the belly do it? According to the doctor, it was not likely. See, it's back near the spine. More likely it would come from a sudden increase in blood pressure. And that gave me my case."

"How do you mean?"

"See, this Ish-Tov had been a student at the university where Grenish was a member of the faculty. And he had a fight with him. Grenish was on the Scholarship Committee, maybe head of it. Ish-Tov lost his scholarship and attributed it to Grenish. He had to leave school as a result."

The rabbi nodded.

"You knew about that?"

"I heard something of it," the rabbi admitted. "But how do you—did Ish-Tov tell you?"

"No, the Shin Bet got it, by way of Mossad, I suppose. They work closely with the CIA, who would be willing to do them the favor of checking with the local police."

"I suppose that's why my friend Adoumi got out of the

186

case," said the rabbi. "He decided it was the result of a personal quarrel."

"Oh, that's right, you know Adoumi. I suppose he was originally involved because the man was missing from his hotel. Anyway, I had my case."

"How do you mean?"

"Well, it's obvious. Grenish comes to Jerusalem and spends his time wandering around the Old City. We know that because he didn't have dinner at the hotel Friday night, nor all day Saturday, except for breakfast. He had to eat, didn't he? And on the Sabbath it could only be at an Arab place, which means East Jerusalem or the Old City. But he's had a couple of days of it. It's natural. The Old City is colorful. It's where tourists go. So for a change Sunday he goes around the new part. Ish-Tov sees him, recognizes him, and there's a quarrel. Maybe there was some pushing and shoving. Maybe a blow was struck. Or maybe Grenish just gets terribly worked up. And that does it. His aneurysm ruptures, and he keels over. And then it's my guess that Ish-Tov panicked. The man was dead and he would be held responsible. So he hides the body in a most convenient trench and fills it in."

"But you say that Ish-Tov claims he never saw the man."

"Oh, sure. That's practically the norm. Defendants never admit guilt. Why should they? What will it get them? You try to explain that if you knew exactly what happened, you could plan a better defense. They don't believe you. Or they can't see how it would work. Or they think what you really want is an excuse if you lose. Or they are not so much interested in the trial and what the judge will think, but in what their friends, family, associates, in this case the yeshiva will think. See, if they deny it all, then all these might think even though they were found guilty, it might not be true, that they were framed, or that their lawyer was inept. Get it?" He halted in his stride momentarily. "Hey, maybe he'll tell you. I'll see if I can't arrange for you to be alone with him for a little while."

187

"Oh, you're here, too," said Ish-Tov as he entered the room where the rabbi and Greenberg awaited him. He slouched in his chair, his long legs crossed at the ankles stretched out in front of him as he answered Greenberg in monosyllables.

Then Greenberg asked, "Now, look here, you quarreled with him, didn't you?"

"I didn't even see him. I didn't know he was in town."

"I mean back in the States."

"Oh. Well, I went to see him at his house."

"To get him to change his mind on your scholarship."

"Yeah."

"Loss of the scholarship meant you had to leave school. Right?"

"That's right. I couldn't ask my folks for the tuition money."

"And you threatened him."

"Well, yeah, I guess you could say I threatened him. But that was years ago."

"Threatened to kill him?"

"No, just to get even."

"So when you saw him in Jerusalem—"

"I never laid eyes on him."

Greenberg glanced significantly at the rabbi and then rose and went to the door. "I've got to talk to the captain for a minute."

It occurred to the rabbi that again and again, Greenberg had led the young man to the point, and each time he had shied away from admitting that he had ever seen Grenish in Jerusalem. And yet he knew that his fingerprints had been found on the shovel that had interred him. So when they were alone together, instead of asking about Grenish, he asked, "Why did you fill in the trench?"

Whether it was the way the rabbi framed the question, or the urgency in his voice, the young man's attitude changed. He even smiled. "Because it was there."

The rabbi also smiled. "Do you go around filling in potholes in the streets?"

"All right. My friend Yitzchak and I were on the roof and saw the trench from there. We were up there because—well, never mind. The point is, we saw it. And Yitzchak had overheard Kahn—he's the secretary—talking to Rabbi Karpis about how it might be an archaeological find, and *they* were worried that it might extend to the yeshiva grounds. And that it might even be an ancient cemetery. Well, I don't have to tell you what that would mean. But Yitzchak is a Kohane, and he takes it seriously—I mean about a Kohane being in the presence of a corpse. He's fanatic about every little regulation. He even gave away all his clothes that didn't say one hundred percent cotton or one hundred percent wool for fear he might be transgressing the law of mixing fibers, you know, *shatnes*. That was before I came here, but he told me about it. And he's very proud that he's a Kohane, so he was pretty worried.

"Well, we saw Skinner and the Arab guy take off in the car, and from what we'd seen before, we knew they'd be gone all day. And the old lady, she's never there on Sunday. So we snuck over there to take a look. There was nothing there. It was just a hole in the ground, maybe four feet deep. We didn't see anything that looked like an artifact, or maybe we didn't know what to look for."

"Did you get down into the trench?"

"No, we just looked at it a little. So I said to Yitzchak, 'How about we fill it in?' See, the shovels were there. Well, he was worried and wanted to get out of there. After the trouble they had a few months back, and after Karpis took over, we were told not to trespass. So I said we could do it after *maariv* when it was dark, but he was afraid there might be some bones still there.

"So after *maariv*, I went out there myself. And then a little later he joined me. I guess he realized I was doing it more for him, because I'm not what you might call meticulous about observing every little rule and regulation. And we finished in about half an hour."

"Weren't you concerned that the trench must have been dug for some purpose and that Mr. Skinner might have to dig it up again?"

"Nah. The hell with him."

"And the Department of Antiquities, did you know that they were involved?"

A shrug. "A bunch of ghouls. We don't care too much about them." He eyed the rabbi speculatively. "You planning to tell my folks about this?"

"I won't if you don't want me to. I think they ought to know, though."

"No. If they hear about it, one or both might feel they've got to come over. And they'd want to hire a lawyer instead of this joker the yeshiva gave me. And they can't afford it."

At which moment Greenberg walked in with the guard, and with a tilt of the head to the rabbi, said, "We've got to be going now.

"Well?" he demanded when they were outside. "Did you get anything out of him?"

The rabbi reported his conversation with Ish-Tov.

"It's not bad," said Greenberg. "Absolutely useless for our purposes, of course, but not a bad effort. You see, what they do is weave a story that covers the evidence against them, work it out in their minds, embellish it until they almost get to believe it. In that way the guy clears his conscience, see?"

"So how will you proceed?"

"Since Ish-Tov refuses to play ball, I'll keep him off the stand. I think on cross-examination I can get the medical expert to admit that death could have been accidental. And then I'll argue that Ish-Tov simply panicked. The judge might see it as illegal burial and failure to report a death. With luck, maybe a fine, which our organization would pay."

"You think it will work? You think the judge will go along?"

"Of course, in this business you can never tell, but I think there's a good chance."

"But look here, why couldn't you present it to the prosecutor? Maybe he would agree to drop the case."

The other smiled. "A lawyer always tries to keep a little something back, Rabbi. And what might work if I spring it in court might not work if I tried it on the prosecution in his office over a cup of coffee."

33

ON WEDNESDAY, AL BERGSON CALLED FROM TEL AVIV. "THIS is your president speaking," he announced.

"Al? Al Bergson? Where are you?"

"In Tel Aviv, at the Sheraton. We'll be here through tomorrow, and come up to Jerusalem Friday morning."

"How many of you are there?"

"There are twenty-six of us. I had thirty lined up originally, but the Moscovitz family—Ed, Emily, and the two boys—dropped out at the last minute. We'll be staying at the King David. Present plans call for going to the service at the big synagogue, but some said they preferred going to the Conservative synagogue on Agron. In any case, we'll have our Sabbath meal at the hotel. Could you and Miriam make it? As our guests, of course."

"I'm afraid we can't. We're expecting company here."

"And Barney's Bar Mitzvah at the Wall the next morning?"

"I don't think so," said the rabbi. "It's a pretty longish walk to the Wall from where we live."

"I'd try, if I were you. There'll be a party afterward at the hotel, but if you haven't gone to the Bar Mitzvah—"

"Then I hardly think it would be proper for me to go to the party."

"But you've got to meet the group sometime, David. I mean, here are a couple of dozen members of your congregation, some of them on the Board of Directors, and their rabbi is right here in the city—"

"How about Saturday night? I could come to the hotel in the evening," suggested the rabbi.

"I'm afraid that won't do. They'll all be scattered. They all have relatives or friends. Look, plan on Sunday morning. I've arranged for a guided walking tour of the Old City, the Jewish Quarter, the Cardo, the Wall. It's probably old stuff to you, but it will give you a chance to meet the gang."

"Sunday morning is fine. I think Miriam has something scheduled, but I can make it. How about you? Do you have relatives to go to Saturday night? If not, how about coming to us?"

"You're a hard man to help, David," said Bergson as they sat in the salon of Gittel's apartment. Gittel and Miriam had gone off to a movie, and the two men were alone.

The rabbi smiled faintly. "You've been trying to help me, have you?"

"Uh-huh. The Levinsons got back from Israel and reported that the Goodman boy had been arrested for murder and that you fingered him to the police and that you almost got them involved as well."

"I merely gave the authorities Goodman's name, and the Levinson's, as being from Barnard's Crossing. It was a matter of identifying—"

"I know, I know. But the Levinsons don't like you, so in the telling, there was a suggestion that there may have been something more to it than that. And by the time it had been repeated and made the rounds, there was a general conviction that you were acting as an agent of the police. And some pointed out that here, too, you were awfully friendly with Chief Lanigan with the implication that you were somehow connected with the police."

"But that's ridiculous. I—"

"Of course it is, and it would be obvious to anyone if you were generally liked. But you're not, you know. So anything that can be thought to discredit you is seized on and accepted without further question. And now you've alienated Barney Berkowitz, and that means his friends. He could understand— not easily, to be sure—why you might give up a free trip to Israel in order to get here earlier and have more time to spend here, but not to come to his Bar Mitzvah when you were already here, and a couple of dozen of your congregants were along as well—"

"How did it go?"

"Oh, fine. Without a hitch. He'd had the cantor record his haftarah on a tape, and he played it over and over. I have the room next to him at the hotel, and I could hear it and him repeating it sentence by sentence, the night before. At the Wall, he choked up at one point, but someone nearby whispered the word and he went on. Then afterward back at the hotel, there were lots of high jinks. 'How does it feel to be a man, Barney?' That sort of thing. And several of the fellows managed to get hold of some of those old-fashioned fountain pens. He must have got half a dozen of them. I gather that used to be the usual present to a Bar Mitzvah boy. Before my time, but I'd heard of it. And Sophie Katz presented him with a prayer book in white leatherette on behalf of the Sisterhood, and I presented him with a matching Bible, as we do to all the Bar Mitzvah boys. And then afterward we toasted him with champagne—Israeli champagne, but nevertheless champagne. I wish you had been there."

"So that I could have made my usual speech to Bar Mitzvahs about his now being responsible for his actions?"

"No-o, but to show them that you were part of them, that they were your people. I can't understand why you were determined not to. It's not such a terribly long walk."

"Because it was foolish. I don't mind foolishness as such. It's even encouraged sometimes—on Purim, for example. But—"

"But you're his rabbi."

194

"Sure, and I was performing my rabbinical function."

"By not going?"

"That's right. In America, the rabbi is rarely if ever permitted to perform his traditional functions of sitting in judgment on civil cases brought before him, or of rendering a decision on a halachic matter. The one function that he can and that his congregation expects him to perform is to act as teacher and guide in maintaining the tenets of the Jewish tradition, and to keep them from straying from the traditional path. Now in our tradition, a boy becomes a man—that is, an adult—at thirteen rather than at eighteen, as in secular society. As a man, he is presumed responsible for his actions; he can give testimony in a law court; he can sign a contract; and he can serve as one of the ten required for a minyan. That's all there is to it, although we ceremonialize it by having him take part in a religious service. If there is no ceremony, he is still Bar Mitzvah simply by having reached thirteen, the age of maturity.

"As teacher and guide in the tradition, isn't it my function to try to prevent a member of the congregation from perverting this halachic rule to something else, to a kind of confirmation, as in the Reform Synagogue? If he had come to me I would have tried to explain it to him, but since he didn't, I could only disassociate myself from the action. And that's what I did."

"Yes, but in doing so, you antagonized some powerful people in our congregation. They've got it all mixed up, your failure to come to the Wall this morning, not showing up at B.B.'s party later, and now the business with the Goodman boy. You've generated hostility, and that doesn't do the congregation any good, and it doesn't do you any good. Your contract comes up for renewal—it was you who insisted on an annual review of your stewardship—and they might use the occasion to express their feelings by voting against you. This business with Barney might blow over, but I hate to think what would happen if the Goodman boy goes to jail."

"Why, what's his situation got to do with mine?"

"David, David, for a smart guy you've got some of the damndest blind spots. In fact, it has nothing to do with it. And his folks aren't even members of our congregation. But our people shop with them, and talk with them as they stand around waiting their turn at the deli counter. People are always happy to hear of anything reprehensible of someone in authority. It makes them feel good about themselves. It doesn't have to be anything specific, you understand. Just a suggestion of something. Now you did what anyone was apt to do. The police came to you and asked you to identify a man from a photo because he came from your hometown. You couldn't, so you suggested someone else they might see who was familiar with the town. That's all. But if that someone else gets into trouble as a result, you're going to be blamed for it, maybe not directly in so many words. No one is going to accuse you directly. But they'll think it, or feel it. Look, I really think it's important that you go on that walk with us tomorrow."

When Miriam and Gittel came home, the rabbi told them about Bergson's visit, and after Gittel had gone to bed and he was alone with Miriam, he amplified his account by telling her of Bergson's gloomy outlook.

"Are you worried, David?" she asked.

"No-o, not really. I think Al Bergson is exaggerating the situation." Then quite suddenly, he was exasperated. "If the Board refuses to renew my contract because I didn't attend Barney's phony Bar Mitzvah, or because I did what any one of them would have done on the Goodman boy, then maybe I ought to look around for another congregation."

"You've had trouble with the Board before, David," Miriam observed, "and you've fought it. Why would you give up now?"

"This is different. It was always a matter of principle, of something I was strongly opposed to, or some action I had taken that they objected to, and it was the principle I was fighting. This is just a matter of popularity. I know I'm not particularly well liked. I suppose I don't have the warm personality that makes for easy friendship. Well, I don't care. What I want is not love from the congregation, but respect. And if I do all the silly things that people would like me to do, I wouldn't even have my own respect."

"Yes, I understand," she said. "You're really bothered about young Goodman."

Startled, he stared at her. Then with a sheepish smile, he said, "Well, I can't believe he actually murdered the man over some old quarrel. I've seen him twice, and I wasn't particularly taken with him. I certainly don't feel in any sense responsible, and still—"

"You're probably thinking of his parents," she said matter-of-factly. "If anything happened to him, they'd never forgive themselves for having asked you to look him up."

34

MANY, PERHAPS MOST, OF HIS CONGREGATION DID NOT NOR-
mally see their rabbi except on the New Year, Rosh Hashonah,
and the Day of Atonement, Yom Kippur, when he sat in his
traditional place beside the Ark, and even the more devout
were apt to see him only when he presided at the Friday
Evening Services, which normally were suspended during
the summer months. So Rabbi Small did not interpret the
coolness with which he was greeted when he met them at the
King David as being critical of his behavior.

"Hello, Rabbi. Feeling better? Glad you could make it,"
was the usual form of greeting. From which he concluded that
Al Bergson had let it be known that he had been ill, presumably as explanation for his failure to appear at Barney
Berkowitz's Bar Mitzvah. Barney himself was most solicitous.
"These summer colds, they can develop into something serious, Rabbi." And because to deny that he had been sick would
give the lie to Al Bergson, he merely smiled and nodded.

But he did express his annoyance to Bergson when they
were seated together on the bus that took them from the King
David to Jaffa Gate in the Old City, where the walk was to
begin.

Bergson was not at all abashed. "Sometimes, David, a
man has to be protected against himself," he said. "As pres-

ident of the congregation, I'm not going to let a split develop over something as silly as B.B.'s Bar Mitzvah. No matter what you think, a lot of the guys have the idea that it is a religious ceremony that every Jew has to undergo, even women. Mollie Berkowitz was going to do it, too, until she heard if they did it at the Wall, there was no service on the woman's side. It has become a tradition, and there's no accounting for traditions. Look at all those youngsters, and older men, too, who walk around with those little crocheted yarmulkes held in place with a bobby pin. Try telling them that there is no commandment that dictates it. As far as they're concerned, it indicates that they are observant. It has become a tradition, and you're not likely to laugh or argue them out of it. And now what's the story on the Goodman boy?"

The question was repeated again and again by various members of the party as they trudged behind the guide, usually prefaced apologetically with, "See, Rabbi, his mother heard I was going to Jerusalem, and she asked me . . ."

To each of them he explained that the system was different here from in the States, that arrest did not have the same significance in Israel, where it was apt to be the beginning of an investigation rather than the end. He explained, "The police have the authority to hold anyone for forty-eight hours without a warrant. After that, if they want to hold him longer, they must appear before a magistrate and ask for a remand. In the case of a young man like Goodman, unattached, without a family or job, who is free to come and go as he pleases, he is apt to be remanded, and the magistrate will go along if they have any sort of evidence against him. It is while he is safely in custody that they work on their case. Only a small percentage of those remanded ever come to trial. The vast majority of them are released."

One of them began his inquiries by saying, "I know you've got some connection with the police, Rabbi, because back home you're pretty chummy with Chief Lanigan, and some of the guys think that's not entirely proper, but as far as I'm concerned, I'm glad my rabbi stands in good with the authorities, and I tell them if the rabbi's got a drag with the police here, it's all the better for young Goodman, on account of the rabbi will use his influence for him."

While the congregants did not confront him as a group, for which he was profoundly grateful, their attitude, as he sensed it from individual remarks, was most disturbing. They seemed to feel that he was in some way responsible for young Goodman's arrest, or at least was in a position to do something about it. The facts of the case had been kept out of the newspapers, so they knew little about it, not even what he had been charged with, but the belief was strong that it was something very serious, perhaps even murder.

Curiously, they did not appear to be concerned as to whether or not the young man was guilty. The feeling seemed to be that it could not be terribly reprehensible because "we know his parents." Perhaps the general picture they had evolved was that there had been a fracas of some sort in which the students of the yeshiva—and, of course, Goodman—had been involved. They had heard that yeshiva students did become rowdy on occasion in spite of or even because of their religious dedication. Something serious had resulted, and the police had latched onto Goodman because—because he was an American and a foreigner. "But most of the other boys are American. It's the American Yeshiva."

"Yes, well, I'm sure his being an American has something to do with it, and the rabbi as a fellow American should do something about it. At least he knows the language and can talk to the authorities."

They trailed after the guide, clustering around him whenever he stopped to point out something of special interest. They nodded to show their approval, or that they understood, as he took them from the Tower of David through the streets of the Old City to the Western Wall and up through the Jewish Quarter to Mount Zion, where the bus was waiting to take them back to the hotel. They came abreast of a couple of Arab masons sitting on the ground patiently trimming blocks of stone, occasionally getting up to fit the stone in its intended place, removing it to break off another chip, and then inserting it once again.

"I don't get it," said one of the group.

"What don't you get?" asked the guide.

"The whole business. Here you've been showing us a whole bunch of buildings and each one was built on top of another, and that one was built on top of another."

"So?"

"So how come if someone is planning on putting up a building in a special place and there's already a broken-down building there, or part of a building, and say he doesn't want to use the walls that are left, so wouldn't he just knock them down and at least use the old cellar? I mean, why would he fill the cellar with all kinds of junk and build on top of that?"

"Oh, I see what you mean. You're wondering how a city can be built on top of another, older city. Well, it doesn't usually follow immediately after. What happens is that a city, or a section of a city, is destroyed by an earthquake, or by an invading army, or it may be a series of floods. The inhabitants escape or move away, and the place lies neglected for years, perhaps centuries. Sand and dust from the desert blow in and cover the area, and by the time someone comes along and decides it's a good location to build, there's very little showing except that it seems to be a little higher than the surrounding territory, which usually is regarded as an advantage. So they lay their foundation on the new surface and—"

"Wouldn't they go down to bedrock?"

"Sure, they put down a footing, and if they strike part of an old wall, so much the better."

"But why wouldn't they excavate?"

"What for? It's easier to build from the ground up. We don't run to cellars much here, and when I was in the States, I noticed that a lot of houses there were being built without cellars."

"Yeah, but the government or whoever is running these digs, they dig out cellars."

The guide laughed. "Oh, you mean archaeological excavations. But that's a new science. To the archaeologist, a potsherd, an old copper coin, a bit of broken glass can be of enormous significance, but to the man building a house it's just junk, like a broken soda bottle or rusty tin can would be to you."

"Yeah, I suppose."

"There's the bus," Bergson called out, and to the rabbi, "You coming along?"

"The bus? Oh, you mean to take you back to the hotel." He seemed to be curiously abstracted. "No, I think I'll walk back."

"It's a long walk, David."

"Well, if I get tired, I can always take a bus."

"Okay. Hey, but look, we go to Eilat tomorrow. How about you and Miriam and your aunt if she wants, coming to dinner at the King David, or someplace else if you'd rather, tomorrow night?"

"No, Al, I'm more or less a resident, and you are a visitor. You come to us for dinner."

"Okay."

"Around seven."

"Fine."

The rabbi set out briskly, but no sooner had the bus passed him, the group on his side waving to him, than he slowed down to a leisurely stroll, his eyes focused on the sidewalk, deep in thought. He made the sharp descent from the Old City and the long upward walk toward the Rehavia section. It was only when he reached the top of the rise that he realized he was tired.

Just ahead was the Hotel Excelsior. It occurred to him that he might stop off there, and perhaps if Perlmutter was free, he might have a cold drink with him. He entered the lobby, looked around, and approached the front desk.

"Is Mr. Perlmutter around?" he asked the clerk.

"Aharon? He went up to Haifa for the Shabbat. I took his morning duty for him."

"Oh. Then he won't be coming in today?"

"Oh, sure. He should be in around one. Is there a message—"

"No, no. I'll be seeing him later in the day, I expect."

35

THE TELEPHONE CALL CAME JUST AS THE RABBI FINISHED
the lunch that Miriam had left him. It was Rabbi Karpis.

"Rabbi Small? Er, Rabbi Karpis. Er, something has—er—
just come to my attention concerning er—the matter we are
both interested in. I have asked our attorney, whom you've
met, to come and see me about it. I thought that perhaps you,
too, might be interested."

"When is he coming?"

"He should be here shortly."

Although the day had been hot and he was tired from his
long walk, he said, "I'll come right over."

But he had to wait for a bus, and it was half an hour before
he arrived. Shiah Goldberg was already there, and he greeted
him with a wide wave of the arm. Rabbi Karpis brushed aside
Rabbi Small's attempted explanation of why it had taken him
so long.

"Sit down, Rabbi. Sit down. I can have coffee brought?"
he suggested.

Both his guests shook their heads no.

"Well, I'll come to the point. I have heard through—well,
no matter. Let's say it has come to my attention that the
medical examiner has some rather startling new evidence. As
I understand it, Dr. Shatz was away when the body was found,

and the preliminary examination was made by a young and I gather inexperienced assistant. He attributed the death of the unfortunate Professor Grenish to a rupture of an aneurysm. He found no signs of—er—violence on the body. No marks of blows having been struck. That sort of thing. I gather that the public prosecutor was going to take the line that since the death had not been reported and the body had in fact been concealed, the rupture of the aneurysm had been due to a fight or that some kind of violence had been done to him. And our position was that since there were no signs of violence, death had been due to natural causes, but that our Ish-Tov had panicked and had buried the body for fear he might be accused of having killed the man."

"That's right," said Shiah.

"Well, then as I understand it, Dr. Shatz made a more thorough examination and found evidence that the man had been bound and gagged. A patch of adhesive tape had been put over the victim's mouth. There were microscopic traces of the adhesive substance, as I understand it. And also his hands and feet seem to have been bound with the same material."

"Oh, the son-of-a-bitch," Shiah exclaimed.

"Are you referring to Ish-Tov?" asked Rabbi Karpis, surprised at the attorney's vehemence.

"He may be one, too," said Shiah, "but I was thinking of the prosecutor." Then with a bitter laugh, he said to Rabbi Small, "You remember, I told you we lawyers always try to keep something back? Now I've got to rethink my strategy. This Shatz has a good reputation, but he's a nervous little man, and I might be able to tie him up on the witness stand. I'll see if I can get permission to have our own expert make an examination of the body. If the man was tied up, then Ish-Tov probably could not have done it by himself. I've felt all along that he wasn't alone in the business."

"You mean you'll implicate others, other students in this?" asked Karpis. "I don't think that would help us very much."

"No, of course not, but—look, if I don't put him on the stand, then if he had an accomplice, it wouldn't come out. I mean, the only way they could find out about an accomplice would be in cross-examining Ish-Tov. Right? So I don't put him on the stand. Then I argue that he couldn't tie him up single-handed unless the man was already dead, or at least unconscious."

"But that in itself suggests that others are implicated, and that would broaden the affair," said Karpis. "We've got to consider the political implications. The Labor Alignment has been putting out feelers to us for the next government, but if there were a suggestion that this might be anything other than an individual—"

Rabbi Small rose abruptly. "I think I should leave now," he said.

Startled, Rabbi Karpis looked up. "Oh, I see. Yes, perhaps this part of our—er—discussion should be limited to— er—well, thank you very much, Rabbi Small, for coming over. I'm sorry I was the purveyor of bad news, but I thought you'd like to know."

The lawyer favored Rabbi Small with a broad wink.

As he made his way out of the building, down the walk, and to the street, Rabbi Small wondered if he was being fair to Rabbi Karpis. After all, he was an administrator, and his first duty was to the yeshiva. From his point of view, if the Alignment was interested in associating the tiny segment of the religious establishment that ran the yeshiva with the formation of a new government, that had to take precedence over any sympathy he might feel for young Ish-Tov. It would mean additional funding for the yeshiva—expansion, perhaps; greater influence, in any case. And from his point of view, Ish-Tov was merely a wrong'un they had tried unsuccessfully to help.

When Rabbi Small reached the Skinner house on his way to the bus stop, he heard his name called. He stopped, looked back and then up, and saw Skinner waving to him from his second-floor window. He paused uncertainly, and a moment later Ismael came running out.

"Rabbi Small, Rabbi Small, Jeem wondered if you wouldn't like to have coffee with us!"

The rabbi considered and then said, "Why, yes, that would be very nice." He followed Ismael up the staircase to Skinner's office.

"We were just about to have our coffee when I spotted you, Rabbi," Skinner said. And to Ismael, "Do we have anything in the way of cake or—"

"Just those cookies Martha baked last week."

"Those were pretty good. Why don't you see what you can rustle up to go with our coffee." To the rabbi he explained, "Martha doesn't usually prepare anything for Sunday. And Ismael and I usually eat our meals out on Sunday."

Ismael was not gone long, and when he reappeared, it was with a tray on which there was a thermos pot of coffee, cream, and sugar, and a plate of cookies as well as one of buttered toast. "It was all I could manage," he said apologetically. He served Skinner and then set two cups down on the coffee table, one for the rabbi and one for himself. It occurred to the rabbi that relations between Skinner and Ismael had improved much since his last visit. There was no sign of the embarrassing servility he had noticed in Ismael before. He now addressed him as "Jeem" rather than as "Mr. James," and he was not only joining them for coffee but also participating in the conversation.

They talked about the political situation in the country and of the fighting that was going on in Lebanon. Skinner asked about Miriam and Gittel, and when he suggested that he would like to see them again, the rabbi readily agreed and said he would talk to them and see if he couldn't arrange to have Skinner come to dinner some evening.

After an hour or so, when the rabbi rose and said he would have to be going, Skinner said, "Ismael, why don't you drive the rabbi home. It's awfully hot out and he might have to wait a good twenty minutes before that bus comes." The rabbi made polite demurral but permitted himself to be persuaded.

Miriam had returned by the time the rabbi got back to the

apartment. In response to her asking how he had spent the day, he told her about his visit to the yeshiva. He tried not to sound bitter as he explained the concerns of the yeshiva authorities. "I suppose it's natural for him to be concerned for his institution. When you consider the sort of person whom they are apt to attract, young men, many who have led rackety lives, one who gets in trouble with the law is not so unusual. But the fact is that their concern is not so much with Ish-Tov as with the reputation of the school. And the lawyer they engage will naturally have the same attitude."

"Oh, dear, is there nothing that can be done for him? Isn't there anything you can do?"

"Like what? Hire a lawyer for him?"

"No, but—look here, all those people who came for Barney Berkowitz's Bar Mitzvah. I gather they were all concerned. Well, maybe they could make up a pool and—"

"And hire a lawyer for his defense?" He laughed. "They're not really concerned about Ish-Tov except as something to beat me over the head with. Al Bergson is coming here tonight. Why don't you ask him?"

"I will."

"And if they got a lawyer, what could he do?"

"Isn't there anything, anything at all that could be built up into a defense, David?"

"Well, there is one thing. Perlmutter didn't recognize Grenish from the photo. That could be worked up. If I could get hold of Adoumi or whoever is handling the actual investigation, I might just possibly."

"How about Gittel?"

"What about Gittel? What's she got to do with it?"

"I'll bet she could get Adoumi, and if he's not actually handling the case, she might be able to get him to get the one who is."

And the rabbi, who had seen Gittel in action before, said, "It's worth a try."

"Oh, David, do you think there's a chance? Do you have some idea—"

"Nothing very much, I'm afraid. But maybe I can delay things a little. As near as I can judge, the way the matter stands now, they're all set to bring the boy before the court and get him sentenced one, two, three. They won't put him on the stand. It probably will be a deal of some sort between the prosecutor and the defense. Maybe a shorter sentence. Something like that."

"Then how can you stop it?"

"Well, there's Perlmutter's testimony. They've got to explain that. If Gittel manages to get Adoumi down, I'll call Perlmutter and have him come, too. His testimony will be more effective if he's here to tell it than if I just recount it."

"Will you call Bergson and tell him not to come?"

"Yeah. Maybe I should. On the other hand, I don't see any harm in his being here. It might even help."

36

On the telephone, Gittel was formidable. When Adoumi explained patiently that he was no longer involved in the case, that he had given it over to Yaacov Luria of the Police Department, she said, "So bring him along with you. Maybe it would be better if both of you were here."

"But Gittel, I can't get Luria to come to your house to discuss a police matter. There are lines of authority, and we don't cross them."

"Look, Uri, he's Tzippe Luria's boy. I was in the Haganah with her. We were close, like sisters. So, do I have to call her in Tel Aviv and ask her to call her boy here in Jerusalem, he should do his old mother a favor and go and see her friend Gittel?"

"All right, Gittel," said Adoumi wearily, "I'll call him."

She replaced the receiver and said, "Believe me, they'll be here."

Sure enough, shortly after the women had cleared the dishes of the evening meal, the two men appeared. Adoumi began to make the introductions, when Gittel stopped him. "No, me you don't have to introduce. I knew Yaacov when—when—I attended his Bar Mitzvah."

"Hello, Gittel. You're looking well. I heard you were in

Jerusalem, and I was planning to drop around someday and—"

"But you were busy. I forgive you. This is my niece, Miriam, and this is her husband, Rabbi Small. From America."

"Rabbi Small was very helpful to me some years ago," said Adoumi.

Bergson arrived shortly after, followed a few minutes later by Perlmutter. As introductions were being made, Adoumi said, "You look familiar. I've seen you somewhere before."

"I work at the Excelsior Hotel. You interviewed me there. At least, you showed me a photograph and asked if it was anyone I recognized."

"Oh, yes, Grenish's photo. You said you didn't recognize him."

"It wasn't Professor Grenish," said Perlmutter firmly.

"What's that?"

"You knew him?" asked Luria.

"I had never met him before, but when I saw him at breakfast that Sunday morning, I got a good look at him, and I'd know him if I saw him again. Let me explain. I am an accountant by profession, and I work in the accounting office at the hotel. But because I am seventy-five years old—"

"Really?"

"You don't look it."

"Thank you, but it means that I can't afford to stand on my dignity. I fill in for others when it's necessary, on the front desk, or checking of guests for breakfast against a list. Well, the first thing I did when I took my place at the little table at the door of the dining room was to go over my list."

"Why?"

"Because we have many foreign visitors from places all over the world—Scandinavians, South Americans, French, Italians. So when they give me their room numbers and their names, I don't have to ask them to repeat them or spell them out. The guest comes in and says, "Smith, six forty-four. I look it up on my list, check it off, smile, and say, "B'tayavon, or bon appétit, Mr. Smith."

Luria glanced at Adoumi and said, "He hasn't absorbed the Israeli attitude yet, has he?"

"Well," said Perlmutter defensively, "so many, especially those who come on tours, are so used to being herded about and ordered around by the tour guides and hotel clerks that they appreciate being treated as guests and feeling that they are welcome."

"Okay, sure, but—well, go on."

"Well, when I saw the name Grenish, Professor Abraham Grenish, I took note of it. I even made a little note of the name and the room number—"

"Why?"

"I come from Poland. Our town was overrun by the Nazis, and my entire family was wiped out. I escaped the slaughter because I was in Switzerland on business at the time. My wife's family was also wiped out. Their name was Grenitz. It means 'border.' So when I saw the name Grenish on my list, it occurred to me that it might originally have been Grenitz. The *itz* ending suggests Russia or Poland, so I could understand someone coming to America changing it to *ish* or *ich*. There is no point in tracing Perlmutters. It's meaningless, thought to be a pretty name—mother-of-pearl—like Goldberg, mountain of gold, or Rosenzweig, rose branch, and adopted when Jews were required to take surnames for official records and for a census. But a name meaning 'border' would be likely to be taken only by someone living on a border. You'll find Perlmutter all over Eastern Europe, but Grenitz is comparatively rare.

"So I thought when the professor checked through, I would engage him in conversation, and ask him perhaps if his name had originally been Grenitz and if his folks had come from our town or near there."

"And?"

"I rehearsed what I would say and just how I would say it. I thought I might pretend to have a little difficulty in finding it so as to give me a chance to study his face and see if I could see any family resemblance. And then I would find it and remark that my wife's name had been Grenitz. And that's what happened, except that before I could say anything about my wife's name, the hotel manager came hurrying over to ask me to go to the front desk, where there was a guest who was Polish or Russian, and they needed an interpreter. He took my place, and I went to the front desk. But I lingered at the door for a moment and watched the professor go to the buffet table and begin loading his tray. Yes, I got a good look at him, and he was not the man whose photograph you showed me."

Curiously, the first question came from Al Bergson. "Where did you learn to speak English?"

"In Canada, where I lived until I came here."

"That accounts for it. Your English is very good."

"Thank you."

Luria glared in annoyance at Bergson and then turned to Perlmutter and asked, "You saw him only that one time?"

"That's right. One of the Arab employees checks out on the Sabbath."

Luria turned to Adoumi. "Did you show the photo to the Arab checker?"

"Of course."

"Did you go back to see if he was still in the dining room—after you got through at the front desk, I mean?" Luria continued to Perlmutter.

"I did, but he'd already gone. I wasn't too concerned, because I had asked how long he'd be staying and was told he had registered for a week. But that was the last I saw of him."

"But look here," said Luria. "Ish-Tov identified him, both the photo and later the man. And the photo was a good likeness."

"And people make mistakes on identification all the time, especially if they've seen the person once," Adoumi added.

"I did not make a mistake," said Perlmutter.

"Then that means—" the rabbi began.

"Yes, Rabbi," Adoumi challenged. "What does that mean?"

"It means that if the man in the trench was Professor Grenish, then the man who slept in his bed at the hotel

Saturday night and gave his name and room number Sunday morning was someone else, an imposter. So the question is, how would he have gotten his hotel key? Grenish could have given it to him, or more likely it could have been taken from him."

"Why is it more likely to have been taken from him?" Luria challenged.

"I can imagine that Grenish might be indisposed and, needing something from his hotel room, he might give his key to someone and ask him to get it for him. But then, would his messenger spend the night there and have breakfast at the hotel the next morning? Much more likely, the key was taken from him."

"It still wouldn't explain why he'd want to spend the night there," said Luria.

"No, it wouldn't," the rabbi admitted, "unless he might have thought there would be a message, a phone call. . . ."

Gittel sensed that the rabbi was uncertain and was floundering. She sought to give him respite to gather his thoughts. "Let us have some coffee," she said briskly.

"No, Gittel," said Luria. "I want to get this over with."

"When you talk to your mother, I'm sure you will mention that you came to see me. And if I know Tzippe Luria, she will ask you what I served. And you will say that you had nothing in my house? Miriam, bring in some fruit, and put on the water for the coffee."

Luria glanced at Adoumi and then, with a shrug, he said, "Maybe we could all use a cup of coffee."

As he sipped at his coffee, Luria said, "All right, let's assume that Mr. Perlmutter is right and that it was some imposter who slept in Grenish's bed Saturday night and had breakfast at the hotel the next morning. So that means that after breakfast Saturday morning, Grenish, the real one, went to Abu Tor. How did he get there? Did he take a cab at the hotel? We can check that easily enough. Or did he decide to walk? In which case, did he ask one of the hotel clerks how to get there? Or did he just start walking aimlessly and—"

"How do you know it was Saturday?" asked the rabbi.

"Because we know it wasn't Friday. He spent Friday in the Old City."

"How do you know?"

"We-el, since he didn't have dinner at the hotel, he had to have eaten in the Old City, or at least in East Jerusalem, since all restaurants in the Jewish section are closed on the Sabbath. Then one of our men thought he recognized the photo of Grenish. Someone asked him why one of the stores was shut down, and he tried to explain to him. And—oh, yes, what's his name, the fellow on whose land he was found, Skinner—he was shown the photo, and he made a positive identification."

"Skinner knew him?" asked the rabbi in surprise.

"No, but he came along as the policeman who speaks no English was trying to explain in French, and Skinner translated. So he was definitely in the Old City Friday, which means he couldn't have been in Abu Tor. It's quite a distance from the Old City, and there's no place in Abu Tor where he could have had dinner."

"No place in Jerusalem is very far from any other place in Jerusalem," observed Bergson, "unless Gilo, perhaps."

"All right," Luria conceded. "So it could have been on Friday." He turned to Adoumi. "Is there anything to show that he wasn't at the hotel Saturday?"

Adoumi shook his head. "As I told you, I questioned the Arab clerk who checked breakfasts Saturday morning. He didn't recognize the person in the photo."

"Did you mention his name? Did you mention Grenish by name?"

"Of course not," said Adoumi. "When you hold an identification lineup, do you give the names and professions of the people in it?" He thumbed through his notebook. "Here it is. This is the Arab clerk: 'I may have seen him, but I do not remember. I see so many. . . . I go by the room number. They give me the number and I check it off.' The only one who knew the name was the manager and—oh, yes, the security guard, but then *he* was part of the investigating team, you might say. As a matter of fact, he almost saw him. Here it is: 'So I'm behind the desk . . . and somebody says, "I think there's something for me, Room seven-thirteen." So I look up, and sure enough, there's a letter in the seven-thirteen pigeonhole. I glance at it and I say, "Grenish?" and he says, "That's right." So I give it to him. I didn't look at him—maybe his back as he turned away.' "

"The letter. That must be it!" exclaimed the rabbi.

"What about the letter?"

"That could be why he took Grenish's room, to get the letter. And it would explain why, if he came Friday night and found nothing, he stayed on through Saturday. There is no mail on Saturday, so he stayed until Sunday. Did your policeman say he asked about a particular store?" he asked Luria.

Luria knit his brows as he tried to remember. "I don't think he was too clear about what Grenish was saying. But that's the only store in the area that's apt to be closed on Friday. The owner is a Druse. The other stores are Christian and would be closed on Sunday rather than on Friday."

"And is that particular store suspect in any way? I mean, has it ever come under official scrutiny? Was your policeman stationed there for any special reason?"

Luria shook his head and looked at Adoumi, who said, "Well, when our army was in the Bekaa Valley, where the Lebanese Druse live, we thought—well, we kept an eye on it every now and then. Our Druse, who live mostly up in the Golan, are loyal. They serve in our army. But of course some of them might feel that their ties to the Lebanese Druse outweigh their loyalty to us. So we kind of watched that store from time to time. Why do you ask?"

The rabbi laughed shortly. "Of course, it could be pure coincidence, Grenish being there and Skinner being there. But it's also possible that Grenish went there because he expected to deliver a message, or a letter, or that it was why Skinner thought he was there and was so concerned when he found it closed."

216

"Skinner, that nice man who helped with your bags?" Gittel was shocked. But Miriam only smiled, sensing that her husband was trying only to suggest possibilities, so that the investigation that had narrowed down to Ish-Tov might be broadened.

Luria laughed, but Adoumi's eyes narrowed and he said, "Are you serious?"

"Why not? By its very nature, coincidence is a lot less likely than no coincidence. Suppose Skinner followed Grenish." He faced Adoumi. "You said you had Grenish on a list because he was friendly with a distinguished Arab professor at Harvard. All right, suppose that professor asked him to deliver a message, a written message which would be mailed to him, to someone in that store in the Old City. Skinner might have heard something of it. He might have had someone in the hotel lobby watching for him. In any case, he may have followed him, and when Grenish seemed so concerned over the store being closed, he might have assumed that the reason for his concern was that he would be unable to deliver the message with which he had been entrusted.

"So Skinner explained, and then they walked on together, looking at shop windows, talking. Maybe they went to a restaurant and had dinner. Maybe Skinner invited him to his home for dinner. Or if they ate in a restaurant, then perhaps to come home for a nightcap. They could have walked there. It was a pleasant evening. Or they could have taken a cab from the Old City. Or Skinner might have had his car parked nearby. If he did, my guess is that Ismael, his Arab manager, was nearby, because I gather he's the one who does the driving. In any case, I'm sure he would be in the house."

"What makes you so sure Ismael would be there?" asked Luria.

"Because he lives there. The housekeeper comes early, serves breakfast and lunch, and cleans the house. Then she cooks dinner and leaves around five. But Ismael is there all the time. He would be bound to know what was happening. Besides, for what happened, two were necessary."

"What happened, David?" asked Miriam.

"I suppose Skinner asked him for the letter. Perhaps he resisted, or pretended he didn't know what they were talking about. He may have tried to leave and they restrained him. Or he may have told them the truth, that he didn't have it and expected to get it by mail. In any case, when they searched him and didn't find it on his person, they decided to search his room at the hotel. Even if he were entirely cooperative, they wouldn't take a chance that he wouldn't cry out and call for help. After all, it was next door to the yeshiva. So they gagged him by putting a piece of adhesive tape over his mouth."

"How did you know that?" demanded Luria.

"I heard it today from Rabbi Karpis, the head of the yeshiva. How he found out, I don't know. But then they'd have to tie his hands to keep him from ripping it off, and perhaps his feet as well. It takes at least two men to do that, one to hold him while the other puts the tape on."

"And then this Skinner guy went to the hotel?" asked Bergson.

The rabbi shook his head. "No, I think what happened next was that they discovered Grenish was dead. He had an aneurysm of the aorta, and the struggle, or the straining against the tapes, or his fear and indignation, caused it to burst. I'm sure they ripped off the bandages and tried to bring him around, but when they realized he was dead, they had to dispose of the body. And they finally decided to toss it in the trench and cover it over with just enough dirt so it wouldn't be seen."

"Why wouldn't they just pile it in the car and then drive out and dump it somewhere?" asked Bergson.

The rabbi smiled. "Back in the States, especially in our general area, you can drive out a few miles and find dense woods lining the road. You can dump a body a couple of yards from the roadway and it might not be found for days or even weeks. But here, even where there are trees, as on the road to Tel Aviv, they're sparse, and there's no underbrush to speak of, and you'd probably have to climb a rather steep hill. If they had dumped the body on the side of the road, it would have been found by early morning, maybe even that very night."

"They could have kept it in the house," Bergson pointed out.

"Not if he had a housekeeper coming in next day," said Miriam.

"You say they just covered the body with enough earth to hide it," said Bergson. "It would seem to me that if they had filled the trench immediately, he'd be completely in the clear. It would never be found."

"Ah, but he couldn't," said the rabbi. "The Department of Antiquities people were coming Monday. If they found the trench filled in, they might let it go, but on the other hand, they were more likely to dig. And if they dug, they'd unearth the body. But if they just covered it with enough earth so that it wouldn't be visible . . ." He hesitated, and then it came to him. "Don't you see? Because they were planning to unearth it. Once he had the letter, they could dump the body. It wouldn't make any difference then if the body were found."

"So what do you think happened?"

"The letter wasn't in the room, so he could only hope it would come in the Sunday mail. It did, and he didn't have to go back to the hotel Sunday night. My guess is that he went someplace to hide it, or to show it to someone, or to try to sell it."

"Haifa," said Luria. "He said he went to Haifa Sunday morning and was gone all day. Then he said he had to go to Hebron, but he stopped off at the house at night before going on."

The rabbi nodded. "Of course, I have no way of knowing, or even guessing, what his business in Hebron or in Haifa was, but I'm pretty sure he came back to his house Sunday night for the purpose of unearthing the body and taking it someplace to dump."

"And?"

"And he couldn't because the trench had already been filled in. By Ish-Tov, alone or with a friend. I saw Ish-Tov at the police station. I went with the lawyer for the yeshiva. When I was alone with him for a few minutes, I asked why he filled in the trench. After an initial reluctance to talk to me at all, he said he had done it for a friend at the yeshiva who was a Kohane and was afraid it might be part of an ancient cemetery and that the bones of the dead would pollute him—"

"You're kidding," said Bergson. "Or he was pulling your leg."

"I'm not, and he wasn't. He himself was not terribly concerned, but he knew his friend was. When I suggested that his neighbor, Skinner, might get in trouble with the authorities over it, he was not in the least concerned. In fact, he was quite pleased at the idea, since Skinner was a Gentile and hence an infidel."

Gittel made deprecatory noises and murmured, "The things they teach them in the yeshiva!"

"I'm sure that's not what they teach them in the yeshiva," said Miriam stoutly. Then, "Is it, David?"

"I doubt it. But some of the students there, and that atmosphere that is engendered . . ."

Bergson addressed himself to Luria. "Well, does that let young Goodman, or Ish-Tov, or whatever he calls himself, off the hook?"

Luria considered and then smiled. "It's a very interesting scenario," he said, "but that's all it is. There's no proof of any of it. I could discuss it with the prosecutor, and he might order further investigation, but—"

The rabbi emitted a little apologetic cough. "There's a way in which you might get the proof you need," he suggested hesitantly. "If Mr. Skinner should meet Aharon . . ."

"You mean get him to the Excelsior?" Adoumi shook his head. "He'd smell a rat immediately."

"I told him we might need his evidence," said Luria. "I could send for him, and if Mr. Perlmutter were there—"

"At Police Headquarters? He'd claim it was a frame and

any judge would agree," said Adoumi. "No, some neutral place is necessary. Tell you what. First thing tomorrow morning, before he's likely to go off somewhere on his regular business . . ."

They discussed the plan at length, and when they finally broke up, it was almost midnight. As Bergson went to the door, the rabbi said, "You go to Eilat tomorrow, so I won't be seeing you until I get back to the States."

"Hell, no, David. I'll have my regular tour guide take the group down to Eilat. I'm staying over. I want to be in on the kill."

Luria studied the map spread out on his desk. Then he picked up the telephone and spoke to Adoumi. "You've got a clear view of the area, Uri?"

"No problem."

"And everyone is in position?"

"That's right. I've got two men at the bus stop across the street, and we've got two men in the car parked right near the yeshiva. You got a car down the street?"

"I've got a truck. He could get around a car. Or he might get excited and ram the car and do some damage."

"Good thinking."

"And Perlmutter is in place and knows just what he has to do?"

"Sure. He understands. If he doesn't recognize him, he just walks on, but if he does recognize him, then he comes forward and greets him with a big smile."

"Then I'll make my call. Look, hang on, and I'll make the call from another line."

Luria hung up and reached for another telephone and called. He spoke in a peremptory, official tone that would brook no opposition. He listened, spoke again, and then said, "Very well, I will await you," and hung up.

Once again he spoke to Adoumi. "He should be starting out immediately."

"Good. Ah, I see Ismael bringing the car out . . . . He's

waiting at the curb with the motor running . . . I can just see the door of the house opening . . . Here he comes down the path, and I've signaled Perlmutter."

Perlmutter began to walk down the street as the figure on the path approached the waiting car. When the two were a yard from each other, Perlmutter's face broke into a happy smile and he came forward with hand outstretched. "Why, Professor Grenish!" he exclaimed. "How nice to see you!"

"Who—what—"

"Don't you remember me? At the Excelsior Hotel?"

The two men waiting at the bus stop began to cross the street. Seeing them, Ismael put the car into gear and with motor racing shot down the street, only to have to put on his brakes as a truck came into the intersection and blocked his way. Men from nearby doorways came running over.

Skinner, now surrounded by the men who had been in the parked car in addition to the two who had been waiting at the bus stop, saw his car stopped and men pulling Ismael out from behind the wheel.

"Oh, the damn fool!" he cried out. "The goddamned fool!"

37

ADOUMI AGREED TO MEET WITH THE RABBI AND BERGSON AT the latter's room in the King David. Adoumi accepted the inevitable cup of coffee and said, "Well, it turned out to be my baby after all."

"Did you get the letter?" asked Bergson. "What's it all about?"

Adoumi pretended not to hear. Instead he turned to the rabbi and said, "You didn't work all that out last night, Rabbi, now, did you? You've been thinking about Skinner all along, haven't you?"

"He's confessed?"

"No-o, but we've been questioning him and the Arab separately, and we have a pretty good idea of what happened. We're letting both of them stew for a while, and then we'll question them again. When did you first think of him?"

The rabbi smiled. "I wasn't really thinking of Skinner so much as I was of Ish-Tov. I was not very much taken with the young man, but I still found it hard to believe that he would renew a quarrel after so many years to the point where it would lead to Grenish's death, even granting that he was extremely vulnerable by reason of his aneurysm. Then when I heard that his mouth had been taped, and possibly his hands and feet, I knew it couldn't be Ish-Tov. That's the sort of thing that would have to be done indoors, or with ready access to a house. Would he be likely to be carrying a roll of adhesive tape around with him? But if he didn't do it, how did he get his fingerprints on the shovel? He admitted he filled in the trench. Then why didn't he see the body lying there? Then I went with Mr. Bergson here, and other members of our congregation, for a walk around the Old City. Someone asked the guide why one would build one building on top of the ruin of another. If you start to lay down a foundation and you strike what is obviously an old wall, why wouldn't you excavate and make use of the old cellar? And the guide explained that it was easier to build on top of the ruin."

"It was about then that you left the group and said you were going to walk home," Bergson remarked.

"Yes. You see, it suddenly occurred to me that if someone had covered the body with enough earth so it could not be seen, someone else could finish filling the trench without knowing it was there. I wanted to think it through. Frankly, I didn't get very far. The thought that it might be Skinner just didn't occur to me. This affable man who had helped me with my bags at Lod Airport, who had driven up to Jerusalem with us, who had invited me in for coffee, he couldn't be involved in anything like this. And then, in the afternoon, I went to the yeshiva, where Rabbi Karpis told me and the lawyer about the evidence of the adhesive tape. In walking past Skinner's house to the bus stop, I was hailed, and Ismael came running out to invite me in for coffee. Now, the first time I had had coffee there, Ismael had been deferential toward Skinner to the point of being obsequious or even servile. He brought coffee for only Skinner and me, and practically backed out of the door as he left us. It was, 'Yes, Mr. James.' 'No, Mr. James.' "

"Not unusual for an Arab talking to his boss," said Adoumi.

"True, but this time, he called him 'Jeem' and he joined us for coffee. Of course, this might merely be because of Skinner's embarrassment, as an American, at the display of servility, especially in front of another American. But I got the impression that they were no longer master and subordinate, but rather that they were now partners, equals; that Ismael had no fear of being fired, no matter how unsatisfactory his work might be. In other words, it was as though he had a hold on him. And then I thought of something you said."

"Something I said?" asked Adoumi.

"Yes. Something to the effect that in ninety percent of the cases, it was the obvious answer that was the correct one. Well, if something is buried in the yard beside a house, who is the most likely one to have buried it if not the person living in the house?"

"I see. Yes, I did say that."

"So I spoke to my friend Perlmutter when I saw him at the minyan. Then I decided that instead of telling you about what he saw, and arguing with you about it in the hope you would then be able to convince Mr. Luria, I'd try to arrange for him to tell it to both of you."

Adoumi sat silent for a moment while his fingers drummed the arms of his chair. Then he got up abruptly and said, "I've got to be running along. Thank you for the coffee, Mr. er— Bergson. Nice to have met you. And thank you, Rabbi. Once again you have been most helpful, and I am indebted to you. You may have . . . well, never mind. We'll see each other before you leave. I'll have Sarah arrange it with Gittel." Ceremoniously, he shook hands with them and left.

"So that's that," said Bergson. "We didn't hear anything about the letter. I asked him but he didn't answer."

"No, he wouldn't. It's something involving security, I suppose. He's not of the police, you know. He's Shin Bet, something like our FBI."

"Yes, I know. Look, what do you suppose will happen with young Goodman?"

"Oh, I'm sure they'll release him."

"I know, but afterward. Will he go back to the yeshiva, or will he go home to the States? I thought if he wants to go home and is short of money, I might be able to work out something with El Al—a free ride, maybe, or at least a reduced rate. Lord knows, I give them plenty of business."

"I'll talk to Rabbi Karpis at the yeshiva tomorrow, and I'll let you know."

"I'll call from Eilat."

38

IT WAS NOT UNTIL A WEEK BEFORE THEY WERE SCHEDULED
to leave that Adoumi called. It was the rabbi who answered
the telephone.

"Rabbi? Uri here."

"Uri?"

"Uri Adoumi."

"Oh, of course. How are you—er—Uri?" It was the first
time Adoumi had referred to himself by his first name in any
of their conversations, and the rabbi thought it was an effort
to show his friendship.

"My Sarah tells me that Gittel told her you people are
leaving next week."

"That's right. Monday."

"I thought you'd be staying longer."

"Well, I have to get back to work, you know. I have a
wedding scheduled for Saturday."

"So how are you getting down to Lod? Have you made
arrangements yet?"

"Not yet. I figured on going by *sherut*. I was planning to
drop in to their office in the next day or two."

"Don't. I'll take you."

"Well, that's very kind of you, but we leave very early in
the morning, around six."

"So? I'll pick you up at six."

The rabbi sensed that the offer was by way of apology, and so he did not offer the usual polite demurrals but said, "Very good. We'll expect you around six."

There was no problem with the baggage, since Adoumi appeared with a large beach wagon. He had the rabbi sit beside him on the front seat, while Miriam sat in back. No sooner had they left the city and were on the road to Tel Aviv than Adoumi said, "I suppose you've been wondering why I hadn't gotten in touch with you earlier, as I promised. Well, it was because the affair was finally settled only in the last week or so."

"I saw nothing about it in the newspapers."

"Of course not. You didn't see anything about Skinner's arrest, or even of that yeshiva boy's arrest when he was taken in. It was all a matter of security, you understand. But it's been in the papers the past few days—"

"Really? I must have missed it."

Adoumi chuckled. "You couldn't have. It was the feature story. In yesterday's paper the headline was 'DRUSE THRUST TOWARD BEIRUT.' Do you realize you changed government policy?"

"I did?"

"Uh-huh. The letter that was sent to Grenish and that Skinner got hold of was a map and a set of directions leading to a huge arms cache that the PLO had buried in a cave in the Bekaa Valley. As it turned out, there was enough there to equip a small army—small arms, machine guns, mortars. When we translated it—it was in Arabic—and saw what we had, we handed it over to the chief of staff. It was debated at the highest level. You see, it was right in the middle of Druse country, and it was the opinion of the army that it would cost us from thirty to fifty casualties to get it out, and it wasn't worth it. On the other hand, if we just left it there, sooner or later someone would get it, probably the Syrians. You see, it was the plan of Skinner and his Arab buddy Ismael to sell it to the highest bidder. Well, if nothing happened, there would be another letter sent out. See? Or someone might come across it by accident, like the boy who found the Dead Sea Scrolls. So it was finally decided to send it on to the Druse. We should have teamed up with them rather than with Jemael's Christians from the very beginning. The Druse were grateful. It enabled them to protect themselves against the Syrians and the Shiites and the Christians. They couldn't admit to having been helped by us, of course, because that would unite all Arab forces against them, but they're aware of what we did for them."

"And that's what's behind their thrust toward Beirut?"

"Uh-huh. Figure it out yourself. These are the first weapons they could get with no strings attached."

"I see."

"Er—look, this is still secret, Rabbi, so don't go telling all your American friends what a big shot you are."

"David never would," said Miriam indignantly.

"And what happened to Skinner and Ismael?" asked the rabbi.

Adoumi shrugged. "Who knows? Ismael says it was Skinner's plan, and Skinner says it was Ismael if anyone was the cause of Grenish's death. Maybe there was some kind of deal made with Skinner. It wouldn't surprise me if part of the deal didn't involve the sale of his house to the yeshiva. After all, the minister of the interior belongs to one of the extreme religious parties. One thing I'm sure of: On your next trip to Jerusalem, you probably won't be offered coffee by Skinner."

Adoumi pulled up in front of the entrance to the airport lounge, and while the two men wrestled with the baggage, Miriam went to get a luggage carrier from the row beside the door. They loaded the bags onto the carrier, and as the rabbi turned the carriage toward the door, Adoumi said, "Oh, by the way, Rabbi, would you mail this letter for me when you get to the airport in Boston?" He reached into his inside jacket pocket and held out an envelope. "It's got an American stamp, you see. All you have to do is drop it in a box at the airport."

The rabbi glanced at the address. "Professor El Dhamouri? Oh, he's the one you said you had on a list—"

"That's right. It's just a clipping from the *Jerusalem Post*. I thought it might interest him—and maybe puzzle him a little, too."

Although the rabbi had decided to sleep late the day after his return, and recite his morning prayers at home, he found that he was wide awake at five o'clock in the morning and could not get back to sleep. So while Miriam gently snored, he got dressed quietly and went downstairs. A little later, because there was no reason not to, he strolled leisurely in the cool morning of the late summer day to the temple to participate in the minyan. He was the first to arrive, but shortly after, he was joined by Al Bergson.

After the initial greetings, Bergson said, "You know, David, when I rejoined the group in Eilat, I told them what had happened. And do you know? When I told them that young Goodman was going to be released in a day or two, the first one to speak up was Barney Berkowitz. He offered to pay the young man's plane fare back to the States if he wanted to come."

"That was very decent of him."

"Wasn't it?" He hesitated for a moment and then said, "I wish you'd tell him that, David. I know he'd appreciate it."

The rabbi studied his face for a moment. "All right. I will, next time I see him."

"You'll have a chance this morning. He'll be coming to the minyan, I'm sure. He hasn't missed a session since his Bar Mitzvah. You understand, he didn't actually pay for Goodman's passage. I was able to arrange with El Al for him to go as a 'dead head,' but the thought was there, and if I hadn't been able to arrange it, he would have."

"All right; as you say, it's the intention that counts. And does young Goodman come to the minyan, too? And does he still call himself Ish-Tov?"

"You know, I haven't seen him around. He's probably out of town visiting old friends, but I haven't seen him, and he sure as hell hasn't been to see me." A thought occurred to him. "Why did you think he might not come to the minyan? Did you see him? Is he kind of soured?"

"I didn't see him. I went to see Rabbi Karpis, the director of the yeshiva, though. I gathered from him that Ish-Tov felt the yeshiva had not been too diligent in effecting his release."

"And you think that might have soured him? Ah, here's Barney now. Hello, Barney."

"Hi, Al. Oh, and Rabbi Small. Welcome back. When did you—"

"Yesterday afternoon."

"Did you see the Goodman boy after—after—"

"After he was released? No. I went to the yeshiva, but he'd gone. I understand you offered to pay his fare back. That was very nice of you, Mr. Berkowitz."

"Call me B.B. I tell you, my wife shops there practically every day. So how would it be if Rose were pining away for her son? It could sour the cream cheese." He cackled at his own joke.

The rabbi grinned. "That's a consideration." He looked around and made a quick count. "I see we have ten. Would you like to lead, er—B.B.?"

"Nah, you do it. You're the stranger today." And he laughed again.

"All right." The rabbi took his place at the reading desk, facing the Ark. He turned his head momentarily to where Bergson was sitting. Bergson gave him an elaborate wink, then opened his prayer book.

After the service, the rabbi stood around with some of the others, receiving their expressions of welcome, gossiping, shmoozing. Then he started back home. As he approached the Goodman market, he saw that it was on the point of opening for the day. Louis Goodman was engaged in pushing a line of shopping carts out in front of the store, where customers could take one before entering. Goodman jiggled the file of nested carts to get them flush against his store window. Then he wiped his forehead and said, "It looks as though it's going to be a hot day. Oh, hello, Rabbi. Just get back?"

"Yesterday afternoon."

"Well, you picked a nice day for it. Yesterday was the first good day we've had in over a week. It was raining all last week." He paused, embarrassed. "Look, I heard you helped our Jordan when he got into a spot of trouble over there. I want you to know Rose and I are grateful."

"How is he?" asked the rabbi.

"Oh, he's all right. He called us and said he'd be along in a few days."

"You mean he's just coming home? I thought he left some time ago."

"Yeah, well, he came back to the States, but he stopped off in New York. It was from New York he called me."

"There's nothing wrong, I hope."

"Oh, no. He gets off in New York, see. And he's in the lounge at Kennedy waiting for a plane to Logan. And three or four of those guys, you know, Hasidim from Williamsburg, come over and start talking to him." A note of exasperation became noticeable in his tone. "And they persuade him into coming with them to this place in Williamsburg. And he's been there ever since."

"But he'll be home in a few days?"

"It's what he said."

"Well, perhaps he'll come to see me when he gets here."

"I'll tell him, Rabbi. Believe me, I'll tell him."

The secretary slit the dozen or so envelopes that had come in the morning's mail, then brought them in to Professor El Dhamouri. He had been away in Spain for almost a month and had returned only at the beginning of the week and still was wrestling with the mail that had accumulated during his absence. She stood in front of his desk, awaiting his instructions on the letters she had just brought in, for there was

232

much of his correspondence that she handled on her own. She saw his face drop.

"This is terrible!"

"Bad news?" she asked.

He held up the clipping from the *Jerusalem Post*. "Professor Grenish died. In Jerusalem. You remember Professor Grenish? Of Northhaven? He evidently had a heart attack while he was in the city." He opened the envelope wide. "There doesn't seem to be a note. Just this clipping. It didn't fall out on your desk, did it?"

"I'm sure it didn't, but I'll look." She went out, looked on the desk and on the floor underneath. She came back. "No, that's all that was in there."

"I examined the envelope. No return address. I wonder who could have sent it. It was mailed here, but someone there could have given it to someone coming to the States to mail. I wonder . . ."

He seemed abstracted. Quietly, the secretary left the room.

The Lanigans had come over for coffee. They talked of things that had happened during the summer, and Miriam told Amy about keeping house in Israel, and Amy in turn told of the difficulties of shopping while the town was so full of tourists.

Then Lanigan said, "Hey, David, you remember we talked about the Goodman boy before you left? You said you were going to see him."

"Yes, I saw him."

"Well, a funny thing happened about that business I told you about, you know, the broken window and the complaint against him. There was an inquiry about that. From the FBI, no less. A feller from the Boston office came down to see me and wanted to know all about it. What do you think of that?"

Before he could answer, Amy exclaimed, "Oh, look, Hugh. Look what Miriam brought me. It's a Jerusalem cross."

Lanigan reached for his wallet. "What do I owe you, David?"

The rabbi shook his head. "Nothing. It's a gift."

"Gee, thanks."

"Oh, thank you, Miriam, David. It's just what I wanted."

"You didn't have any trouble buying it?" asked Lanigan. "I mean, it wasn't any bother for you, was it, David?"

The rabbi shook his head. "No bother at all."